The Arthuriad Volume One: The Mystery Of Merlin

Zane Newitt

First published 2017
by Rowanvale Books Ltd
The Gate
Keppoch Street
Roath
Cardiff
CF24 3JW
www.rowanvalebooks.com

A CIP catalogue record for this book is available from the British Library.
ISBN: 978-1-911569-25-1

Morgana, Morgana, M... ... ...

ANOTHER BOOK ABOUT KING ARTHUR?

Rejecting the accidental view of history as folly or intentional deception, it is paradoxically of great import and little surprise that no figure save Jesus Christ has been given more attention in the written, theatrical and cinematic domains than the legendary King Arthur.

As a student of history, literature and theology, I shelved for a time the passions of my youth for the great King of the Britons. Returning to the vast body of historical, literary and romantic works, it was found that any objective study of the available material proves the existence of a very real King Arthur. Moreover, a conjunctive study of the Occult demonstrates that both actual and embellished events of the Arthurian period are used as a portal to an ancient heresy.

Indeed, growing up, Arthur was my Christological archetype. Mystically conceived, fully human and yet somehow transcendentally divine, Arthur was the slain and risen lord, the Sacral King. Gwenhwyfar was the Bride of Christ. Dogmatic, structured and strong; yet in the end, she, like the Bride, would betray her faithful Bridegroom. Lancelot, full of light and grandeur, was the Deceiver, Satan. Moreover, Arthur, like Christ, would be felled by his own kinsmen and carried away by the women closest to him. In the hour of his nation's greatest need Arthur, like the Son of Man, would return triumphantly to establish a heavenly kingdom on earth. The Britons (Welsh), like Israel, stumbled and fell and, typologically, the blended New Man (Welsh, Norman, Saxon, Mercian) of the present dispensation would arise, thanklessly and oft unknowingly benefitting from the work of a great man, warrior and king that they had retired to the corridors of myth and superstition.

Benign as it all sounds, not all that glimmers is gold with making a Christian allegory of the Matter of Britain. We, living in the Dispensation of the Grace of God, having God's full written revelation, have no need of an archetype; nay, we have the real thing! We need no Arthur to celebrate or explain Christ when we have Christ, even the complete record of the Lord Jesus Christ. So-called Christian allegories, then, when fully deconstructed, are distractions at best and occultist tricks at worst, leading the reader down a path that slowly pecks away at the veracity of literal truth and leading the unwary not into the arms of our precious Saviour but rather into the talons of His enemy and counterfeit, the Anti-Christ.

This does not take away from our love of Arthur or the Arthurian period, or from the value of other archetypes in our lives. What Man means for evil, God can use for good. In the crest of the rekindled Merovingian Heresy now masquerading in books, movies and documentaries aplenty, the Arthurian medium (the Scriptures notwithstanding) is the best forum with which to counter an error burgeoning in popularity.

Additionally, the Faerie Lore and cosmological 'myths and legends' from Ireland and Wales have been seemingly hijacked by atheists whose objective is to render mankind 'believing in nothing'. This they often accomplish by separating the Christian faith from the indigenous folk religions and pagan roots of the Isles.

There is more than meets the eye on this subject as well.

When a careful Bible student begins to overlay the legends and worldviews prior to (and after) the Flood of Noah, a world of Giants, Gnomes, monsters and hybrids emerges; God's word validating legends and legends validating God's word.

Instead of "Christianity vs. Mythology", the correct worldview is rather a created order that was perfect and then corrupted by fallen beings, resulting in fascinating, woefully and miserably damned heroes, demigods and other creatures.

The Arthurian body of literature is replete with Giants, Witches and Faeries, and with good reason; they have their part in the Great Conversation.

And so: for the Welsh from whom Arthur of Glamorgan and Gwent has been stolen; for those I grew up with who loved the story with me; to reveal the real secret of the Grail; to wrest away that now dead Wizard turned saint from the enemy's boast; to teach on matters precious to believers in God's undiluted Grace; and for Arthur the Silure, Pendragon and Protector of Britain, I submit my work to the Arthurian body.

ON LINGUISTICS PLACES AND NAMES

Ninth grade Creative Writing class.

With salivating anticipation, we had finally reached a segment on Arthurian Literature in the curriculum.

I was an Arthurian and "Celtic" radical at the time. While the potheads would visit "Stoner Hill" and the jocks would cut class to eat amino acids like captive sharks at feeding time, the vice of my youth was stealing away to the library to ingest as much Arthur, Lancelot and Merlin as I could get my hands on.

When the teacher, reading from a poorly rendered text book summary of Mallory's *Le Morte*, opened class with the words "Arthur, King of England", all at once feelings of isolation, betrayal and subject-matter-specific arrogance consumed me.

"How could Arthur be king of a country that did not exist?" I demanded.

An alligator's death roll rant followed.

"The defeat of the Angles, Jutes and Saxons are the primary focus of Arthur's military campaigns! England would not exist as such for some two centuries later than the Arthurian period!"

With one final gasp, I pronounced: "Calling King Arthur the King of England would be tantamount to making Geronimo Chief of the United States! You have ascribed to the King of the Britons the very title of his enemies."

I learned that day that there are two distinct camps when it comes to students and fans of matters Arthurian:

1. Students/readers who care very much about Arthurian accuracy.
2. Students/readers who care very little about Arthurian accuracy.

Over the ensuing years, I have observed a great spectrum amongst readers in general and Arthurian fans in particular.

Some, moved by the romance of Arthur, care little that the knightly and ecclesiastical orders described in medieval Arthurian literature did not exist in 6th century Britain.

Contrastingly, the opposite extreme exists. The contemporary obsession with Celtic primitivism, of long-haired naked warriors running to and fro in skirts screaming in mania, has no place in legitimate Arthurian history.

The ancient British culture was the most advanced, perhaps save Rome, of the Ancient World. Men, though styles were diverse, wore their hair "high and tight" and, for functions of health and cleanliness, had no body hair. As for armor and attire, the Cymry worked in fine silks, decorative crests denoting tribe, cantref (similar to our 'county'), sub-kingdom and nation. They wore a diverse range of battle arms, depending upon the situation. The ancient British were sophisticated and it was the Saxon who was bankrupt of culture, virtue, or God, in the Arthurian setting. That modern academia has turned this truth on its head is historical revisionism that would shock and anger any objective inquisitor.

For this piece, the writer has endeavored to have a balanced approach, combining fidelity to the linguistics, culture, places and names while at the same time providing some minor synonyms and modernity for ease of reading. This is primarily found in the use of the word Cymru, which is nowadays rendered "Wales". The term "Walles" is a Saxon pejorative that means "foreigner". This crude, if not callous and ingenious, form of racial imperialism whereby the invader renders the invaded as the "foreigner" remains a grave national insult to the ancient and glorious people of Wales. Thus, Wales is rendered as Cymru.

Other terms such as Britannia, the Isles of the Sea, and the Blessed Isles are also used. As for its people, "the Cymry" or "Britons" is used throughout the story.

The Vale of Glamorgan (South East Wales), named after King Arthur's son Morgan the Courteous, has been left in its modern form as such for ease of pronunciation by the reader.

With regard to personal names, it is important to understand that many Welsh names are titular, some are descriptive, and others given at birth. To fully bring forth the rich and powerful names in the Matter of Britain, the book toggles back and forth between nomenclature.

For example, in history Morgana Le Fay is Arthur's sister, Gwyar (mother of both Gawaine and Mordred). In the book, she is presented as either Gwyar or "Morgaine", depending upon the "circumstantial punch" needed.

Bedivere has been rendered Bedwyr and Guinevere as Gwenhwyfar. Gawaine will be found as Gwalchamai. Arthur is unchanged.

As for the historical model, this piece is set against the skeletal framework of the Arthur of Glamorgan and Gwent position, of which the greater portion seems, in light of current scholarship, to be most accurate.

At issue for uncovering the Historic King Arthur is not a lack of documentation, but an overabundance of it. Welsh translators and historians continue to release the outcomes of their labor, working from documents suppressed for centuries by British Authorities and the Vatican.

One of life's greatest joys is to travel to majestic, mysterious Wales and stand next to the sarcophagus of a person that the English claim "never existed".

'The shiny silver of armor. The errand of mounted knights. The mysteries of Britain. The famous Wizard and the Boy King. The Sword and the Cup. The romance and ideal of Camelot. The betrayal of a friend. The Grail Quest... All seduction veiled in grandeur – if not grounded in the word of truth. History and lore's most powerful lure to drag some, unwitting, into an old heresy dedicated to the premise that Jesus Christ is not God and in its aim the preparation of a watered down and inclusive world for a Second Messiah which is called Anti-Christ.'

Dr. Zane Newitt
Winter, 2016

PROLOGUE I
68 AD

Paul, the prisoner of the Lord and the apostle to whom was committed the simple good news of Christ and the dispensing of the Grace of God, desired greatly to journey to Britain: to preach unto the heathen and to the dispersed children of Israel who rejected the message of Peter during his administration (for, by divine accord and binding agreement, Paul could go to unbelieving Jews who were uncircumcised in heart and mind as well as to the Gentiles).

While yet under house arrest in the regal Palace Britannia, the Apostle grew to greatly love the Silures, the royal clan of the Britons who were fellow political prisoners of Rome.

King Caradoc, comely Eurgain, pious Linus and other Britons had become his dear brothers and sisters in the Lord; their conversation so Godly, in nationalism zealous, in wit fiery, and in kindness, of no equal. Paul yearned to see their homeland for reasons both emotional and theological, wanting to see the mettle of the nation who whipped Caesar and who would not yield to the imperialism of Rome.

The bloodlines that constitute the Britons, specifically the great Royal Clans of the Cymru and Lloegyr, are the resultant mixture of two major migrations; firstly, of Albyne, the daughter of Diocletian, from the Near East; and secondly of Brutus of Troy, after whom the Isles are most commonly named.

Add a sprinkling of Hebrews fleeing to both the Continent and the Islands during the second dispersion, and also as a result of Paul's terror upon the Messianic followers when he was yet Saul, and indeed the stock of Britain was a unique assortment.

A visit was important to him beyond cultural curiosity (for Paul was a man of letters and of culture, knowing how he ought to interact with Men from all parts of the known world). The divergent origins had produced dangerous doctrinal predispositions that greatly worried Paul.

The original Jewish immigrants did not bring the truth of the God of Abraham, Isaac and Jacob. Instead they were idolaters and progenitors of dark doctrines passed infectiously from their Babylonian and Assyrian captors. For their part, the British Isles became awash with the errors of dualism, relic worship, veneration of tradition, emanationism, angel worship and Gnosticism. The Jewish colonies had much stained their spiritual identity with devilish compromise and deep betrayal of their Most High God through the blending of truth and error, which is iniquity. They intermarried with the local tribes and, through intrigue and political maneuvering, became, over time, the wise men. In dress, identical to the native Druids; in manner of life, foreign to all that is called good.

Paul had dealt with the Traditions of the Fathers and their corrupt priesthood structure. He oft battled and overcame the tendencies towards legalism and reversion to the Law by his own countrymen. James, the brother of the Lord, had ever been his adversary, calling Paul a liar, and wicked, at every turn.

Moreover, Paul had masterfully deconstructed the empty conclusions of fatalism and nihilism, the folly of philosophers, effactually presenting the hope of the resurrection to atheists, Neo-Platonists and the pantheists of Greece. He possessed the ability to meet foe and friend alike on a common ground from which to share the truth of God's existence, power and love, even to those who exalted human intellect above all and who worshipped and adored the creature in the stead of the Creator.

To the aged Apostle, those campaigns seemed – at this he both laughed and sighed within – immeasurably less taxing than overcoming the superstition, idolatry, sincere confusion (for Peter's message was ministered to remnants of his little flock in the Isles in the Sea during Boadicea's war. Thus, Paul would take great caution to only visit those for purposes of fellowship, refusing to build upon another's foundation lest the saints increase in disappointment and confusion about the delay of their promised Kingdom), and sacred wisdom possessed by the Britons.

When thinking of the task at hand, Paul quickly reminded himself that it was the word of truth that did the saving – that he didn't need to help the Gospel, only to boldly preach it.

Years before his imprisonment and long before he had written to those at Rome, he had deployed his friend Aristobulus to the British Isles to teach the Pauline Mysteries. Now, at last, during his final season of liberty, Paul himself went to the British Isles.

Landing first upon the Isle of Wight, he then made the mainland, receiving great reception at the hill which is called Ludgate (each gate of the small port city of Londinium bore the name of a warrior, king or hero of great fame).

The Tribes of Lloegyr met and hosted Paul for a space of three months until, finally, thirty-five years after the Passion of the Lord Jesus Christ, Paul ventured to Cymru. There he found, amongst wondrous valleys, rolling hills and shades of green his eyes had never seen, the kingdom of his friends, the Silures.

Paul would even half-jest that Cymru was more beautiful than the third heaven, and Paul had now seen both.

Assembled within the crowded boat-shaped circle hewn into the earth, roofed only by the stars of heaven at the place called Llaniltud, Paul preached unto the Druids (of which there are two primary and several minor divergent sects), and unto the Kingdom Saints taught by Peter.

Mary, the Mother of the Lord, and her company, had reportedly stayed in Gaul for a time, then exiled herself on a tiny island to the west of the northern Isle called Ynys Mon, fearing that men would swear by her. However, Anna and many who had been with the man who provided his tomb for the Saviour were amongst those who came to hear Paul.

Doing all in his might, he labored to fill up that which they were lacking.

Paul preached Jesus Christ according to the revelation of the Mystery which was hidden in God since before the foundation of the world. Within its tenets were divided out those things which belonged to Israel versus those unique blessings and positions belonging to the heavenly body; under grace Christ became Man's sin and imputed His righteousness unto all Men, especially to those that believed, through the Cross. Man's flesh, being dead, therefore, could do nothing to please God. Thus was vanished the necessity of works. There was no tithing system for profiting, no ritual to be administered by priests, no levers of guilt and reward, only the simplicity of Christ reconciling the world unto Himself and the free offer of salvation on the merits of His shed blood.

Those with a Jewish ancestry rejected him with audible and violent rumblings, each and every one. The Druids listened with respectful contemplation as they do to all men, and then informed Paul: "Little Pause," as the Druids translated his Greek name, "we know already the secrets of the One True God."

To conclude his preaching, Paul warned against misappropriating the kingdom promises and principles that belonged to Israel (to her times past and to a time yet to come), and against reading Paul's good news back into the message of Peter and the Eleven. Paul focused on the 'but now' of human history where God was erecting a heavenly body with spiritual blessings.

Other than the kinsmen of the Silure and Princess Eurgain (who was also present), the Apostle's message was rejected by all save one Druid, a prince from the area of what history would call later call the Vale of Glamorgan.

Adjusting his white robe to cover the midnight-blue enamel-scaled breastplate so that it wouldn't bruise the old Apostle, he embraced Paul heartedly. The trees surrounding the circle funneled and intensified the clamor and debate, the wrangling. Saying nothing (for the embrace said what was required) save "so, then, faith cometh by hearing", the Druid hooded his robe, attempting to leave the starlit assembly.

Victory is not measured by numbers of converts, but by the quality of each convert and Paul knew that just one man could turn the world upside down – for good, or for ill. Paul used elbows and dodges to stop the Druid ere he was fully outside the Cor.

Thanking the armored warrior-priest, Paul gifted him fourteen single page letters, rolled and bound beautifully with camel leather and metallic buckles. The 'book', Paul fastened on the Druid's body using the straps of his own robe. With only minor protestations at the intrusion the Druid began to query Paul, but the Apostle placed a finger to his lips, staying his voice.

"In these letters are words that bring eternal life. Thirteen are to you and one is for you. Study." And now it was Paul who quickly left the Druid's side and returned to the center of the wooded meeting place.

Understanding the great potential for good, and for evil, of these coveted Isles just beyond the outstretched fingertips of Rome, as his last act before leaving Britain, Paul reached out to Anna, cousin of Mary, and begged the Cup that she bore.

Paul sized up the man who was of Anna's company: a kinsman of the Lord who bore a resemblance to the Saviour, yet with dishonest eyes. Paul did not like this man. Returning to Anna, he looked up at her, imploring: "They will worship the Grail at the expense of the One whose blood it bore. And there is no salvation in it to save them in their day of trouble."

The Jewess declined. "We will see that it remains guarded and, if meet, we shall hide it as we have the Lady and the coffin of the Law of Moses."

"Nay. Give me the Cup that I might destroy it."

"Nay," said Anna.

Eurgain raised her voice in an effort to support and help Paul but was put down swiftly.

"Nay," said Anna.

PROLOGUE II
484 AD

Regal, red and raging, the seven-tailed dragon orbited over the Blessed Isles, announcing his dominion o'er the white heaven above and the green earth below.

The head of the winged serpent was constant in flight, position unchanging. His seven tails, or rather one tail with seven spikes, moved in a chaotic dance, dragging behind and beneath the head, crackling in and out of the low cloud cover and making Christ-Mass morning a flash of yellows and reds, creating brightness as if there were two suns.

Merlin knew the stars, the luminaries, and their courses of traffic. His own little dwelling place, near a chapel outside the great mountain fortress of Caer Caradoc, provided a special high place for observation. Merlin cared for his ailing, elderly mother, with whom he dwelled, and had made haste early in the morning to ensure that she was well so he could spend the sum of the day posted near a large standing stone, just up the mountain from their home, and study the red serpent's path.

Leaning back, arms folded, head cocked to the right, the robed Druid said within himself: *A vision of perfection save the tail, which doth worry me.*

Meanwhile, another wonderful dragon was far too busy looking down to look up.

King Meurig, who was the Senior King, the Uther Pendragon, Protector of the Tribes and Royal Clans of the Cymru, and his young bride, Queen Onbrawst (a powerful woman, always of a soft and temperate disposition but one not to be crossed by scheming or dishonesty) were about to be delivered of a precious gift: their first son.

Kings held several plenary courts, manors and fortresses from which they managed their administrative, military, legal and residential responsibilities of governance. Often their Queens would live only in the residential manors, and sometimes alone, receiving their husbands to bed but periodically. However, this was at the discretion of the couple and there was no law or custom demanding the same.

With relative quiet (for Saxon invasions were rare in winter), other than the shared trauma and turmoil of a first pregnancy, they spent most of the winter in their residential mansion in the South East of Cymru. The men of the Cymru loved their wives and, from beggar of lowest station to king of the purest royal lineage, the great majority of couples were friends, partners and protectors of their spouses; the union was considered sacred.

The couple mutually enjoyed the manor, as it had family ties for Onbrawst and was very near to where Meurig had received his schooling as a boy.

The mansion home was near the coast but

securely surrounded by a small ring of fortress watchtowers that could, through the sparking of a simple fire, send an alarm through a spiderweb of interlocking towers in a matter of seconds. Merlin had designed this and many other ringed fortress 'webs' that, like interlocking wheels, provided maximum protection with minimum investment of the Cymry's most valuable resource: its men.

From the most ancient times the place had been called Caer Bovum, which is "the Fortress of the Bull.". The palace's position and name, like many of the Mysteries of the Druids, had multiple meanings. Looking down from the ceiling of heaven, Caer Bovum aligned identically with the most prominent star within the constellation Taurus.

Unfamiliar or apathetic to this fact, to King Meurig and Queen Onbrawst it was simply their favorite place of dwelling; romantic, near the sea, full of memories and love.

"What troubles you, my son?"

Even with Merlin sitting poorly postured against the monolith, he towered above his mother, standing before him, offering him a cider and a concerned, maternal reckoning.

"You should be resting." Merlin's smile blended great respect with a little grumble of interruption. But he welcomed the scrumpy sup. "I can follow its course, can tell with great certainty that this great portent will traverse far to the East, turn on itself and return once more to our land. I believe I can even predict the timing of its return."

"One more time we shall have such a visitor, brighter than the noonday Sun! That is joyous, my jeweled prince! Why such pause?"

"In the dragon's grandeur, dancing along heavenly skies, no looking glass known to man, nor any means of divination, of science or observation, can know the detailed form of his ethereal body. We can see it flying far, far up there." Merlin drew its path with his left hand upon a firmament canvas of nothing. "Especially on clear winter nights and on mornings when the mists recoil. But now that it is within the heavens where the birds fly, this dragon's tail has at least one broken spike and should it prick the earth below, I know not what it would do to creaturekind and land alike; nor can I allow myself to imagine thusly. The position of the dragon's head is perfect and will herald the birth of our future High King. Pray that the tail touches not the earth."

Merlin was a man who taught and spake mostly by riddles, and his candor and plainness of speech worried his mother. Due to his sober expression, she too now hoped that Merlin's foretold dragon would light up the Christ-Mass sky, but then be quickly away safely to its starry home.

Morning became midday and the comet passed safely over the kingdoms of Western Britain, to great celebration of Merlin's prophecy. However, tragically, one small splinter of the comet's tail did fall out of formation and touch down just to the east of the center of the Isle in the kingdom called Lloegyr (tribes and clans who were of the same blood as the Cymry).

Where the comet touched, men melted within themselves and all life died, the land becoming at once a great wasteland. Only a small share of the Island was affected. The spike of the dragon's tail singed a border between East and West. For tribes and small kingdoms within the shadow of the tail's touch, a pestilence and disease took first the virility of the men and livestock, followed by their lives.

Merlin saw only a small mushroom of dust and yellow-hued clouding far to the east. Far and away from the kingdom he served, he hoped against hope that none perished. When the pomp of Meurig's firstborn's entrance into the world of Men had abated, Merlin would go and investigate and warn his people of what might happen if the tail of the dragon made direct impact with the kingdom of the Silures on its next visitation, which Merlin knew to be fifty and three years from the day of his first visit.

And thus, on the day of the Christ-Mass, under the banner of a Red Dragon, under the Sign of the Bull, was born King Arthur, the Bear of Britain.

PROLOGUE III
An Ancient Rite

"My cock works fine, My Heart, I just can't fight anymore." Meurig, trying to suppress panic, eyes begging confirmation of worth, clasped Queen Onbrawst's fingers.

It is a timeless tactic, primal and dark, practiced by all Nations and Tribes save the Cymry: to pierce the king or an important chieftain through his loins with a spear, arrow or sword poisoned with a special concoction that destroys his virility; with his virility the perceived fertility of the Land; and with the perceived fertility of the Land, his Crown. And, should a drought follow, even his life.

Even with the Saviour come four hundred and ninety-eight years now, the Tribes and Clans held fast to this custom, fully believing that yield and harvest were connected to he who was head of the Dragons (High King). The same practice applied for he who held the Spear of Lugh in Eire.

A raid near the northern borderlands in Gwynedd (far from the King's palace in Glamorgan) had escalated the need for Meurig's personal presence. It was alleged that one of the

Sons of Cunedda (the Royal Clans of the North of Cymru) was under suspicion for treacherously giving the Saxon raiders passage, in exchange for future conquered land in the South. The metallic anxiety of civil war was in the air, heightened by burgeoning raids.

Whether by chance or by design, a young Saxon found the King's thigh before any investigation amongst his own Countrymen could occur.

A Saxon chief and Witan (member of the loose Germanic Confederation's High Council) called Hortwulf had slain Meurig's father, King Tewdrig, also during a raid, with a fortuitous spear. Now the horde seemed on the verge of celebrating the killing of a second Pendragon.

It was not to be so; Meurig lived.

Bloodied and soiled as if he were a spring lamb baptized in shepherd's dye, the midnight-blue under-tunic of the proud King was now black and thick with his own blood.

Returning to Caer Bovum at last, to his great bed with Onbrawst kneeling by and cradling his head with her shoulders while giving him both hands, the King managed to cough up familiar words often heard when emergencies and distresses were escalated.

"Bring me the Merlin."

Merlin, with two healers, began to address the poisoned wound.

"You are not here for nursing."

"No?" The towering Druid stood and yielded, yet motioned for the women to continue their work.

"No, not for nursing, for politics." The King

coughed a broken expulsion from the deepest part of his lungs. "It is early spring and I am felled. The people will want a sacral, but the young Bear is only fourteen. He is too young."

"Do you think the crops rise and fall with your loins, my lord?"

Meurig mustered a laugh, always puzzled at Merlin's moments of sacrilege against any and all faiths (but 'twas the humor that accompanies respect, not disdain).

"I don't know, but the people believe so."

"Too long have we labored to unite the South with you two," Merlin started, winking at Onbrawst. Their marriage was strategically ingenious. It enjoined the kingdom of Gwent with the lands of Gwrgan Fawr, the lord of Ergyn. This fused together the great Royal Clans of the Silures, the Island's most powerful tribe.

One people under one future king under one purpose.

Kingdom matchmaking aside, Meurig and Onbrawst were no political pawns. Rather, the people enjoyed the glow and shine of living in a country where their leaders were actually and passionately in love.

"Your son has experienced a season of fostering in the North with Cai, has had three winters here in Llaniltud and has already forged key relationships in Nevern in the West, in Powys and in the Midlands. At this moment, he is dazzling friend and foe on the field of battle in Little Britain, aiding our kin and becoming a young man of renown. He is well embraced by all of the Britons. The spark in that boy is brighter than the comet that hailed his birth!

The crown must not pass to an uncle, nephew or cousin. Nor can we split the High Kingship into King and Wledig. No. The wave of war coming to these Isles demands a Pendragon, even if he is but fourteen, to lift and engage the spirit of the nation."

Merlin sent the healers away and drew closer.

"As you are Christian, you may consider retirement as did your father Tewdrig, in the stead of the Sacral Rites." Merlin was a hard man in matters of military strategy, soft and conciliatory as a friend. "I am so sorry that you will not officially wield sword and spear again, my friend. But we need you. We need your wisdom and your council and your love. Retirement, and not sacrifice, my Lord."

Meurig now felt the rush of an involuntary stream of tears run at once from his left eye. He blinked repeatedly. He preferred death in battle to the hermitage he faced; but in the end he concurred with the Druid's words.

Three days later King Meurig, under his own power, was able to stand a little and move around of his own accord. The high thigh wound severed many nerves where the leg attached to his pubis bone. This caused his weight to shift to his knee and calf on the wounded side, resulting in a low, awkward limp.

Clumsily, he made his way to a dining hall where he sat for a cider with Merlin.

The conversation regarding his office and successor resumed, less emotional and more head-driven after three days of rest and healing.

"He is so young. How will they accept him?"

"It is Spring." Merlin paused and posited his

face for an uncomfortably intrusive query. "Did your boy's eyes and heart fall upon any damsel whilst at school?"

"Would a teenaged boy tell his parents of schoolyard love, Lord Merlin?" Onbrawst was always inserting wisdom and wit – a truly timeless Queen, and mother.

"He is a virgin then?" Merlin's cheeks crimsoned at the asking.

"What does that have to do with a young man's eyes or heart?" Meurig bellowed with laughter. "Rather to worry about his loins!"

That Meurig could muse about what was now an unmentionable subject informed the Druid that either the poison in the King's male parts failed or that he had come to terms with it. Either way, Merlin reckoned Meurig to be a remarkable man.

"Stop, you. And he is surely pure, but don't speak of it again!" scolded Onbrawst. Upon further contemplation, she added: "Well, he had puppy-eyes over some dark little thing for a while. He and that treetop-tall whelp from Gwynedd whispered about her more than a few times." Onbrawst's humor, which matched her husband's, returned. "Meurig and I used to think it odd that he doted on one that looked so much like his sister."

Merlin consumed that information. He then repeated, "It is Spring. And this is my recommendation." The Druid requested more drink, which he consumed in two swallows. "There will be no sacral rites. You will offer your sword to the Llyn Fawr, and your kingship will die."

Words hard to utter.

"But the young Bear will rise in your death of retirement. He will be the primary actor in the Spring rites, he will hunt the White Stag to show his virility and strength, and then he will join his spirit with the land through the Sacred Rite." Merlin paused to interpret the expressions of the boy's parents.

Queen Onbrawst's visage was as that of any parent confronted with the thought of their child having intercourse. That it would be in a ritualistic context layered shame atop shock. Merlin wanted to provide words of comfort, but Meurig's unspoken gestures made it clear that the effort would be vain and that he should just press on with the information. "Get on with it, Wizard" might have been said, or at least heard, by the Merlin.

"The rites will appease our countrymen, who yet cleave to the old gods while we continue our gestation as a Christian nation. If Arthur returns from Brittany now, this can all be done in perfect coordination with both the rites of Spring and with the Pentecost celebrations, letting him come on the scene with pomp and ceremony to bring joy to men of both faiths.

That your boy, the Bear, was born on Christmas day and announced by a heavenly messenger will satisfy the sign of his coming. Add to it the timing of his ascent and they will in no way refuse him on account of his youth."

Meurig agreed, but still doubted. "Will this ritual alone convince men that they should have a Boy King, Merlin?"

"It will go far, but not of itself."

"What more?" asked Onbrawst.

Merlin's thoughts again returned to the sad deeds soon at hand relative to his friend's abdication of crown and glory. He placed a comforting hand upon the King's forearm.

"What more? A Sword. You have a sword to return to the waters and I have a sword to go and raise from the same, my Lord," said Merlin.

Meurig first went up to Llyn Fawr. He wore simple beige clothing with just two or three golden torques looped round his arms and a tight leather band about his neck. Scarred but handsome; humble.

The injured Pendragon struggled to maneuver around but managed at last several paces into the lake. The cold still waters were now disturbed, splashing upon his wool tunic in protest.

Meurig winced when the short waves lapped over his injury; the war wound was ablaze in returned protest. The water and the wound worked in concert to afflict the day, but he appreciated the pain as it reminded him of the validity of his purpose. He could not defeat the coming horde; the people could not place their trust in a lame King. Focusing hard, he prepared himself.

Then he saw her.

A nearby swan-shaped barge undulated gently, docile and lazy upon the lake. Next to it was a platform that led deep down to a mysterious cavern beneath the Lake. Turtles circled the barge and diverse birds made symphony above.

Accompanied by percussion and strings played not by the hands of men, the Lady of the Lake rose from the waters.

Hair as late summer straw, bound with golden crown plated with hundreds of diamond-beaded threads. In blinding brilliance, she shone from the diamonds kissing the face of the water and the diamonds glistening in alternating notes within her headpiece. Add to this the rays of sun drawn to her dress and the Lady was as a luminary being, a star resting upon the center of the Lake.

Through the light, the drawn back locks revealed a long neck, freckled cheeks and a pointed, simple nose resting upon thin upper and thicker lower lips. Her eyes were soft, light blue, and sparkling.

She wore white-scaled armor made of a light, unknown material that seemed like leather but with some metal composition. Around the armor flowed a silky white garment with pillowed sleeves and hand pieces of samite.

Her declaration was as though the waters themselves were sing-speaking, projected towards the King by the acutely directed winds.

"Paramount King Meurig. Greeting. You are a great king, a dear friend, an encouraging and selfless father and, above all things, you love your wife as you love yourself. The Clans, Tribes, Cantrefs, Kingdoms and Nation of Cymru give you our deepest thanksgiving.

"I accept your return of the agency of your power and throne to the source of all life under God's creation. From the waters first He called forth life and to the waters your life now returns. This in an honorable rite. May the Lord of heaven and our great goddess guide and succor your next life cycle. Meurig, cast me your sword."

Meurig's sword was resting upon both palms. He looked at the shaft that had been his ever companion throughout a generation of war and unavoidable bloodshed. It was not customary for him to speak during this ceremony, for the dead ought not to speak. The hilt he clasped hard with his left hand and he slung the blade high, arching end over end.

The Lady of Llyn Fawr the sword did catch, and she retreated into the lake, seamlessly, leaving only the barge, and silence.

Meurig was officially abdicated, retired as High King of the Britons.

Next, a short time later, the Merlin of Britain visited the same location. While he was at Llyn Fawr seeking a far more unique weapon from the one who possessed the authority to give and to repossess it, he was wholly unaware of the details and arrangement for the Spring rites. And most acutely, who would be selected to represent the Land and the Moon as Arthur's counterpart in the ceremony.

A sixteen-year-old, petite, with raven's hair and the eyes of a Persian cat, was chosen. Local whispers declared her possessed at times or rather having some mysterious accord with a goddess, or even with the primal witch. Though promised to Llew son of Cynfarch, she was in her office for this deed anon and she was indeed a virgin. And that innocence she would give as a willing actor in the theatre of sacred fornication to validate a too-young king; for she, though yet sixteen, was a radical patriot.

And, though of royal blood, never at any of the three courts but ever at Llyn Fawr, elsewise on Ynys Mon, or tending the orchards in the Isle of Apples.

Some say she was only fostered by mortals.

Some say she was of the Fae....

CHAPTER 1
A Typical Raid

The brave warriors of the Trinovates were in pursuit of German raiders, following them from the eastern shores north into Iceni territory.

It was the Lord's Day and the village was unprepared, caught unawares. Though they did give chase well, the lay army forgot to leave a rear guard band in position for a second wave. The Saxon diversion worked and the village was left defenseless.

A woman's station in military matters was as diverse and numbered as the Tribes. In several Tribes they were raised to fight alongside the men and were equally lethal in combat. In others, they assumed more domestic roles. In all Tribes, women owned property, enjoyed rights of inheritance and were active in commerce and trade.

In this particular Tribe, the men were giving chase and the women were very brave but simply were not fighters; neither were the elderly, nor the children.

A flat platform boat kissed and hissed and crackled against the pebbly shore.

And then another; a third and a fourth.

A girl of twelve, holding a straw-made doll wrapped in green plaid wool of remarkable skill and craftsmanship, didn't want to look up at the pungent heap of tar- and dung-smeared muscles with hair arching over her. The Saxon's double-headed ax beneath her chin made forced their eyes to meet.

His dirty fingernails raked flesh with garment as he tore her clothes, and then tore her. Blood and innocence were spilled right there on the pebbles, with only seagulls to scream protest. Her brother came sprinting to her aid, ghostly white, now the witness of things none so young, or old, or any person at all, ought to see.

That invaders take time mid-battle to rape and violate is but befuddling on the surface. In truth, it makes every sense. For what is invasion but the imposition of will?

Invasion is rape, in every way.

To mock the boy's horror the Saxon twisted the boy's arm, turned him over a felled dead tree along the beach, yanked his trousers about his ankles, bent him over, and punished him without mercy from behind. The boy screamed a deathly rattle, but the scream only encouraged more. And yet his young sister, during her identical torture, had given not a sound. That the boy rewarded the villain with his screams whilst the girl did not infuriated him.

She just lay upon an elbow on her side, with a glazed, dead look in eyes that should have been alight with life.

Seeing the object of her torture, covered with blood (while two hundred more invaders were sprinting and many others engaged in like deviancy) at her eye level, the distant eyes at once regenerated. With the bravery of her glorious ancestor Boudica, the freshly violated twelve-year-old girl swung at it with a large branch. The blow to his groin dropped the Saxon; the siblings stood and rallied, sprinting for the village.

But too soon, the Saxon rallied also.

Much faster than the children, he caught their stride quickly and shoved them both down violently, but three feet from the village chapel door. A simple circular structure with a modest cruciform hewn through the eastern wall, the humble wooden building was warm, friendly, welcoming and nearly salvation for the ruined children.

Locked in their own private war, the freckled siblings did not notice that the chapel was ablaze from the hinder side and that women and old men were being butchered sloppily. There was no precision in the killings, only malice and barbarism.

The brave girl stood again, blood and urine glazing and painting her naked thighs.

"You cannot kill us!" She screamed with authority at the Saxon until her voice was nearly gone.

He understood none of these things. Her Brythonic language was an affront, profane ringing in his Germanic ears.

"You cannot kill us," she rasped. "We are not soldiers. Our elders teach that soldiers only kill other soldiers. You cannot kill us."

Whether he deduced some of her meaning, and her impugnation of his cowardice, or whether he simply grew tired of her screaming, he thought to stop her tongue by removing her brother's.

The grimy man with poorly made black leather armor jerked the wailing boy up by his hair and clasped his jaw so tightly that the lad had no other choice but to open it; teeth were cracking and falling from the side of his mouth, causing the tortured boy to bleed, now from both ends. Gasping, his tongue waggled out.

The Saxon swiftly dropped his axe and drew a dagger and cut, nay sawed, the boy's tongue off; then he made a mechanical turn down and to the left, showing the trophy to the resilient heroine. Now tears came as she looked upon her brother, but she remained brave to the end. She arched her back and found the black eyes of the Boar, whispering with the residue of her voice.

"In the West Country, far from here, lives a great king. Some day, be it today or ten years from today, he will send all of you bad men home, or into the ground. He will avenge us. He will save our people!" She found one more scream within her mighty and shattered soul. "*King Arthur!*"

The Saxon knew this name, as did any living at the time, in any language. The double-headed axe cleaved her forehead, leaving a red-haired and green-ribboned scalp upon the ground. The brute yanked the green ribbon from the lifeless locks it complemented, a trophy of his conquest and power-mad perversion.

In addition to murder of the defenseless, the Saxons raped old women and children, and committed sins against nature with horses and sheep.

The party of male warriors later returned from

what they believed to be a successful expulsion and small skirmish to a village charred black, bodies stacked and burned. Some had been burned alive and then thrown into a nearby pond, for the invaders to watch the screams of "hot then cold". Those bodies floated, bubbled skin and eyeballs separating from the corpses.

To be raided on the eastern shores of Britain, even now giving way to the phrase "Saxon Shores", was not a light matter, nor a political matter, nor a controversy. It was cancer, an open and overt cancer seeking to devour and remove the existence of a People Group from the earth, forever.

And although it was only in the early years of the Saxon Wars, it was already moving west.

CHAPTER 2
The Battle of Mynydd Baeden and Waiting

Several years, eleven major battles and over sixty minor clashes later, a brisk December dusk found the Round Table knight, selected by lot for the aridity of waiting alongside his king.

And waiting yet more.

The strategy demanded waiting.

Finally breaking the long silence, seeking to ease the moment with his best friend, he said: "What chance has a boar versus a bloodhound and a bear made of iron?"

Arthur gave no answer.

The Iron Bear above, the Bloodhound Prince below.

Merlin was right; even the ignorant heart of the Saxon can be crippled through the use of terror. Merlin was also absent.

The mighty King Arthur's horse, a mare called Llamrei, jostled restlessly beneath him, sensing the uneasy rhythm of her master unsuccessfully laboring to stare stoically at the mound called Baeden.

Arthur's thoughts flinched, even if his face did not betray it. The terror inflicted, the thrashing of enemies along trails and in gullies in the valley of Maesteg that opened up below Baeden hill, the escalating brass of screams as hungry men with foreign tongues died within ear-shot did not give the just King pleasure. But he yearned for when it was finished; it would give the nation peace.

The three nations of Germania were finally come, setting aside intrigue, false witness and the cowardice of raiding to face him in his very own lands as upright men, as an upright army. Should these three hundred thousand invaders have calculated that The Ravens from the North would flank and funnel them through a field of slaughter… That Maelgwn and his famous blood-soaked Hosts would use unconventional tactics to establish a rear guard position that forced the invader to either ascend up Baeden Hill on foot to face a heavily clad, well-fed, professional equestrian army led by Arthur, or instead face the Bloodhound Prince in the valley below, or lastly, hold their ground and starve… Should they have known of this triad of doom masked as choice, they would have greatly preferred the death of the cruel winter and famine plaguing their homeland and simply stayed home.

The Western Sea feeds the heads of three great rivers that converge near the battle site. The winds press upon the confluence, regularly producing a thick and ethereal mist, as it did this day, creating a shadowy canopy over the whole of the valley. Arthur and his knights had to peer down the slope, and could see only shadows, and glimpses of blackened snow below.

The screams of the Saxons made many of the mounted cavalry atop the hill retch. Others were moved to forget the discipline of a Cymry warrior. Bloodlust overcame them, and these abandoned the ranks and joined the battle below.

As Merlin had mentored Arthur on the power of both words and song, the King countered the influence of the death cries with melodic Bardic songs and hymns of victory, attempting, through polarity, to neutralize the field. Moreover, the leadership of Awwn Ddu, Owain the Raven, and Arthur's young son, Llacheu, held tight the line of restless warriors.

The strategy required that they remain still, and still they remained.

This was no easy feat. The full complement of the British confederacy numbered twenty-four groups of three thousand. They were positioned throughout the interlocking wheels of fortresses that sprawled like a great tent over the whole of the seven cantrefs of Glamorgan and several thousand warriors lined the top of Baeden in groups three lines deep.

"Hold!" bellowed through the mist. Horses expelled their breath in concert, and here and there one complained with a whinny. If a Saxon raised his dreary eyes above the shelf of mist, he would see a quilt of wonderfully colored killing instruments, each defined first by their royal clan and secondly their tribe.

The Silures, the Royal Clan of the South East, maintained with careful and studious pride the traditions of their ancestors and donned an efficient armor, gilded in midnight-blue enamel, designed for speed, defense, and killing while mounted. Upon their shields were the double chevrons. The northern tribes wore black like ravens, or black and red, had a single chevron and were less armored than their kinsmen from the South.

A marriage by Queen Marchel, aunt to Arthur, to an Irish King called Coronac had ended Irish raiding and produced a sub-kingdom in the South through Marchel's son, Brychan. This brought Arthur's Irish allies to Baeden, whose warriors dressed in speckled green.

King Hoel from Brittany, familial allies with the Silures for generations, carried a brilliant blue plaid, honoring their heritage from the Silures.

Banners, flags, plaids and colors of many other tribes from the remnants of Lloegyr to the Midlands were also present.

Each warrior attached a small dark blue shield to the left shoulder; engraved upon the shield was the image of the Woman, sometimes called "The Compromise of Arthur". Although she was the Mother of the Lord, the artistry and style of the image left her identity vague. Though he revered her greatly, the King left her identity to the individual's perception and perspective and beyond that, spake of it not.

Trumpet, drum and stringed instrument continued and singing was perpetual. The Saxons battling below were at all times surrounded by sounds of triumph and power in a language they knew not but understood nevertheless.

The tongue of the Cymru; the language of heaven.

"Hold now!"

"Steady, brethren!"

Had Merlin calculated the taxation of waiting? King Arthur peered left, then right, surveying his men.

"Have you found him, Urien?"

"I find him not." Urien had been charged to abandon the battle and to find Merlin who, as one of Arthur's three principal counselors (and the young King's closest friend save Bedwyr), would not be truant for the sentinel event of his people's history, lest it be by some as yet unknown treachery.

Urien, younger than Arthur but already with two strong teenaged warriors dominating the fields, was in a foul mood as his oldest, Prince Owain, would bathe in much killing while he was out hunting for an old Wizard.

"Then again to it," said Arthur, who now fiddled with the hilt of his legendary sword.

Excalibur would saturate the soil with Saxon blood soon enough. The strategy was to wait. The young King, not yet thirty and three, and (were it not for retirement caused by injury), not even the most senior king in his own household, used the pains of pause to reflect on the strategy.

The strategy…

CHAPTER 3
The Strategy

Across the stone bridge o'er the Usk River, a short ride northeast leads to the walled megalopolis that includes Caerwent and Caerleon.

Protected by the hilltop fortress called Lodge Hill (the ingenious design of which made it so that just two watchmen could survey the whole of the Vale of Glamorgan. Also, the place most frequented by Arthur himself when he desired solitude), in the heart of the city, surrounded by springs and natural baths, assembled all the great companions of Arthur's Britain in a great circular amphitheater.

They were come to his court for official discourse, debate and preparation for the battle of Baeden, only two night's winks hence.

It being a bitter December night, the hard cider, drink of the Cymry Warrior, was replaced with spiced wine that was prepared in large iron casks and stirred slowly, producing a pop, sizzle and hiss that contributed to the symphony of Bardic song, loud clamorous debate, a dash of laughter and not a few of the lewd words that are precursor to pugilism.

The great Royal Clans sat in a circle within the amphitheater, no one tribe greater than the next. The kings and princes, with their Bishops, Druids and women of renown, formed the second ring. Each king had twelve Bards (Maelgwn brought twenty-four) forming the third ring. Behind them, and arranged by rank or by role, were the warriors. Some clans and tribes had professional warriors and others served both as farmers and spearmen. Depending upon the local tribe, the landowners who were not warriors formed the outmost ring.

There were no slaves amongst the Britons. All men were deemed of royal descent as sons of Brutus, and the purpose of a king was to administrate, not dominate, the people. To this all kingdoms, to include Powys, Morgannwg, Dyfed, Gwynedd and Deheuarth, agreed in each of their several customs and ancient laws.

The kingdoms in Eastern Britain, collectively called Lloegyr, depleted in times past by Roman treachery and recently by key losses during the Saxon Wars, also sent what remained of their armies and joined the rings of attendees arranged by their customs.

There were no Picts present at Baeden or the preceding councils, for Maelgwn Gwynedd trusted them not (though they would have him to be king over them).

Lastly, at the very center, there was one circle, inside even the ring of the kings and Bishops (although this circle could, from time to time, include both).

The circle was a great stone table with golden and brass rivets, a set of six interlocking rings crewed by four knights apiece that formed one large round circle with a small circle of one with two seats in the very center. And each of the locking rings or circles could both rotate, and orbit. Thus, twenty-four knights plus Arthur and Maelgwn were seated at the Round Table (a table of the same design was found in a place called Cwbbor at Caermelyn, Arthur's legislative court). The Knights had arranged their seating to show the people that how they met privately matched the manner in which they spoke openly: nothing was held back from the armies, or from the public.

As dusk gave way to nightfall and all guests were assembled, Arthur's father, the Uther Pendragon, stilled the fighting, fellowship and song, bringing the conference to order.

With a booming, deep and paternal projection that filled the whole of the amphitheater, he said: "Blessings and welcome, kinsmen."

As Uther addressed the assembly, King Arthur, a young man with a sense of his own place in history, stepped outside of himself. He looked upon the special collection of thousands of Britons and considered, *There are not enough Bards, books or scribes to record the deeds and constitution of the heroes, and perhaps villains, who stand here.*

In this time, this perilous time, this special dispensation of radical change and radical courage, he thought, *I am not great. Rather, I am surrounded by the convergence of greatness.*

Pious bishops such as Bedwini, Illtud and Dyfrig (who would pray over the armies), mystical women with the power to command men's hearts, minds and loins, sat or stood side by side with the men; Onbrawst, Marchel and Vivien amongst them.

Catching a glimpse of his father, Arthur stood and then reseated and swiveled back towards the center of the Round Table to hear the Uther Pendragon articulate the agenda to the gathered stadium of Britons.

Meurig, the "Wonderful Head of the Dragons", wore brilliant blue enamel armor and held his helmet (blue and silver with red horse hair, similar to the Roman style but closer in fit and shape to a Corinthian helmet; molded and tightly formed to the face of the warrior) securely beneath his left shoulder. Though retired for a decade and eight years, this red-caped Silure Warrior was yet fierce to look upon and few would desire to combat him, wounded or whole.

"Three are the topics for homily tonight, kinsmen and allies.

"Merlin has crafted a battle strategy that differs from our campaigns in the North. Never before has the Long Knife [the term, in addition to "The Boar", most ascribed to the invaders] consolidated for a singular assault so near our capital and strongholds. As Merlin will explain, we have let them come this far west with minimal resistance by design.

"Second: we will discuss a policy for Saxon residency after our victory with options ranging from expatriation to annihilation. Or, for those with merciful disposition, grants of citizenship after the ninth generation may be considered."

Any notion of quarter resulted in expected grumbles. However, Saxon settlements had already been long established in the East and no Briton would uproot and kill innocent children now born in Britain (albeit with foreign blood), without first exhausting all other considerations.

"And lastly, after military and political discussion, my oldest companion and advisor Dyfrig will look to the care of our souls, praying for the armies, the families and our nation. Then, when finished, shall the Bishops discuss the mode of Baptism and the Saxon policy for worship and congregational membership."

All of a spiritual ilk knew that the mode of baptism for Saxons that survived Baeden was just another thorn to prick the ceaseless quarrel between the new Religion of Romanism, which was gaining some following, and the long established British Primitive Church. The doctrinal differences were minor, save one, the ceremonial differences vast (and the disputes and fighting over them, vicious and often violent).

The one doctrine that could be taken advantage of, could undo a nation, was the belief and practice that kings give great portions of land to the Church of the Britons near retirement or death (or after some great sin). As only the Royalty were allowed to be clergy, this maneuver was a shell game; a means of doing penance whilst securing land influenced by a patriotic Bishop's family or tribe, forever.

The Catholics had no such demand for gifts of land or property, no need for a "mansion given here or a mansion given up there". Rather, and more overarchingly, they interpreted that the True Church possessed temporal power to occupy all land it touched anyhow, until the Lord come again. Thus they made treaties, behaving more like a government than an ecclesiastical body, whereby converted church land would be absorbed and owned by Rome, whilst private holdings would be left to sovereignty of the land holders.

Because the British Church held such large and strategically located tracts and grants of land, conversion to the popular Roman Religion was, to some, the equivalent of giving away Britain to Rome.

Meanwhile, the Druids, Gnostics and those who followed the paths of old gods also had a place at the 'round table' to discuss their concerns and the survival of their faiths, waxing old like a garment thrown to the rear of a closet, well in the shadow of rising Christendom.

After three songs moved the assembly into an animated spirit, it was time for Merlin to speak.

Gwenhwyfar ferch Cwyrd of Gwent strode awkward with a bobble and a hobble. No longer upright with shoulders down and bosom proud, she held her left elbow fixed and her head tilted, a woman whose very body bore the outworking of the grief within her broken spirit. With a morose tug to the King's elbow, Gwenhwyfar took her seat next to Arthur. Though garlanded in an emerald dress to match her foresty eyes, she may as well have worn the widow's black at all times. Truly the Queen was a crimson-haired white phantom.

"How many will come home, Bear?" spake a wife and mother, dead though she lived and beyond consolation. No soft oratory by husband, priest, kin or king could comfort the shattered and shadowed heart of a widow, yet worse than the widow, for she had not been robbed of a husband before his season; rather, taken from her were sons.

"Only Llacheu will fight at Baeden, Gwen. Amr has already been sent North, part of the ancillary units to prevent scatter raiding. He is with his cousin at Ynys Mon and not called to the fight." Arthur was a soft and sensitive man. Gentle. His voice broke twice as he tried to say, "If I could do more –"

The Queen, who possessed no other natural station than to be a mother, stayed his speech and tried to be understanding whilst the madness continued to rise in the tide of her eyes. "Our nation sends boys to war at fourteen and princes must be willing to do that which they expect of their men." The response was cold, but the soft kiss upon Arthur's brow warm. "I cannot endure talk of war and religion this night, sweetheart. I have greeted those whose pride needed greeting and the requirements of hospitality are met. I am leaving now."

Gwenhwyfar departed from Arthur.

In her crippled walk, long ceasing to be regal, she found Merlin ten or twelve rows up from Arthur. She pulled him into an arched corridor.

"I am a Christian Lady, Lord Merlin. Two of my boys sleep in the ground at the Long Knife's hand. I am a Christian Lady, Lord Merlin." The Queen was several spans under Merlin's great height yet somehow, in this moment, with eyes on the same level, she peered into the old Wizard's face. "Whatever dark arts will protect my boys – do them."

Merlin gave a strange answer that none heard

save Queen Gwenhwyfar, only it seemed her countenance fell yet further.

Whispers rumored of Merlin acting most peculiar of late.

Arthur gave a last look upon Gwenhwyfar as she evaporated in a sea of kinsmen.

The inner rings within a ring rotated outward from the center to the North, South, East and West, creating a singular point within the circle from which Merlin could address all seated in the amphitheater.

Starting from the corridor where he conversed with the Queen down to the center, two rows formed, making an archway of men; one side with sword, one with flame. To onlookers it appeared that, from any vantage or position, the hooded Druid walked beneath an escort of flaming scepters, making his way with supernatural authority to the center of the Round Table.

"The old man gets more pomp than I do!" Old Meurig was famous for his humor and mused privately with a poke to his wife, the great Queen Onbrawst. "I brought the lad into the world, not Mer–"

"You paced around, stumbling over oak barrels half drunken on cider; I brought the boy into the world of men, my love. Your work to beget Arthur was much shorter in duration than mine." Onbrawst was always equal to the task when a verbal joust was at hand, and she kissed her husband hard upon the lips. The retired monarch's warmth could thaw the most frigid of winters. "Now listen to the Merlin, love," she concluded.

"What is greater than eleven?" Merlin opened.

None of the several thousand attendees knew how they ought to answer a man wiser than Solomon and endowed with a wit and propensity for riddle. Even young Taliesin the Bard opened his mouth to speak, cocked his head and shut it once more, declining response.

King Arthur felt no intimidation, for he knew well that when Merlin appeared to say something complicated, his aim was, in reality, simplicity.

"What is greater than eleven, Lord Merlin, is –" Arthur counted his fingers with a grin "– twelve."

A smile, revealing he was pleased, curled. Merlin became a pointed nose with a grin and no eyes, like a wrinkled squash. "And the Iron Bear is…" The pregnancy of Merlin's pause caused all to lean forward, whether seated or afoot. "Correct!"

Merlin looked up at the assembly with a laugh, chased soon by a scold. "Now don't go a-roaring with mindless yawps yet, Britons. You know not why he answered as he did." Merlin smiled once more and then changed temperament to a serious and proud tone.

"Eleven times we have met the Long Knife in battle. With apologies and grace to those honorable progeny who remain and are amongst us, Vortigern the traitor brought the Boar here. He slew our Northern Princes through intrigue. He was hunted down and butchered by the great Wledig, Ambrosious…" Ambrosious and Merlin had been friends, closer than brothers, and when the great battle leader died he bade Merlin move North to Dinas Emrys to manage his own estates. Upon the death of Merlin's mother, this he did. "…And by Uther Pendragon, with the allied support and skill of the spear of Budic and Hoel, our kinsmen across the sea in Little Britain.

"Eleven times we have soaked our native land in the Boar's blood. The Long Knife has crept in unawares through the Northern Kingdoms. They have slashed through the forests of Caledonia, have met us on water and in marsh.

"Three campaigns spanning twenty years, eleven major battles and countless minor raids. Eleven!" Now Merlin raised the clenched fist of victory, his robe falling down his arm but a little, revealing two very old blue serpents, painted forever into his skin. At the erection of his victorious arm, the assembled royal clans of the Britons broke into a deafening cheer that could be heard two cantrefs away.

"Eleven!" Merlin returned his clenched fist to join his right hand upon his staff and the crowd's roar ceased.

"A War King was needed to guide you, proud heroes, to corral your interests of Self and put our survival above ambition. Ambitions of cloth and o'er men's souls. Ambition of lands and of quests. We live in an Age of Saints, of gilded warriors. It was imperative that we not fall in upon ourselves with the weight of our own greatness, for as it is written, Pride goeth before Destruction."

Merlin looked directly at Maelgwn, the greatest of all warriors since Achilles who, for now, had given up crown and conquest to serve Arthur, with a special measure of gratitude. Upon Maelgwn's spear rested the unity and hope of the entire Island Kingdom.

"Whatever Providence each of you worship, give praise, for a War King was needed and the War King was given. Praise God for King Arthur, the possessor of the two swords, and by the authority of the three swords! Praise the one who will overcome the Dragon whose sigil is that Dragon. Praise the one who unites our land. Praise the Bear Exalted! Praise for Arthur and for eleven, but –"

It was more difficult to gain the praises of Merlin than for Arthur to push a boulder up Mynydd Snowdonia with a dry piece of straw. The young sandy-haired king was ready for the "but" and braced for further expectations, corrections and improvements demanded by his Merlin.

Instead, the word play ensued.

"Eleven is great, but alas, one more time, boy, we need one more, we need TWELVE! What is greater than eleven?" Now the crowd followed, chanting "twelve" with the rhythmic harmony of Illtud's famous choirs.

Next the cheers and chants shifted to "one more, one more" in that special and heavenly tongue of the Cymry. It is said that angels joined in the singing and chanting (for they spake the same tongue) and that the Constellations grew jealous and, for just one evening, altered their circuits to get closer and listen.

This time it was more difficult for Merlin to quell the noise he had created. When at last it relented, he continued.

"But how will we defeat them? How will we give our whelps and babes a chance to grow up in a Summer Kingdom of peace?"

The assembly quieted. Still. Ready to hear "the how".

Merlin in an instant transitioned from

riddles to direct, patient teaching. He wanted the men who would die over the ensuing days to understand why, and he wanted this for their wives and mothers as well.

"A fortnight ago," he began, "the Saxon kings sued us for peace and we conferenced with them at great length. Our emissaries in Little Britain and on the Continent informed us three weeks ago that a fleet of ships such as never was assembled had already left Germania ere the conference began.

"Moreover, separate Saxon tribes and princes who could not be under the same tent together without putting knife to gullet had demoted their sigils and flew one united battle banner. Remarkably, if only temporarily, the Germanic peoples are coming, united."

The Merlin cleared his throat.

"We have learned that only the Vandals held out, and why would they not? Africa is under their dominion and the Black Boar is at present content to leave our Islands alone. But not so for the Angles, the Saxons, the Jutes and the tribes of Dan.

"Thus, the invitation to discuss peace was a delay tactic and one well-known. We played the part, courteous and firm, and soundly rejected the Long Knife's empty terms of eastern homesteading and harmonious integration. As if a Fox would integrate with a Hen!"

Merlin continued. "We gave safe conduct to the Saxon Princes and intentionally gave appearance of weakened defenses all along both the old roads east, and the outlying trade and watchtower villages. Although raiding occurs under every moon and season, there is an unspoken agreement amongst all kindreds that no battle campaigns occur during Winter. For this cause, the Long Knife sought further to deceive us, making their winter visit falsely appear all the more benign. We countered by making our defenses look equally benign.

"The nature, my beloved kinsmen, of their assault is a 'one-time', sentinel event with all lots cast. They are invading in Winter, they are united, and they think that we are being true to our character of war-time honor and wholly unprepared. They will annihilate us, or they will be lost for a generation as every boy who can carry a stick is with them."

Merlin's tone made the imminent danger grave. Then his disposition lifted.

"As always, the Saxon is a dullard, a dribbler and a *fool!*" screamed the old Wizard excitedly under the starry winter night at the table round in Caerleon. "The strategy." Merlin's head tilted here, then there. "The strategy, my brothers and sisters, is to simply let the Boar in–" Merlin here began talking with his hands, shrugging his shoulders, and lightening his tone as a confident child does when at play "–let him starve, then make him climb."

Merlin went on to say how the Saxon horde would receive little interference landing, making ready and then marching west from Lloegyr all the way into the Vale of Glamorgan (this they had already begun to do).

The Saxons would come as far as the Maesteg Valley, with her gulches, winding paths and open, hilly fields. Then the real differentiator of the strategy would activate.

In most cultures, the rulers build defensive structures that remove them from the masses and afford maximum protection with minimum effort. The Cymry did not view the king above the pig farmer and thus mitigation of loss of life and property for the common man was, to Princes, paramount. To this end, from ancient times, fortresses were built high atop mountains, near caves where feasible escape routes for children, women and creaturekind were well-known, exercised and rehearsed.

When attacked, the armies would descend from the fortress hilltop, escort the people to safety, lob preliminary volleys, and meet the enemy in open combat, typically and with hope that the open warfare would occur ere they reached even the outskirts of the tribe's lands and homes.

The technique of scorching the harvest, killing the livestock and starting over anew if the battle was won was not an option in the mind of the Briton.

This time, the strategy was very different.

"Let the Boar in, starve him, make him climb." Merlin's words would be immortal.

The people would be long retreated to the hill fortresses atop and around Baeden hill, far away from the thousands of marching soldiers come to destroy them. The exodus would be intentionally slovenly; some livestock would be left, hearths still aflame and a general illusion of a hasty departure projected.

The three Kings of the Saxon armies would undoubtedly call for the slaughter and immediate consumption of the livestock and the burning of any habitable living structures along the roads, knowing that more bounty would be available upon victory in an open battle.

Instead of the descent of an entire army and a massive conflict where the Royal Tribes would be outnumbered, the Britons would instead surprise and harass the Saxons from the sides of the Valley and ultimately trap them at the foot of Baeden Hill.

Instead of Arthur's remaining troops descending upon the plain, they would simply wait atop the hill in frightening and disciplined formation and then, when starving and desperate, the Saxons would climb to their deaths from an untenable low-ground position.

CHAPTER 4
TᏂe Po|icy

After Merlin had articulated his brilliant strategy for triumphing in the sentinel event to come, the congress of Britons shifted to how they might manage the surviving Saxon populations in Lloegyr.

This level of planning was not one of arrogance or assumption, but rather of necessity.

There were well over twenty diverse tribes of unwelcome Germanic invaders and many of them had inhabited hides of land, illegally and immorally, on the Blessed Isles. Most of the men occupying these lands would take up arms and drive westward, right into Merlin's trap. If the magnitude of victory matched Merlin's predictions, that would mean thousands of Saxon children, women and aged to deal with, in just a few days.

A reasonable person would think that this topic would ignite grand debates of every philosophical persuasion.

But Religion is a far heavier stone than Reason.

Quickly local chieftains, major cattle owners, clergy and all of the Cymry agreed that Saxon women and children would be treated with mercy and respect; that deportation back to the Continent would be safely conducted, sanitary, well planned and with protection. Those born on Britain's soil could stay but not own land for nine generations; and only those political prisoners who were of the most extreme danger would be executed.

"Well, that was easy," said Cai.

"Of course it was; all the more time to argue about Religion," mused a metallic and vibratory voice that belonged to Maelgwn Gwynedd. He gave his foster-mother, Vivien, a comforting look of support, knowing he could leave and enjoy mead and meal but that she would suffer sitting through the entire session of old men about to argue about how to save souls, or rather, increase their power and position over them.

Determining the policy of water baptism for the new Germans would not be so easy!

The primitive British Church predated Rome, significantly. When synods or councils were gathered, the seating was based upon primacy. The clergy of Cymru and Eire were seated first. The beliefs of the native church eschewed Statism on a centralized or federal level (although a local Bishop had come to supplant the place of a Druid in many cases, settling minor disputes, and adjudicating land grants along with other small scale administrative functions). By contrast, the Roman Church declared itself the Pillar and Ground of Truth for obedience by the Nations. The Britons were finding themselves increasingly overwhelmed.

And the Roman Church had gold. Excessive, immeasurable amounts of it.

Because of this, they could plant priests amongst the Britons, influence major farmers, cattlemen and landowners and lob volleys of pressure over to the Isles all the way from Rome.

Some of the influence was finding fertile soil. During the Saxon Wars, for example, the Church at home attempted to levy a tax for protection of chapels and relics and was beginning, like those in Rome, to make tithing compulsory.

Arthur refused to levy this toll on an already distressed people, instead insisting that giving be voluntary and that the ecclesiastical organism make use of its existing revenues.

He would say, "A man who own cows must defend his herd; why should a bishop be any different with his flock?"

The controversy became so inflamed with a Bishop called Padarn that Arthur stripped the vestments from the saint's back and banished him from his assembly. Bishop Bedwini took his Bishopric.

Other principal Saints and Patrons of Cymru such as Dyfrig, Illtud and young Dewi appreciated Arthur's position and respect was reciprocal in times of both agreement and discord. The Roman Church (ever positioning for a cut of the collection plate) did not. For Rome fancied itself the Seat of the Universal Church. And the Catholics were positioning for the Bishop of Rome to be officially designated as the all-father, or Pope.

This greatly concerned the old British church (and ancient assemblies in other nations), pagans and heathens alike.

For his part, Merlin could see that Imperial Rome was slowly and methodically giving way to Holy Rome. In his travels, the Merlin witnessed intimidation, absorption of pagan belief into the burgeoning traditions of the Church, and ever-increasing forced adoption of Latin at the expense of the native written language of the Britons and the script of the Irish.

A man dedicated to pursuit of spiritual truth and societal justice, the Merlin never hated Christianity. He did recognize, however, the dangerous blend of Church and State, having seen a measure of corruption and imposition by his own Druids when given similar opportunities. "Power corrupts whether you follow Christ or Rhiannon," he had said.

The Romans never took by sword what they would now take by crucifix. Left alone Britain would inevitably follow Jesus anyhow; 'twas the method more than the outcome that concerned the Druid. And the extinction of free thought and critical thinking skills.

In the Isles, the common man could read, he could look at nature and make a personal decision regarding his beliefs. Literacy was strong with regard to the native language, and the 'Latin game' bothered Merlin immensely.

"It's easy to render a country ignorant when their official language is officially foreign," he would often protest. The imposition of an official language and other such presuppositions, in the Merlin's view, were not for the Pulpit to determine.

The Lady of Llyn Fawr, a Breton called Vivien, had waning and vague influence in political matters. Christians still viewed her as having some ancient magick as old and as cherished as the Island itself. In some Christian sects, her veneration gave way to that of the Virgin Mary.

None knew her age (and not even a fool would inquire) but she fostered Maelgwn, and he was two winters older than Arthur. Her blonde hair now shared space with some silver locks but it still featured indescribable entrancements and fell well beneath her thighs. Her garb was silver and white and even the most pious Christian opened themselves to the notion of a real-life goddess standing amongst them when they looked upon her.

She compressed authoritative thin red lips. *I am called the Virgin as well, married to the god. Indeed, when recognized as King of Glamorgan and Gwent, Arthur honored the king-making rites, but he did so in a private grove, his Apostolic and Catholic coronations carried out in public splendor,* she thought, listening to the Bishops and Priests beginning their rant about how to cleanse the souls of the invaders.

Of those rites, she recalled how, just two months later, she had visited court and witnessed the Church's perversion of a festival dedicated to the Babylonian goddess Astarte, now repurposed for their goddess, Mary.

She lashed out openly at the Bishops. "You have your risen King, he was made so at the rites! And his name is Arthur!" Too popular to kill at present, Vivien was tolerated at the table of political Britain.

And besides, 'twas Vivien who taught Maelgwn his martial arts and, by extension, the whole of the army that had also adopted it. The Lady ever featured armor as part of her ornate and creative attire and gently reminded the males that she could kill most of them with ease, via technique in combat or enchantment, upon her whim.

Outside of fear, the Bishops were simply too busy to deal with the Lady of the Lake. They had the Catholics to contend with and the Catholics with them. Yet, her friend – her lover, as the rites made requisite – Merlin, the man she respected above all others, had sought her counsel and presence. He felt she was greatly needed in light of the great changes coming in the 'Summer Kingdom' of peace that would now be an imminent reality, should Arthur and his Companions adjudicate Merlin's strategy at Baeden Hill.

Truth is not afraid to compete. Truth is not afraid to tolerate. Factions were healthy, checking their rivals and rendering taut the sinews of public discourse.

Factionism was deadly, Merlin and Vivien postulated. Diverse beliefs and gods were safe; a diversity of common law was deadly.

Rome's hatred of the competing Christian and Gnostic groups concerned them. The Church tried to convert the pagans. All faiths evangelize. But the greater concern was that they had aggressively begun to cannibalize their own dissidents, though they claimed the same Christ.

Such was the concern for the remnant of influential pagans that they worked extensively with the local Apostolic Britons, who had roots in the Isles dating back to the thirty-fifth year of the first century, and other Christians of local influence (such as the followers of Pelagius), constantly gauging the strengthening political power of Rome.

Borrowing in part from the height of successful republics of antiquity, the Merlin and the Lady of the Lake favored a nation where freedom of religion flourished. The young King Arthur agreed. And he was politically brilliant in this arena. Where the old Wizard mentored the Bear of Glamorgan on many matters, the sandy-haired young King both agreed with and perfected their stance on this most defining topic with an intangible gift that could be cultivated but never taught.

Vivien remembered one rainy day before an overtly tense tussle between twenty Roman Catholic priests, a hundred and seventy Apostolic presbyters, the British Church's Great Bishop, Dubricius (who was also called Dyfrig in the language of heaven) and not a few influential pagans. Arthur had interrupted with boldness and grace.

"Merlin–" he looked up at the towering Druid "–I think you are trying to say this." Merlin, taller than any Briton save Maelgwn but Briton to his core, sat down, smiling at his young liege. Old Meurig smiled too.

"No society can operate when divorced from a common set of norms. From a single moral fabric. To this end, Britain should be a Christian nation in principle, namely that we should, by enforcement of the common law, and executed amongst the Confederacy and in every Cantref: not kill, nor breach a covenant, nor defraud a neighbor, nor rape. Neither shall we steal, neither shall any principality or power do any of these against any citizen, and of the rights that are their obverse, from encroachment refrain.

For without its counterpart in responsibility, no liberty can long sustain.

"And this shall be the end of the law, that men may worship what gods they will, only that they do not kill their neighbor for it."

In a few words, Arthur both enforced the Christian foundation of his realm and protected the liberties of all men, even those who disagreed with it.

Facing the real peril of a theocracy, Vivien and Merlin could both acquiesce and support Arthur's vision of a Christian government.

But now there were to be new subjects and, with them, a renewed effort for the policies of Rome to yet again bleed and burrow into the policies of the local ecclesiastical structures. Vivien, Merlin and anyone with a salt's pinch of common sense knew that any policy made for Saxon citizens could be used as license for later use against the Britons. Forced baptism per the sacerdotal system of the Catholics for them could be forced baptism per the sacerdotal system for all. Land ceded to Rome in Lloegyr today would be land ceded to Rome in Cymru tomorrow.

And so the debates and clamor droned and droned.

The Briton Bishops were adamant that a man should be baptized after conversion to the Faith and then again, for kings, before death. And the mode of this baptism should be by immersion.

The Catholics viewed this method as 'incomplete' and insisted that an infant be ceremonially washed to remit Adam's Original Sin. Subsequently the individual would do works, affirmations and confirmations. The baptism, for the Catholic, or those of Catholic leanings, was an ordinance in replacement of Abraham's circumcision. The mode was sprinkling.

"They fight like this over which day to observe Easter too," heckled Meurig. Onbrawst laughed aloud.

The arguing was intense and the hour growing late.

The assembly began to disband and revelry turned to fatigue. A full stadium empties slowly, and warriors and women alike sought slumber.

"We have a battle to rest for and many, many Clans to organize down at Ogmore. This goes too long," Arthur protested.

The Lady of Llan Fawr interjected, "And if a Saxon sees not the Light of your Christ and His Church and prefers Odin and Loki or other deities of their fathers, what then?"

"We honor the diverse beliefs of those born here, Lady," said a Saint of extreme influence. "But," he continued, "the Saxon is come to annihilate us, to remove our lamp and to stamp out our people, forever!"

He had a point and Vivien absorbed the words.

"Thus, for those children who are allowed to settle here, they must be Christian of some denomination or sect, they must be baptized, and if their parents allow this not –" the Saint paused "– this will be rare, I assure you, for most of the Germanic horde dies in two days!"

"Not if we're still here talking about this!" Meurig delivered more well-placed levity, bringing interruption.

"I shall cut to the quick, my Lord."

"Please do."

"We will baptize the children and execute the non-consenting parent. That will be the policy."

That the non-consenting parent would be removed from his head met no opposition. After all, these were the invaders who would rape, kill and assimilate every Briton, were they able. But the response gave Vivien great pause.

The arguing about 'mode and timing' kicked right back up again.

King Arthur rose.

"Retire from the amphitheater and continue this back at our great hall or your privy chambers. All of Caerleon has had enough debate tonight over sprinkling versus dunking. It is the same God we serve, after all."

An irritated King gave a polite nod and exited the Round Table.

The arguing continued for a short space even after their dismissal, as emotions were running hot and the embers were still red and orange. Suddenly Merlin, acting very passionately about some matter, with great conviction seemed to command the paused awe of every clergyman. And of Vivien.

Arthur had already paced out some distance between himself and those still engaged. He could see something different about Merlin's disposition, but of the nature of the post-conference bantering, he knew not. His mind had returned solely to the war strategy and all that must happen next. His confederacy assembled, the strategy articulated, it was time for history's greatest king to lead a war to end all wars; at least for a generation. A generation of peace.

And yet, that something strange had just

happened with Merlin twanged his ribs twice or thrice, and then was dismissed.

To himself, he said, "I need a cider," and he sought out Bedwyr for the same.

CHAPTER 5
The Victory at Hand

"Hold!" Cai yelled, breaking Arthur's contemplation.

"You steady that horse, boy!" Cadoc hollered.

The Battle of Baeden started at the noon hour and lasted but three days.

Exhausted by Maelgwn and his bloodthirsty hosts at once striking and withdrawing, and three days bereft of food, drink or sleep, at last the Saxons, who knew not how to make war upon steed, began to climb the mountain as their final, fatal recourse.

Like a statue come randomly to life, "Let the Boar in," said Arthur, and his head snapped sideways at Bedwyr.

Finally breaking his stoic silence, he said: "Starve him."

"Make him climb!" Bedwyr stole the King's line and remarkably, spotted a smile from his Sovereign. Spotting a light moment that would soon be gone, Arthur's first knight continued. "To what do we set the trump, my Lord? We dare not issue an attack, what shall we signal?" Bedwyr laughed aloud. "Is there a trump for 'here they come, look down at your feet, go to it?'"

Excalibur was already swinging high above and picking up the last shards of light breaking through dusk-shadowed trees. "Kill will suffice, Bedwyr. *Kill!*"

With their black leather lacquered armor and wooden shields, the swarm of climbing Saxons looked like cockroaches swarming a dead tree trunk. Their numbers were as the sands of the shore. No horse flinched; no Briton gave ground and the downward slashing from atop their war horses was organized, swift and without error.

No volleys could be lobbed lest the Ravens be shot by their own kinsmen, so archery was used near range and with less volume.

When a Saxon would slay a Briton with stone or fortuitous strike, both rider and horse would topple down the mountain, creating a boulder of flesh, killing as it rolled. The death of one Briton above oft resulted in the loss of three Saxons below. When a Briton felled the Saxon with long weapons, a spear, arrow or from mounted position, it was easier. To kill a man whose eyes are through the helm opposite your own is a far more difficult proposition. And some simply could not do it, could not kill.

To take the life essence of another man, to see the light leave his eyes by your hand, to be around the body of death: this changes and in many ways ruins a man. Nightmares, barriers to intimacy, drunkenness, loss of virility and suicide were the real ongoing disease of war.

Many thought that Merlin and Illtud should counsel and train the young warriors to objectivize the deed; to step outside of themselves and kill for the cause. This, the two men knew, was folly, so both they and other mentors, counselors and strategists trained the young warriors to do just the opposite.

"For politicians it must needs be strategic and cold. For warriors, it must needs be personal," said Merlin on many occasions. "The Saxon is not invading to take soil. He is invading to take *your* soil. The Saxon is not here to take a Cymry woman to wife; he is here for *your* wife, your schoolyard fancy, your sister! The Saxon is not here to be your neighbor. He is here to remove *you* personally, and your sons, from history itself, to take your poems, your ballads, all that is *you* and exterminate it." Then the old Wizard would draw up his authority, usually gazing up and then snapping back down, chin to chest. "It is personal, young men. When you are engaged in close combat you must heed these instructions. Do this and you will both live to see one more tomorrow and mitigate the madness of the kill."

Merlin would then brandish his short leaf, dangerously sharp and knotted with engraved entwined ravens and bears. The top of the hilt featured three lines that looked like an inverted arrow or the rays of the sun. Emulating the lethal maneuver, he would say, "Find the short rib here on the enemy's left, lest he be left-handed, then use diagonal slide step and come to his right." Merlin sounded like his lifelong friend Vivien, the soft-spoken warrior who could have been the resurrection of Boudica, had her people needed her in that capacity. But the people had Arthur (of this she was most glad). "The blade must go through the armor at the rib like this–" Merlin drew a great breath "–and then, without reservation or hesitation, do and say the following."

Merlin's next motion and scripted words were portrayed so frighteningly that the young warriors, professional soldiers all, recoiled in fear.

Merlin looked deep into a phantom Saxon's eyes and growled, breathing inward deeply, "We are not Walles [which by interpretation means 'foreigner'], you are! We do this for defense! We *live here*! WE LIVE HERE!" At conclusion of the final syllable and while demonstrating an upward stab from short rib through top clavicle (this path severing the heart and producing a fount of blood and instant death), he breathed outward in thrice measure of the intake of breath and screamed, spending the entire volume of his lungs. And then, in an instant, ceased.

The combination of the stab with the scream resulted in a Saxon's last experience ere he entered Hell being one of utter and complete terror; but the ritual was not for him, but rather for the Cymry warrior. By bawling aloud, the honorable nature of the deed, a legitimate and audible justification was spoken into existence. The sheer violence of delivery helped the Cymry warrior spill the negative energy as one spills their seed, releases and then sleeps. In this way, Merlin was helping them find a killing ritual to "do it and then let go". The routine had many favorable results amongst young warriors, sent to go and defend their country, sometimes as young as fourteen or fifteen years old.

The Saxons also started picking up some of the phrase in the singing, angelic and authoritative Brythonic tongue of their enemy. Thus, when engaged closely and nearing the moment of the stroke, pre-screams filled the fields and crags of battle.

And so it was at Baeden Hill. The layering of sounds: harp and horn and stringed instruments, choirs of men singing hymns under streamers, fiery female singers blasting imprecatory prose and curses into the sky o'er the enemy, battle drums, the protest of steed and the undisciplined screaming of soldiers in broken Latin, in Gaelic, in thirteen dialects of Jutish, Angle-land and Saesneg. In Cymraeg could be heard in strict and disciplined performance, well-timed through the night, blended with the sound of snow and the soundlessness of snow, with the wind and against the wintery wind, above all and through all, the ritual Merlin taught the young men: "WE LIVE HERE!"

But Merlin was not there.

Arthur scrambled away from the direct action a few times to scout. He identified his son, safe. Llacheu was ascending a ridge well clustered by armed Knights. Gwenhwyfar would be pleased.

Arthur scanned the Vale for Maelgwn and found him not, but given the numbers in mortal clutch, the mist, and the fading light, he was not surprised at his inability to see the great soldier.

The Britons began rotating the front line cavalry and had developed a strategy for fighting in the wintery cold: water.

Merlin and Illtud, masters of aquatics, had developed wooden tributaries that caused great amounts of water to be redirected down the mountain, like three well-organized girthy waterfalls made by men. The water itself was a cold and unyielding adversary and the Saxons found themselves dying in freezing mud.

Meanwhile, skins were thrown upon the warriors who were out of rotation. They were warmed, given hot drink, recomposed and then rotated back into the alignment.

The song and music now increased so that it became one with the rushing winds, masking the screaming. It had become so deafening that time seemed to stop and then alter the speed at which men moved, rendering them participants watching a drama, watching their own theatre.

The panic of the terrorized invader grew and grew as there was no place of retreat: Arthur's sword at the throat and Maelgwn's spear at the heel.

Finally, freezing in mud, blinded by mist, surrounded by death, the Germanic kings – the loose confederation famous for sacking Rome, conquering Northern Africa and much of the known world through numbers and ferocity – realized that they would not have this special and coveted Isle, not today, and not for many days.

Osla I was slain; Cedric the Gewessi hacked his way out of death's pursuit, retreating to the east of the fighting. Aelle, the third king, possessor of the largest divisions, screamed in a Latin tongue (for no Cymry would learn the sounds of the Long Knife) for quarter, crudely offering himself as prisoner to Arthur. Owain ap Urien granted King Aelle's request for mercy but not before he struck him hard with the hilt of his sword, taking the unconscious and defeated king and battle lord into custody.

The Boar. Let him in, starve him, make him climb. Kill the Boar.

Cleaving the head of the adder did not immediately stop the flailing of its tail. The Saxons' panic made them at once easy to kill and hard to compel to simply lay down arms and live. Even as the Britons sought to explain that it was over, the Saxons climbed upwards to their awaiting death.

"They cease not. Will we have to slay all of them?!" screeched Bedwyr, heavy breath forming clouds in the cold.

"Aelle cannot signal their surrender." Owain surveyed the bound Germanic king for alert eyes, but he was yet unresponsive.

At the base of the Baeden, Maelgwn's men had harassed and attacked from behind and funneled the Saxons to either 'climb or die' so effectively that they could now see more Cymry warriors than Saxon.

Like a fist slowly clenching, the invaders were now far fewer than the Island's defenders, and when the fist fully closed, there would be scant few left.

The small plain and three ridges leading up the hill where piles of Saxons went to their god or on to Hell would one day be called 'The Bridge of Slaughter' and 'The Place of the Soldiers' in Cymraeg.

Finally, with the wine press virtually closed and the Ravens now indeed climbing the mountain on the heels of upward fleeing Saxons, the German attack's back broke. They started to drop arms, fall to knees and cry for mercy in their barbaric tongues.

King Arthur, ever 'in office' (as Vivien taught him), tried to be balanced. He was not a cold stoic, neither a jesting fool. When others wept, he wept. When they rejoiced, he was glad-hearted with them. One of the King's greatest attributes was his sense of timing and ability to meet people upon their level and in their context rather than always his own. Balance was slipping and Arthur just wanted to hug his men, to yell joyously.

Nearly twenty years of the Saxon Wars were nigh to a climatic and unanimous victory. In these moments, men hug. Men embrace. Jumping around like boys in the schoolyard kicking a ball, the great companions of Arthur shoulder-checked one, and then the other, frantically looking for the next man to congratulate.

Midnight Blues hugged Black. Black embraced Speckled Green. Blue Plaid mauled Yellow. All the Royal Clans and Tribes and kinsmen rejoiced!

Bringing this confederacy together had not been easy. Although the Round Table Fellowship formed a unique principality (especially when they met at Caermelyn and were under a specific code; a peculiar nation of twenty-four and two within a larger nation of several million), beyond its hallowed halls there was ongoing need for vigilance and discipline in keeping the nation from crackling and splintering into Civil War. Even before the battle had commenced, this was freshly evident.

The collective armies had had to ride directly west from Caerleon to the beach-head at Ogmore, where they organized and finalized tactical aspects of the strategy. From Ogmore to the base of Mynydd Baeden was only two hours, directly north, by horseback.

As Merlin had never arrived at Ogmore, there

were some minor delays and, with the wait, came the tribal skirmishes. Urien was dispatched to find Merlin and much of the management of the Northern Tribes fell to his son Owain (for Maelgwn left in the night for his unit's part in the Strategy).

The tribes had grown so restless that Owain and Arthur tried to calm all by playing an ancient board game called gwyddbwyll. It did not work. Report followed report to both Arthur and Owain of one tribe harassing, fighting and hacking at the other.

Owain, in an error of youth, even threatened to kill some of the men of the South (Arthur's very own Silure tribe). Arthur said nothing at first in response to the threat, but simply crushed a clay game piece. Letting the bits fall to the gwyddbwyll board, the eyes of the Pendragon found Owain's soul.

"Your move."

Owain had settled his Ravens.

Arthur also got his first look at Maelgwn's youngest son, adorned in golden armor (Arthur's own fetching lad Llacheu also favored shimmering in gold armor), and the Pendragon very much enjoyed seeing the future of Britain strolling about the tents together.

All strife was now gone and all the tribes were, at least for this rare, unspeakable savored moment, together.

Still looking for more men to shoulder check, pump fists with, shout to the heavens with and embrace, Arthur found Cai. He hugged him tightly. This was not easy given the height and thickness of the man with whom Arthur had spent two years as foster brother and two decades more as friend. Twenty years of fighting by boat, in forest, on sand and in crags. So much loss of life for love of hope. Cymru would survive, led by history's greatest king, and into the bosom of his steward he could finally breathe.

"We did it, Brother."

Releasing Cai, Arthur clasped Bedwyr's left hand.

Arthur smiled.

Arthur wept.

CHAPTER 6
On Fostering

King Arthur and Cai ap Cynfarch were foster brothers. The practice of fostering in Cymru had a very specific, very well intended purpose.

Well before Arthur and most of his famous Companions were born, a great treachery was visited upon most of the nobility of the Britons. Although the cowardly sin against warfare and honor occurred at the mountain fortress of Caer Caradoc in the southeast, it, in dark and far-reaching irony, forever impacted the kings and princes of Northern Cymru.

A treacherous king called Vortigern had conscripted the Saxons and made them hirelings to ward off raiding from the tribes from the Emerald Isles. The hirelings soon began to devour the flock and would not go home to Germania when finished with their employ.

A conciliatory council was called. The Britons and Saxons agreed to discuss possible co-habitation, a peace accord for slow and regulated migration to the eastern parts of the Isles. This was before the Saxons were exposed as wholly untrustworthy demoniacs.

Instead of honor and reciprocal diplomacy, the Boar waited until the Britons were drunken or retired and then ambushed them with blades concealed. Caer Caradoc was so full of butchery that its beautiful dykes and waterfalls ran red with the foamy life essence of innocent men and women. A fortress celebrating the son of Bran the Blessed now became a place of cursing, the place of mourning. Many royals were laid to rest in glorious burial mounds right where they fell and many Wells (where it was believed that a man's soul could traverse through the Deep, back to its source) were erected.

The incident became known as the Night of Long Knives and, in earnest, launched the Saxon Wars.

Over four hundred princes, chieftains both major and minor, bishops and Druids perished that night due to the treachery of the Boar; the cowardice of the Long Knife. Perhaps the greater loss was the women, who were murdered as well without regard or honor. This left an enormous void of those vessels of honor to give future sons to the Ravens of the North.

What the Saxons meant for evil, however, God wrought for good. By chance, against hope, two rulers from the South East were away in Brittany, missing the conference entirely. And so, by horrific murder of so many princes, the Saxons created the stage that would be filled by the one who would come to destroy them.

The Pendragon, Tewdrig, and his battle commander Ambrosious survived the ambush by their absence. Later in life Tewdrig begat Meurig, and Meurig begat King Arthur.

The resulting void of rulers for the north of Britain resulted in Arthur and the Silures having to establish kings with wives and provide stability. For example, the dismal King Cynfarch survived the Night of Long Knives. The Silures gave him to wife Nyfain, daughter of Brychan. This union gave the world Urien and Llew and Arawan who, downstream, gave the world some of Arthur's greatest allies such as Owain and Gwalchmai.

These remnant Sons of Cunedda, the most powerful senior bloodline in the North, both appreciated and resented the South. Only a handful of chiefs survived and as these married and gave Cymru new sons, and with great sacrifice and efforts from the South, the North loosely began to restabilize.

Feeling like they no longer needed "help", the Northern indigenous kings like Cynfarch and Cadwallon Lahir increasingly fomented and flowered the seeds of resentment, and raiding of the South became frequent. And the Bishops of the North were slowly giving way to Catholic leanings as well.

To combat this dilemma, as ongoing acts of grace, friendship and hope, fosterage became formalized and frequent.

Sons and daughters of the South would spend two summers reared by the North (and not just a "nobility for nobility swap"; often a prince would learn to tend sheep, a princess to work the plow) and the children of the North would do the same, living at the hearth of the Clans in the South.

This forged friendships, reduced frictions, sowed seeds of youthful romance (and thus future political marriages), and greatly aided in fusing together one united Cymru.

Sometimes.

Though a noble pursuit that bore much good fruit, such as the bond unbreakable between Arthur and Cai, there were times where the fosterage had the opposite result. In these cases, a prince from the South would be turned against his own family and become a dormant pawn, just waiting to strike or to betray. The host family would corrupt the heart of their foster child, creating assassins and killers and traitors, leaders of cowardly raids to steal cattle, sheep, precious resources and people.

The national character of the Britons was strong, gilded. They were a moral people. But when the exceptions arose, they arose, sharp as long thorns hiding in plain sight in the rose garden, the tare in the wheat.

For Arthur's part, he enjoyed many adventures with Cai in the North and his love for Cai well exceeded the love of a brother. They were together, and inseparable, from Arthur's twelfth unto fourteenth year prior to joining Hoel on the Continent; then Arthur returned to school near Caer Bovum at an old college that would one day be known as Llaniltud Fawr.

Cai accepted the office of 'Steward' during that tender age and it was an office that he manned with zeal and fervor, as if he had been born for the very purpose. Just minutes after introductions made when just a boy, Cai fondly remembered King Meurig dismounting his horse, kneeling down gracefully to meet eyes with the lad.

Meurig's words were soft in tone but grave in nature.

Noticing a special, loyal light in the boy, the King said, "I give you the greatest tasks of all men, young Sir Cai. It will not earn you much public glory but the Lord God and I, Uther Pendragon, will be watching, and we will be very thankful and very proud." Meurig lightly pushed Arthur away at this point, encouraging him to go play with other boys. The opening remarks of the charge had Cai brimming with excitement and expectation of what would come next.

"At your service, my Lord?" His voice begged Meurig to continue.

"Protect Arthur at all times. This is the sole purpose of your occupation for the next two years. And when I come and visit, I will monitor the execution of your stewardship privily, to see that you give me neither eye nor lip service. Your sole purpose." Meurig increased the gravity of his tone, garnished with the reward offered for the thankless and private employ. "Do this for just two years and you and whatever lass you wed will live in riches at Caerleon all of your years. You shall never want."

The two years were over too soon and Cai petitioned Uther Pendragon to be the Steward of Arthur, not for just two years, but forever. Meurig happily accepted. Cai would do anything to protect his friend and King. His foster-brother.

CHAPTER 7
The Absent Sister

The Princess Gwyar ferch Onbrawst was also fostered.

She was noticeably, yet not unusually, absent at the gathering of the Tribes in Caerleon before the battle of Baeden.

Either the Long Knife will have the day and a dark age of rape, tyranny and annihilation will befall us all, she accurately surmised, *or we will win and our own Religionists will bite, devour and consume each other and then turn to us and do the same thing.*

Fondling the pretty purple floral head o'er the toxic monkshood plant and then jerking it cleanly from the soil, root and all, she said: "Kill me swiftly or kill me slow. In the end, I'm no less dead." Gwyar made an angry smirk, gazing upon the limp stem. "I'm still dead, yes?"

Seagulls cried an ugly song of agreement with the Princess's appraisal, swooping in to feed upon the offerings of the island's coastal shore.

"Why waste time with meetings?" She finished her thought.

As Arthur, Cai, Urien, Bedwyr, Hoel ap Budic, Cadog, mighty Mofran and the rest of Arthur's glorious twenty-four were presently engaged, leading thousands of their kinsmen in the most important battle in her people's (and perhaps any people's) history, Gwyar was pleasantly enjoying the magical little intersection, found on many of the Isles, where the forest lies behind and the beach lies ahead. A gateway between two worlds; from ocean to greenery within seven paces, truly the Isles testified to the artistry of the Creator.

Britain itself was this gateway.

More special perhaps than the rest was Ynys Enlli, the Island of the Currents. The island of treacherous currents. A remnant dot of now long-sunken earth between herself and the long land-end arm of the Llyn Peninsula, Ynys Enlli at once felt like it was at the end of the world, and the center of it.

Unreachable because of undercurrents and tides that ran to and fro in defiance of the observable laws of nature and guarded by a citadel of dolphins, Ynys Enlli could be accessed by neither barge nor boat nor swim from October through springtime. It was December and yet Gwyar traveled here as she pleased and personally stewarded all the permanent residents, providing supplies, wines and foodstuffs during the harsh winter.

Although but a two-mile journey, it was hopelessly impossible; yet she frequented the Island often, and none dared to asked how.

Following a short hike, beach became forest, and forest became a steep sloped mountain. To the west and nearly atop Mynydd Enlli's peak was found a large structure that housed a striking garden and the oldest apple orchard in the world; local legend recorded that a great dragon had brought the first seeds there following a clash involving the Sons of Brutus and a Giant whose son was Gogmagog. Additionally, the unique edifice accommodated living quarters for twenty and four souls and ten guardians.

A stone round table, similar to those found at Caermelyn and at Caerleon, dominated the hall. Differing from those palaces and forts, this table rested upon a floor made entirely of dark blue glass. Wondrous fish and other illuminated swimmers and sea horses spiraled in ethereal dance through what appeared to be a great natural aquarium that spanned the breadth of the hall.

Sometimes the mist enveloped the whole of the dwelling, as if to guard it. Sometimes the Dragon's Breath escorted but shards, strings and beads of sun through the archer's slits in the towers and, on rare occasions, the breath recoiled entirely, showing off the top of the great tower to an unbelieving and skeptical world.

And while the mist guarded this Castle of Glass, the Castle of Glass guarded the Isle of Apples, and the Isle of Apples guarded many mysteries and the treasures of Britain.

Sitting at a grey table in a circular room prominently featuring a curious mirror and two dark-stoned indoor wells, Gwyar put fists under chin and rested atop her elbows. There alone in the Isles in the Sea, she harbored and again and again quelled resentments which were meet and just. Gwyar's thoughts now turned and rested upon her son, who could well be sword to sword with a Saxon at that very moment, far far away in the South.

Gwalchmai, the Hawk of May, son of Gwyar and the Lion (who was Cynfarch's son), was said to bring sunshine wheresoever he trod. It was told that days of incessant downpour would at once open to clouds of happy blue the moment his feet touched the ground of this village or that village.

Gwalchmai's hair was reddish blonde; he favored two slightly curved leaf swords that complemented his motions and could be sheathed efficiently on his back. He, of course, fought in the style of the Bretons. A student of philosophy and the sciences, he respected all Faiths and Religions though himself was a Christian, probably from spending two summers with Arthur, Gwenhwyfar and Saint Illtud down in Glamorgan.

Larger than Arthur and of a gentle disposition, many thought Gwalchmai would make a fine king and, although not near the skill of Maelgwn with sword or shaft, he possessed and excelled in all the intangibles of leadership, critical thinking skills and wisdom, similarly to the great Pendragon himself.

Princess Gwyar desperately hoped he was safe and would return from Baeden with his usual vigor, bringing Sun and Summer to a dark world.

Yet Gwyar too was dark.

The stock of Onbrawst and Meurig gave the world King Arthur, the sandy blond-haired (though most Silures had dark hair and brown eyes with olive-colored skin) and blue-eyed King of kings. The boy King was now a man who could conquer the world and make himself Emperor but who, against the nature of Men, found no drunkenness of power and sought no kingdom beyond the protection of the sovereignty of his own.

Indeed, Arthur put himself under the very laws that he adjudicated and had, by his own imposition, less local power than a chieftain, and a chieftain less power under the roof of a citizen than the citizen. Thus, on a daily basis and in a very real way the common man was, logically, more powerful than the High King, and this by the insistent design of Arthur and the Silure kings before him.

The Law ruled from the Yellow Fortress of Caermelyn. The Law and not Men.

This was the uniqueness of Arthur's Cymru. *But what happens when one faction or denomination homogenizes with the Law?* Gwyar pondered. The threat of Romanism and the invasion of the Long Knife ever threatened what Arthur and Merlin had exhaustively labored for twenty years to build.

Yes, Arthur was a light, but Gwyar was a shadow.

Without controversy Onbrawst and the wondrous Meurig gave the world not only Arthur, but his infamous sister too. And in an age of heroes and villains so plentiful that their legends cannot a hundred libraries nor ten thousand scrolls contain, she was indeed most mysterious, most fascinating, and most to be feared.

Like Arthur, Gwyar too was fostered.

CHAPTER 8
What Is Wrong with Gwyar?

Three alone have knowledge of Gwyar's origin tale, and it is at that speculation. And these three are the Merlin, and King Meurig and Queen Onbrawst.

On a rainy and desperately dark day two years ere Arthur was born, the stately Queen Obrawst, newly delivered of a baby girl, was visiting the Lady of Llyn Fawr. The Queen favored the romance of rain and, to resume health and form after months of pregnancy and the travail of childbirth, she took a walk near the lake. Alone.

Guards for the Queen were quite close and the area was safe. Safe enough… to any foe of mortal coil.

The Isles in the Sea were at one time overrun with creaturekind trapped betwixt this world and the next – the next world for them being the Underworld; and without hope for any alternative destiny, as they were from a time when all flesh was corrupted by Fallen Ones, and abominable spirits begotten. Though often shining and brilliant in appearance and possessing unnatural long days in the here and now, they could not escape their dark nature or their fiery end. As happens by misfortune in the Isles, Onbrawst had wandered into the wrong ring of stones at just the wrong time.

"Dance!" boomed the Twlyth Teg's King. "You are in our circle and yet will not dance?" The Fae lord's eyes were all red with no pupil, and his head inclined with inquisitiveness as he towered over the Cymry Queen (for this race of Fae were very tall, and not tiny as are other races, forms and kinds).

Onbrawst was a pious, yet neither haughty nor arrogant, Christian lady. Disoriented by an encircling funnel of darkness and billows of smoke crackling with spires that enveloped and smudged yet burned not the flesh, she was miserably enchanted, confused and out of place. Her disposition pushed her to a reactive, rude and out of character response.

A brief error with just cause, fated to life-long effects.

Looking up at the ivy-crowned Being requesting she spin and spiral with his untoward mates, she spake before thinking. "Thou offspring of the Devil! I would not justify you by my dance!"

The Fae abhor rudeness from the Sons of Adam. He looked up to the heavens as if the Stars too shared his gaping offense. His knuckles met hard upon the Queen's same cheek. There was a hollow thump and a rattle. The blow rolled her eyes and split her face. Flaccid, she swooned into his cradled upper arm; her head fell back like that of a child's doll. The Fae King opened her green gown and cupped her left breast, enjoying the full shape of it (for she was newly nursing her babe).

In one movement he spun her round, reviving her, and his right hand quickly un-hooded the entrance between her legs. He made sure the Queen's bloodied eyes met his own. Though violating a lady touched only by her husband, loved only by her husband, somehow the Fae made both Onbrawst and the Fair Folk watching feel like *he* was the one offended by her outrageous refusal.

Following one more uninvited painful fumbling, and a pat on her flank as if she were livestock and no woman, the red-eyed creature's voice rose deep from the Underworld. Metallically he spoke.

"Cursings and Blessings from the line of Uther Pendragon."

* * *

Onbrawst stirred amongst shallow reeds near the shore of Llyn Fawr. With unfocused vision, she glimpsed a silver swan arching its proud neck. The swan's head plunged and disappeared, reappeared and then plunged again to fish when Vivien suddenly, no less blurry, replaced the bird before Onbrawst.

"My heart, you have fainted!" Vivien rushed to the Queen's side.

"Where is my baby?" Onbrawst didn't acknowledge Vivien's concerned greeting, a feeling of dread dominating her.

"Oh, the babe does well, Dear Heart; you've been gone but twenty minutes."

"But it was night and now day –" Onbrawst captured and held her tongue before tripping on more confusion. She lightly applied fingertips, as if they were feathers, to her broken face. No wound. Her garment was perfect with no tear and no part of her felt molested.

Was it a dream? she thought.

"You are not a fortnight removed from giving birth." Vivien could assume all of life's most important offices in an instant. At present, she was Maternal Nurse. "You need rest and tea, not walking."

"I'll forgo the tea and accept the cider drink." The endless humor of Onbrawst resurrected. "I thought a walk and some air would help. Baby Gwyar decided to come violently into the world of Men."

"A cloudy cider from the apples of Ynys Enlli it is!" If Vivien knew at the time that Onbrawst had befallen some peril in the Faerie Realm, she concealed it brilliantly, or she simply didn't know.

A young priestess in a lakeside home that would later be repurposed as a chapel watched o'er the babe.

"There, there she is," said Vivien. "Ready for mama to hold her."

Cursings and Blessings from the line of Uther Pendragon. The words at once flooded back at the very instant Onbrawst picked up the dark-haired little bundle.

"Look at those bright eyes!" Vivien was crowding over Onbrawst's shoulders, anxious to take in as much new baby as possible. Then she saw the eyes, which most certainly had been grey-blue upon birth.

Onbrawst saw what Vivien saw. She interpreted Vivien's pause – for she shared it as well.

The baby's eyes had changed to a soft golden color with dark speckles in the gold and hues of bronze around the pupil.

The touch of the baby was different, and not. The scent of the baby was new, yet still Onbrawst's very own. The baby had changed but was yet hers.

Queen Onbrawst, a warm and sweet woman who greeted more oft with hug and kiss than bow and handshake, had felt, against all her might, the seeping loss of natural affection toward the child from that day forward.

Difficulties compounded over the years to follow and, when any person would pose a question to the effect of "what is wrong with her?", Onbrawst would give a public answer to quickly defend the lass; but the deepest secret caverns of her soul gave another.

To herself, she said: "She was changed, if she is my baby girl at all."

Onbrawst did all to love her, even by rote, but was filled with a shameful relief when Vivien agreed to foster Gwyar when she turned eight.

CHAPTER 9
The Watchful Steward

The tears that accompany rejoicing contain extra salt, and find a way into every wrinkle fashioned by so many smiles over the years. Salty tears and blue woad paint rendered the noble king's face a mess.

The Tribes rarely wore facial dyes. They did so for ceremonial reasons, or periodically to honor their ancestors. The bishops constantly lobbed critical quips about body markings, whether under or upon the skin, as 'heathen barbarism', and the practice was diminishing. Arthur favored a handful of different uniforms, armor and appearances and did, to manifest extra ferocity, don the paint from time to time.

On his right cheek was an image like an inverted arrow head or three rays of light. The image was called *the Awen* and represented divine inspiration. To a Christian, the image was viewed as a beautiful picture of the Trinity, depicting light that can be felt but not seen, light that can be seen but not felt and, lastly, light that can be both felt and seen. To the Druids and other sects, it had diverse meanings. Upon his left cheek was a perfectly rendered bear claw; the sigil of the Silures. And so, the decorated story upon his face rendered 'Arthur, the Iron Bear, is divinely inspired to vanquish the invader and save his people'.

This imagery borne upon his visage was messianic and menacing.

Less menacing was his handsome face, now just a smear of blue with a touch of frost and smudges of mud. Some of what was now a distasteful blue paste crept into the corner of his mouth.

"Victory is brackish and makes me look ugly!" Arthur jested aloud, laughing and laughing. Certainly, this was the zenith of his military career and he was filled with elation. He could not possibly feel better.

Optimism flooded over the king. Merlin would be found (probably not in attendance deliberately to teach another of his obscure and treasured, but hard to receive, lessons – this one maybe about learning to rely on others more than the aging Wizard), and he was about to be home for an extended spell after three separate war campaigns. The coldness between he and Gwenhwyfar surely would thaw.

All would be well at this, the dawn of the Summer Kingdom.

Arthur gave Excalibur one final loop into the sky, stars kissing the blade, then sheathed it gracefully. His red cape whirled around, and his blue helmet was cradled beneath his left arm. The night was dark, grimy and filled with death and fright but, in spite of this, the Round Table fellows, archers, and soldiers looked upon their king, inhaling pride at how regal he looked.

Many fires were blazing atop Baeden. There was a sloped plain where pavilions and well-organized stations of munitions, food and provisions were positioned. A short walk up and leftward of the plain revealed a thick, frightful forest. A rear guard assault through the forest was impossible, due to the lack of entry points and the natural positioning of the hill. The enemy would have to go through the plain if they desired to hide in the forest.

Or be smuggled in unawares.

So many torches contrasting against the white of the tents rendered it almost as if it were yet day and not well after midnight. The fighting had stopped below but there was a brief frenzy of disorganization due to the euphoria of victory: a moment of chaos for an always well-ordered army. The king scanned scores of faces amongst the tents until he spotted Llacheu's likeness, several hundred feet away.

Arthur hollered after his son.

"Llacheu! My son, my son, we did it!"

The shimmering knight, yet at a distance, did not acknowledge his father's spirited yell. Rather, he continued to make his way outside the torch-lit boundaries, now very near the forest. The prince walked with a small company of young men and the behavior was not suspicious, given the noise and circumstance. Arthur continued to swim as a salmon, muscling upstream through friends, warriors, choir singers, noblewomen and physicians, trying to get one hug from his son ere he considered respite for what remained of 'victory day'.

After four minutes more of trailing after the boy, Arthur finally caught stride with the small troop encircling Prince Llacheu. They were in the forest, but not the thick. Owls and an adder made protest at the crackling caused by the boots of men. The Pendragon softly clasped the boy's shoulders and gave a fatherly tug, whirling the lad around and finding the eyes of his child.

His boy was still wearing his helmet. It was ornate and the envy of the army: golden with a simple groove inlaid for a crown and dragon wings adorning the sides like fins. Llacheu's chin and eyes alone were exposed.

At the instant the king opened his mouth to proudly greet the Prince, Arthur saw, or perhaps rather felt, Cai's battle club find the back of Llacheu's helmet. A clangor of metal, then dull resonation, long lasting. The blow dropped the recipient's chin down hard against his own chest plate. Head springing back up, likely as reflex only, he managed to turn towards his assailant.

This was Cai's aim. The next swing separated helmet from head, cracking the top of Llacheu's skull. The fatal blow spilled the prince's brains all over his father. Arthur's face was now tears of two kinds: blue paint, and his own son's grey matter, splattered and smeared.

Llacheu's blue eyes now white-grey, he crashed hard and stiff to both knees, then rolled left to wintery, muddy ground; dead. The dagger meant for his father twitched along with nerves still active in a dead left hand.

Horns were sounding above, but Arthur heard them not. Others had seen the action developing and were already furiously sprinting into defensive positions at the edge of the wood. 'Twas not a small circle of youthful soldiers carrying on outside the battle camp that Arthur had happened upon. It was ambush. It was treachery.

Approximately nine hundred Saxons had been carefully and meticulously placed into the woods by twenty villainous Britons from the North. Thanks to his treacherous son, they were positioned within striking distance to ambush the king.

The tactic was obvious when later analyzed.

Nine hundred loosely disciplined infantry could not overcome the thousands of Cymry led by professional equestrian soldiers. Nor was that their aim. Rather, the dodge was to lure Arthur away, slay the king and a small number of key leaders. The traitors commanding the scheme would do this in the forest and then pretend to vanquish or capture the very Saxons with whom they were in league. Arthur would be dead and Llacheu crowned a puppet king.

But Cai, the Steward of King Arthur, had sniffed out the ruse. It was his appointment to watch everything.

At the moment the boy's shattered head met earth, it was three hours past midnight and a mist suddenly filled the forest, as if some great dragon had set his nostrils to cinder the entire wood, joined in outraged accord with the Britons. Arthur had not a moment to consider his own despair. Bedwyr had rapidly readied Arthur's steed and the Pendragon was at an instant mounted, with his spear unharnessed and ready, a long black weapon called Rhongomyniad. He engaged in killing the immediate near threat, the young warriors who were with the bloody corpse that had once been his son. When these were all slain, by the king's own hand, the Round Table Companions paused.

"How will we identify friend from foe in the mist? Even in daylight, some are our own kinsmen," said a mounted knight, dejected and anxious.

"Hawk of May." The call of the king was stone, bereft of emotion.

"Yes, my Lord." Gwalchmai step-jumped forward, ready to receive instruction from the great War King.

"Where your feet trod, the Sun shines." Arthur surveyed his options rapidly and continued. "In the mist, fifty men will seem as five hundred. Bring but fifty and gather all white battle standards." Here, Arthur's natural leadership attributes exceeded those of all men, even the Merlin. At key moments, champions make key decisions.

"The white standard will cast shadow against the dragon's white breath. At the same time, burn the top of the standard, creating bright oranges and yellows. As one banner burns out, have your men rapidly set another alight." As Arthur spoke, Gwalchmai was absorbing the plan swiftly. The hearers marveled at the brilliance of using white against white to produce contrasting shadow. The Hawk of May had the scene mapped in his mind and was ready to act.

"If a cluster of men are not under the Sun you've created," Arthur continued, "then they are not of us. End them." Arthur looked to the lump that was his son, the fostered traitor.

"Know this, friends. We will probably not discover the leader of this plot out here in the cold tonight. Kill without discernment or investigation. We cannot negotiate with treachery. The truth will out in the fullness of its time."

"We are to it!" said several Round Table Companions.

Bedwyr was friend first, Round Table Companion second. Having grown up with both Arthur and Gwenhwyfar, he looked at the king for a fleeting moment, knowing the heartbreak that would rush in when the thrush and thrust of the battle was over. Llacheu's death (compounded by the manner thereof) would ruin Gwenhwyfar beyond redemption. Only one of her sons now lived and he was far to the North sweeping for tertiary raids, significantly removed from the fight, safe amongst monks, priests and Druids up in Ynys Mons.

Would it ruin Arthur too?

Arthur had sent Llacheu for his fosterage to the steady thorn, the cantankerous rebel Caw. He did this as a demonstration of the king's grace and endless selfless and creative approaches for peace. Caw concocted endless superfluous land disputes in all directions, ever hassling Maelgwn, Urien and even suing for tracts as far south as Erging. Although incorrigible, Caw was reputed to be a good father of several sons and daughters, many of whom were radically loyal to Arthur. The Pendragon had visited Llacheu oft during his two summers and both Arthur and the Golden Prince had enjoyed holding Caw's newborn son, Gildas, earlier that very year.

The disputes had not seemed murderous.

Neither treacherous. Yet, apparently, they were both. If, Bedwyr speculated, Caw sought to use the confusion at the conclusion of Baeden to assassinate the king, if he had turned Llacheu indeed against his own father, then what of the other son? What of Amr? Amr was under the roof of Caw as well, the two brothers having been sent North together.

Bedwyr paused his speculation. He, Owain, Cadwr and Gwalchmai took ten and fell in behind Arthur and his ten. Into the thick of the wood they went.

At just after three in the morning the Pendragon gave a softly spoken order, carried out uniformly, with discipline and fearsome perfection.

"Blaze them."

Instantly banners of white became crackling orange, yellow, blue and red. The knights were thigh high in mist and vaulted by banner and flame. The sight was so menacing that even the forest ghosts feared these men and not the reverse. The tactic illuminated the woods and at once differentiated friend from foe. Scores of the black lacquered leather chest armor were made manifest as expected, and not a few of the Ravens from the North.

Arthur opted for Excalibur, putting away his renowned spear, and brandished the Sword of Power, personally leading the advance.

The Britons that practiced Vivien and Maelgwn's methods were not hackers, not undisciplined, not aggressive. Their method was driven by counter-fighting. A diagonal position was ever maintained, except at the moment of the counter maneuver, away from the opponent's strong hand. When, on rare occasion, the Briton would need to strike first, a 'goad' was required, provoking the enemy to move, and to err. The goad took many forms, from a shifting step towards the opponent, to an intentional lazy jab, a head feint or an intentionally weak sword thrust to the foot of the opponent, enticing a drop of high guard or other ill-planned reaction.

With mist confusing belt line level maneuvers and the burning fabrics above creating disorientation, Arthur wheeled Excalibur around high, twice, three, now four times. He then waved down in the mist, well below the belt line.

The 'up, up, up, then down' goad inevitably caused the Saxon's eyes to search for the steel downward below the mist line. Upon their low aggressive strikes, Arthur would move but slightly to the side yet simultaneously forward through the plane of the blow, maintaining his diagonal line, and put Excalibur to the rib cage of the opponent. The union of Excalibur's sharpness and Arthur's technique rendered this a *one move kill shot*.

Up, up, up, then down, slide on the diagonal, kill through the ribs.

Although Owain, Bedwyr, Cadwr and the Hawk of May picked off sundry Saxons, Arthur himself was well ahead of them, tilling his enemy as a plow through soft soil.

There was no mania or screaming, neither was Arthur outside of himself. Methodically and stately, the Pendragon wedged through and annihilated the enemy. It is not known if even one Saxon or traitor escaped the slaughter within the ghostly and frightful wood north of the tabletop-shaped plane at the peak of Mynydd Baeden.

Bedwyr's eyes compassed the high willow and black poplar trees glaring down hard upon him.

"Now there be hundreds more fellows to haunt these woods," said Bedwyr to the trees.

The sun rose on day three after the battle had ensued and King Arthur was finally in his tent for the elusive sleep. The nation had been saved, but Arthur had nearly been felled by his own son. The sum of the matter being too much for even Arthur's balanced disposition, he politely asked Cai to remain awake and guard the tent (yet from afar, so that not even Cai would hear the king).

This Cai did.

Certainly, this was the abyss of Arthur's parenting career. Yet his mind went to Amr and his heart told him the abyss was yet bottomless. He could not feel worse.

Arthur wept.

CHAPTER 10
To Broceliande

A dark messenger clad head to foot in black had bidden Merlin go to the mysterious forests of Broceliande in the land of the Bretons. And Merlin was required to hearken to the call, dreadfully ill timing notwithstanding.

It grieved Merlin mercilessly to miss the Battle of Mynydd Baeden.

The days and events leading up to the epic – and where the Saxons were concerned, final – confrontation of his generation were a swirl of intrigue and change. In addition to being summonsed to this covert congress in Brittany, Merlin's acute, if not supernatural, discernment alerted him that the altercation with the bishops at Caerleon might result in them putting him in the dirt, permanently.

Pious men become corrupt with anger and corrupt men plunge into villainy. Hatred and misunderstanding (or understanding all the more) leads to a path of darkness and evil. Merlin felt he was at dire risk to be thrust into the Deep by the religious and atop this he had to make his mind ready, along with many arrangements, to go before the Brotherhood that had guided his spiritual journey for countless moons.

There were preparations ere he met with them that were not optional.

The dark messenger communicated to Merlin that it was time for him to complete the circle and to compass the square, to learn the Secret Rite. The pinnacle and crown of all esoteric wisdom; the final step in the spiral staircase of becoming. Because Merlin now knew in his heart that he would attend the meeting to learn *about* this mystery but not partake *in* it, he fully recognized that his travels to Brittany might be a one-way journey.

This Brotherhood was not the local orders of Druids, but rather a more enlightened guild several rungs above his local colleagues (whose most sacred mysteries did but approach the outer porches of the Sacred Wisdom possessed by the Brotherhood). They were a Principality not to be trifled with.

The native faith was waxing like a moth-eaten old garment. Beautiful and vibrant in parts, elsewise steadily diminishing. And in no way dangerous.

Merlin had ever been a free-thinker. He naturally eschewed anything overly organized or official when it came to the governance of men's souls. And this extended to men and women of cloth, rank and diadem without respect of persons. From his earliest memories Merlin had intensely hated centralized power and corruption. This, he and Arthur shared with uncanny identical fervor.

There were, at Merlin's time, only a few strongholds of the old Druidic orders (notwithstanding the utter norths of Albion where the Picts ruled). Ynys Mons, where a remnant remained of that fateful Roman purge so long ago, and Lough Derg in Eire. This was the sacred inland island where Patrick did not quite exterminate all of the 'snakes', as is commonly reported. A revival led by the daughter of Gebhan had flowered. Ironically, the very places that tyrants sought to annihilate from history protested violently by and through their obstinacy and existence.

These two locations wielded some influence that could even match and apply leverage with the Christian politicians.

Aside from these, each royal court had twelve Bards (but this was an office and not a religion) and a few tribes still featured two small, local councils, the Druids and the Dynion Hysbys. The Druids were at all times confused with and blamed for the deeds of the Dynion Hysbys.

In Brittany and Cerne, Christ and His bishops ruled but followers of the old gods; sacred Tree and Water cults persisted, and Vivien was their queen.

Although formally attached to none, the Wizard was somehow viewed as Arch-Druid over all. The Dynion Hysbys especially hated Merlin because he had made an open show of their corruption and folly when he was yet a boy during that incident when the coward Vortigern was building a fortress near the town that now bears the Wizard's name.

Yet they too, when confronted, would acquiesce to the Merlin.

Not so for the Brotherhood that had summonsed him.

Truly Merlin coveted the knowledge of the other Adepts, but now he was intent upon communicating to them a secret; a Hidden Thing, of his own. The Catholic priests surely now officially loathed him and the Cymry bishops were in angry contemplation, brooding and stewing about his words. Thus, Merlin faced perils behind him and soon, perils from his own.

It was three days after the beginning of the battle. Merlin's strategy allowed him to make a reasonable calculation that the enemy was now starving and thirsty and had probably made their terminal decision to fight their way up the hill. If the tribes of the Britons had been patient and carried out their part, victory was at hand, if not already won.

Merlin was long past exhaustion from traversing up north of Maesteg first, then through the city of his birth and then winding north yet further again, up past Gwynedd, to his initial destination. Afterwards, he had cut back across the midlands and down south to the port where he would travel by barge to Brittany. Ten youthful warriors could not match the Druid's verve but, on this day, he was sore tired.

A man of great years, he had seen a span of events equal to several lifetimes. Merlin had been eyewitness to the cowardice of Vortigern, hiring and transplanting Saxons to Cymru's shores. He had seen Northern Britain crippled after the Night of Long Knives, had guided difficult and sometimes contradictory policies to help the mighty men of Ynys Mons and Gwynedd in the

Old North not pass into extinction (as was the ever encroaching reality for the tribes of Lloegyr in the East). And now many of those same mighty men resented the Silures, and were leaning religiously towards Rome.

He marveled in his long years at too many examples of vanity and greed in the form of endless raids and land skirmishes; witness to the utter foolishness of men that culminated in the Scots and the Gaels swapping great swathes of each other's countries.

Merlin had been present when a holy well sprang at the passing of one Pendragon, and he had personally consoled a second when his career was cut short by yet more cowardice by the Germanic maniacs.

Merlin enjoyed wine and hard drink, cider and ale; the best in the world, by his unbiased estimation. He lived hard, laughed often and drew upon mysterious authority as and when needed.

Merlin loved his mother and had never known his father.

He had been married once to a wife lost, Gwendoloena, and had lusted for but one woman since her passing: Nimue.

Merlin saw things in the Isles that he loved so dear, and things terrifying. The Wizard witnessed things that challenge, alter and disrupt every man's worldview, regardless of his gods. These were the Blessed Isles and Merlin understood many of their secrets and why they were coveted. *The Coveted Isles.*

And he was blessed enough to see the rise of King Arthur, the Iron Bear and savior of his people.

Through the myriad failures in every person's life, of enterprise and relationship, of family quarrels and failed crops, of mentorships gone afoul, once in a lifetime chance happens and a person gets it right. And Merlin had got it right when it came to Arthur.

Thinking of the thirty-three-year-old sovereign gave Merlin a grin that produced happy, permanent smile-wrinkles.

Arthur was a ready pupil, a focused, accountable and competitive student, and above all attributes, was aware of the burden of his own place in history. Arthur was a living legend and, up to now, with no sign of wavering, managed it to perfection. When he needed to be warm, he was warm. When he needed to be aloof, withdrawn. When anger was called for, wrathful. When forgiveness the needful thing, gracious and friendly.

Moreover, Arthur was a warm, jovial, attentive and wonderful father. Attributes oft not reciprocated by his sons, Merlin time and time again observed. Arthur selflessly handled this sad situation as well, empathizing with and regretful for the long shadow he cast over their lives.

The young king's love life was a tightly guarded vault that not even Merlin could breach. The true love modeled daily by his parents did not translate to Arthur, as if some great fracture lay upon his heart. The king did not walk around gloomy or defeated by this, but his relationship with Gwenhwyfar seemed more of office than romance. Yet the Merlin doubted not that he loved her.

Great was Merlin's regret at missing his pupil

and friend's moment of glory and the more Merlin immersed himself in regret, the more he determined to finish his course, and return to his king, alive. To this end, before leaving in the middle of the night at the conference in Caerleon, the Merlin secured the greatest surety of survival that any person living in that legendary and perilous time could. The Druid swayed Maelgwn to leave Baeden early (and that only if victory was at hand) and to accompany him to and, by the Grace of God, from Broceliande.

They met at a port in Glamorgan later named after Arthur and it was a direct route south into Brittany. Ironically, the Merlin had traveled far from Baeden and then stealthily traversed back near the battle area to leave by boat for Broceliande.

Thus, Maelgwn, the Bloodhound Prince, upon abandoning Baeden near its conclusion, did not travel far.

One never knew the reception they would receive from the warrior greater than Achilles.

Though three hundred orderly vessels stacked the shores and many boatmen bustled about, these two stood out like cedar trees amongst mulberry bushes, two or more heads taller than any of their kinsmen.

For this reason, the salutations were brief to mitigate being seen. Merlin was nearly as tall as Maelgwn, and their moment of recognition created one of those instances where history pauses, and remembers. Two titans, ever used to condescending, exchanged a wordless greeting; eye to eye.

Breaking the silence, Merlin but said: "Lancelot."

Two perfect light blue crystals where eyes should dwell were looking back. A deep mannish voice that shook the leaves yet was somehow soft: "Merlin. To Little Britain then?"

Maelgwn was famous for cutting to the quick and these few words allowed Merlin to fully trust that he would have his shield of protection, his escort.

"To Broceliande."

CHAPTER 11
Follow the Gold

"Bedwyr. Where is he?"

Arthur's face now was clean. His short beard, at this season of life still full of the sandy colors of youth, was groomed and he was as presentable as a man operating on four hours of sleep, after three days of glory matched in equal measure with hell, could be.

A windy winter drizzle had brought back the mists but now there was a morning respite from ill weather. A sunny rainbow had formed, seemingly resting directly upon the Pendragon's tent.

Bedwyr's disposition did not match the break in the weather. His face was ashen; his eyes scanned the frozen snowy greens below.

"Which he?" Bedwyr gazed to the blue winter skies. "Merlin not found. Maelgwn…" No words, or angels from the sky cascaded down to help the great knight. "Maelgwn now added to the missing."

No response was made (or needed), beyond the king encouraging Bedwyr to join him for the first meal of the day.

Shortly after, he went down and reposed with his men, who had also built a valley of white tents beneath the shadow of Baeden. As mid-morning progressed, he found himself losing the great optimism he had enjoyed from the night before. The king was now sensing that a great wrong had befallen his counselor, his friend. The Merlin possessed unparalleled strategic and tactical warfare skills, yet he was absent to see Arthur carry out his strategy with absolute perfection. Arthur wished he could repeat the moment of victory for the Merlin in the same way that a son wishes he could recapture a great fish when his father is away from camp and, by misfortune, misses his boy's great conquest.

Arthur now had his first few real moments to contemplate, consider and begin to investigate.

After the amphitheater assembly in Caerleon, Merlin and the bishops had exchanged words. This was not uncommon and, with the ruckus the Counselor of Britain had created with his speech, it would have been impossible for Arthur to hear a horn blown from his lap, let alone Merlin who, at that time, was far away from the king.

Perhaps the discord had been more than the standard rhetoric and rancor of priests and their competing gods. That was Arthur's only lead, and thin at that. Church offerings and tithes, land deeds, water baptism and Sunday attendance, matters of soul and entry into the next world were not the only 'fork in the road' quandaries now faced by a free nation. *For the first time, truly free.* Unfortunately, matters of sword and tax prevailed as well.

The Pendragon did not possess the largest

army in the known world but it had no peer for skill, vigor, loyalty, will and strategy. But would it continue to exist under its current construct? And should it? Arthur would soon have to congress with his twenty-four Round Table Companions (Arthur, the king, and the Champion Lancelot summing twenty-six) and then send the armies home for the winter – or longer.

The twenty-four Round Table Fellows, princes, kings and mighty men of Arthur's Britain, met on military matters alone. Arthur was the only connection between this fellowship of wartime companions and policy-making for the several kingdoms of Britannia. Each local *Rix* or chieftain served as a type of senator and, along with other representatives, formed a republican monarchy. The local tribal leaders made policy in their own lands. If tyranny arose at the local level and the natural rights of man were infringed, a petition could be made of the king, or, in some parts, of the Druids or of the Church. The Round Table Fellowship was committed to the protection of the borders of Britain and Brittany and to carrying out the wishes of the local tribes. National versus local. Never, declared the Bear of Glamorgan, would the twain mix.

Should the unified army disband, reduce or remain? What was their role in a dawning era of peace? Should Arthur take Rome as his great grandfather had? The proper course of action in imminent peace is as dangerous as when faced with imminent war.

Merlin would certainly know. But he was gone.

Urien, still smarting from scouting whilst his

brothers had got to slay the Long Knife, brought a good tiding for his king.

"The Boar is awake," he grumbled.

Instead of fretting about what he could not control (Merlin's whereabouts), the great king attended to that which he could (deposing Aelle).

"We shall congress with our companions tomorrow, Bedwyr. I go now to see my enemy, alas, eye to eye, held this hour in the camp of King Urien."

"Will you run him through?" Bedwyr asked.

The Pendragon's answer surprised Bedwyr. "Have you not seen enough of it, companion?" His eyes guided them both to pools of blood mixed with snowy, muddy hoof prints littered all around the pavilions.

"Cut the root, that it cease to bring forth bad fruit, my lord."

"You have the wisdom of the Bards, my friend," Arthur responded. "And to that subject, we must swiftly get word to the queen before she hears it as a Bardic ballad first. Will you please personally go and give her the report? That our lands and her father's lands are safe. Safe. Safe from all save the cost paid to earn it."

"To that task I shall presently attend." Bedwyr departed from the presence of Arthur, full of dread for the questions that would ensue about the queen's son on the immediate other side of rejoicing over the victory. And he wagered the sorrow would outweigh the elation. Greatly.

"There is much merit to Bedwyr's sentiment," said King Urien. Arthur and the powerful young king of the Old North paced thrice round the tent wherein Aelle was bound.

Urien's closest men had fought against him personally during the battle. Their report, sure to be a Bard's song, revealed that the aging king of the South Saxons was swift as Lancelot with a sword but forgot himself with rage, resulting in clumsy unbalance, and that Lancelot himself had been needed to undo him.

Aelle had slain ten Britons but moved ahead of his left rear flank in the course of action. Isolated and then cut off from his men, Aelle was defenseless as Lancelot clipped his left knee and right hand with one action. The Champion of Britain did this intentionally when he desired a prisoner instead of a corpse. The motion was effortless, fluid and looked more a short dance than a sword fight. Stunned and wounded, the Saxon warrior was easily subdued after that.

Prisoner of a tree stump within the tent, Aelle saw the flap ripple open. The sunlight kissed the ground and splintered shards of light through the white fabric. The Saxon heard, either in earnest or in his head, the melody of Bardic ballads. A god greater than Odin entered the tent, clothed in the sun, compassed in all glory. Nothing better reflects the measure of a man than how he is seen in the mind's eye of his most hated enemies.

Arthur had no such gilded imagery for the foe before him.

Aelle. Pretender ruler of a sliver of the Isle, earned illegitimately. He had secured the Insula Vectis, a small but important daughter island off the mainland in Lloegyr. This fiend had sacked twenty small towns over many years of raiding and conquest, including an infamous and despicable tale of sore treatment of an entire river village near a place called Adeferas. The village had been abandoned but for an afternoon as its warriors went north in chase instead of staying put. What happened to the women, the children, and the elderly had haunted bedtime warnings and ruined mealtime reflections for two decades now.

Aelle had led them.

Aelle had been first man off the raiders' boat, boasting of this always.

All leaders of merit are first historians, and Arthur knew the history of this man.

The greying leader of the greatest foreign invasion against the tribes of the Britons since before the days of Magnus Maximus was a full head taller than Arthur and half again his mass in muscle (the Bear of Glamorgan himself no small man), yet Aelle was ashamed that he had fought against this man and would have bowed before Arthur save for the bindings that prevented him.

Instead he gazed upon Arthur with defeated eyes.

King Arthur was wearing a simple blue tunic, trousers, with black belt and boots. Crimson caped with a large embroidered ensign aligned atop his left breast. A small silver shield was clasped to the great sovereign's right shoulder, itself covered with an additional sigil. The Saxon beheld the *Walles* warrior, wearing simple cuffs and thin silver breastplate; minimal armor for speed, coverage only upon mortal parts, in design superior to Roman armor, in appearance beautiful like unto their ancestors from Troy.

Aelle's eyes moved now to the king's helmet, tucked snugly in his left arm. Stories had spread amongst the Saxon tribes that Arthur's Champion was engineer of the *Walles* armor, that he found no function in Roman helmets that covered a man's nose at the expense of his vision, that he had fitted the helmet more closely to conform to the face of the wearer, removing any extra weight or distraction beyond that which was necessary to save a man's life from arrow, axe, sword or spear. The German marveled at the Briton. Lacking plume or horn, the simple helmet was fitted roundly to a man's head. Arthur's bore two draconian or serpentine fins above the ear and a special groove whereby he could wear, when the occasion was meet, a simple circlet of gold.

Sandy hair and blue eyes revealed a brain that was always busy. A king of Glamorgan and Gwent at fourteen and surely but a fortnight from being crowned Emperor of the World should he covet such. Aelle beheld a man who was a legend.

Even my people call their children Arthur! he cried within. His eyes panned down to the brand sheathed in the king's belt. *But not known for legendary mercy!*

Excalibur remained yet in scabbard, for now. Arthur knew not if the old Saxon spoke the Cymry tongue. Some of his forebears had been conscripts of Rome and thus, by deduction, Arthur tried Latin.

"This is a time of war and this is no mean country. However, it is not requisite that you be judged under the laws extended to a citizen of Glamorgan, or of the Confederacy of Britons," he began.

"Dragon." Aelle's Latin was broken but

functional. "I know no law but death, no mandate but to wipe the *Walles* from OUR land. If you slay me bound like an animal, then like your enemy you will become. Wherewith then would we be different?"

The Saxon King did fear Arthur. The fear was a poison that oscillated between worshipful reverence and overt hatred, making Aelle double-minded, and very dangerous. Fear was the prevailing mechanism and its agency at last gave way fully to his hatred of the Britons. Moreover, by provoking this god-like king, Aelle might be slain, but not deposed.

Arthur, though anxious, even hungry, to rid the world of Aelle, was not to spring the trap, not soon to let hunger take the bait. And then, a random glance passed upon Aelle's scrip, a simple leather purse. It was worn and soft, revealing a bulge of gold coins.

Illtud had required that Arthur study the economy of gold and, when war campaigns interrupted the course of schooling, Merlin took up the slack and made Arthur do the same.

In times past it had been used as means for exchange on the Isles. At other times, gold was only used for trade and purchasing power at the ports. Presently, the currency of the Cymry was land deeds, livestock, property and rights of inheritance. A complex system which intended to give every man, low or high born, the same opportunity, was not without error or corruption. It led fallen men to manipulate laws and lent itself to raiding (indeed, the theft of another man's horse was a capital offense throughout the Isles) but it spared them from being poisoned with lust for gold.

During one of many discussions considering a policy change, Merlin had taught Arthur about value-based currency founded upon precious metals. But he had also made a warning. A warning turned memory that flew now as a fiery dart into Arthur's recollection.

"Remember this." The old Druid had paused so that Arthur would mark him. "When pursuing the source of a conflict, follow the gold."

In the Mystery Schools, Merlin had been made to learn some legends about men of great wealth, without respect to nation, kindred or culture. These bowed not to any God save themselves, and loaned gold to both sides of a conflict to ensure, regardless of outcome, the wielding of power greater in might than ten Excaliburs: debt. Merlin could see hints and shadows of this practice staining the variant Christian churches, but knew not its source.

Arthur began to deconstruct the situation as if the Merlin were at his side, lecturing, quizzing and provoking. *Who would Aelle be indebted to if today had been his victory at Baeden? Who is he indebted to now?*

"There were legions of Saxons, Angles, Jutes, Picts and some Ravens from the north of my own blood in league with you. Now they lie, fodder for vultures." Arthur evoked the authority of words just as Merlin had trained him. "How did you feed, arm and transport them?"

"Victory fed them, bravery armed them and they were borne here by truth."

"What is truth?" posed Arthur.

Aelle's disposition shifted in the twinkle of

an eye to that of a man who wanted to remove the stones of burden from his chest, for he knew he would not be spared. In these cases, talking can prolong the blade, provided that the talking is profitable. "This Island is the germinating seed of something more terrible than you or your cursed Wizard have foreseen; nay, *can* foresee. Though you were victorious today, you have lost. And would you have lost, you would have won."

"Riddles must come with age," sighed Arthur, now looking deep through the shutters that housed the soul of the aging king of the South Saxons. "You have not my Merlin's wit, however. How now, Aelle, would a defeated chieftain in any wise be rendered a victor?"

Knowing some of the truth of the matter, Aelle conjured a veil and lied overtly. "You would have been co-Emperor of the world with my three sons. Only a fool would rid the world of the great King Arthur. The *Walles* would be subjugated under the thumb of the house of South Saxons, your warriors conscripts, your women planted with the seed of Saxon. Your people who have no value to lift sword or push plow or spread legs – swept aside like Mayflies. But you, young king, would live, though your people be enslaved or perish."

Again, violence was tempered with the Pendragon's unwavering self-control.

"Postulate with all fantasy. The 'ifs' of the future are made irrelevant by the 'ares' of the present. For you, Saxon raider, have lost." Arthur, not deterred, returned to the paramount issue. "This catalyst for evil, who gave it to you?"

The Bear of Glamorgan made an aerial show of the contents of the scrip. The tent rained, for a moment, with Roman gold.

Aelle answered him not.

CHAPTER 12
The Bishops Adjudication
of Merlin

Now, the prominent bishops and elders of the Church of the Britons were these:

Dyfrig (who was also called Dubricious), the Bishop of Llandaff, a See founded by King Meurig.

Bishop Teilo, Dyfrig's chief disciple.

Illtud the Wise, teacher, preacher and philosopher from Caer Bovum, near the palace of Meurig and Queen Onbrawst.

Aidan, disciple of Dyfrig.

Bishop Comereg.

Meirchion, a very old man born at Glywysing in Arthur's kingdom of Glamorgan. He made residence in a palace near Illtud's school. Although from the South, his line hailed from the house Coel Hen, giving him deeply imbedded allies and affinity to the Old North. He was naturally amongst the southern kings placed in authority in the North to help fill the vacuum from the Night of Long Knives. Meirchion, who is also called Mark I, converted wholly to Catholicism and became something unique to the Isles; a sort of Roman Catholic priest-king.

(Being of royal pedigree as qualification for service in the clergy was not uncommon to the Isles. They, too, believed they were a nation of priests and kings. However, they maintained a strict segregation of power and function. Often, a king would retire and become an elder, or a solitary saint. Sometimes a bishop would retire young and become a knight. That Mark did both was abhorrent, and bothered Illtud, above the others, to no end.)

Bishop Cadfan, son of Eneas and Gwen Teirbron from Brittany, but schooled under Illtud.

Bedwini, Bishop of Caerleon and Arthur's great friend.

Not present was David son of Non. He was but sixteen and sent home to Mynyw in the far south west of Cymru.

And so it was that these seven bishops, plus the Priest-King Meirchion, remained long after the armies started their war march to Ogmore to prepare for Baeden. *The bishops and elders were preparing for a battle of their own.*

They met in a small, comely timber home in Gelliwig, which is in Gwent. Queen Gwenhwyfar was lodging in a stately white house nearby.

There was an ancient custom amongst the Britons that required secrecy and safety regarding anything shared privily amongst the clergy (and the Bards and Druids before them). *Secrecy unto the grave.* This custom created comfort and confidence, allowing the elders to speak their minds without fear of gossip, as gossip on spiritual matters could directly result in the separation of one's head from their body.

Knowing this custom, Meirchion, a hideous hybrid of a crone and stork, save with great swine ears, arrogantly spoke first.

"He must die. A dangerous heretic with the High King's ear is a danger to the safety of the Nation, and her soul." Meirchion slumped down on a lounging couch, hungrily and rudely pushing around a charger filled with meats and cheeses.

"You would place the Bishop of Rome at the king's ear in the place of his Druid." Dyfrig was not only bishop of the See located closest to that golden fortress of such fame where met the Table Round Fellowship in Caermelyn; he was also the unofficial leader of the primitive Church of the Britons, and commanded much respect from these men. "And that is your purpose here, Mark the Mad."

"See my sword?" Meirchion unsheathed his leaf blade, showing but a hint of steel above hilt, and then re-sheathed it. "Many have seen the rest of it for calling me that. And it was the last thing they saw. Shall I show you my madness?"

"We've suffered the fullness of violence on our Islands. For a thousand generations. Forever. If we yet have a nation when our boys return home, let us have an end of it. Let us rather endeavor always for peace. And a just peace indeed, not in word only." Bedwini was Arthur's personal bishop and ever spoke with a pleasant voice.

"Blessed is the peacemaker," Meirchion mocked Bedwini, and continued eating.

Dyfrig didn't flinch at the Crone-Stork's boorish threats. Utterly ignoring them, he gracefully took command of the discourse. "I do not like you, King Mark, but I concur on this. He does have our High King's ear. And not his alone. Merlin might be the most influential man in these Isles. His prophecies are honored by men of all religions. His riddles ever create awe and men dedicate whole days to gleeful analysis of them. He dazzles children; he brings joy and then, at an instant, fear and mystery. I cannot find the word." The bishop looked through a window at the heavenly hosts observing them, twinkling with their diverse glories and curiosity. "Merlin is a star.

"Morever," said Dyfrig, "his battle strategies have directly put us at the precipice of winning this war. The brains behind our army's bulk. This is as much Merlin's Britannia as it is our Arthur's."

All nodded at this truth. The men paused for some dining and then Dyfrig resumed.

"Let me tell of you briefly of another man. His name was Marcion and he lived about four hundred years ago. From Pontus, he was once succored by the Church in Rome, but then in the process of time he..." Dyfrig again searched for careful words, "...saw Scriptures and practices differently. He, like the Merlin, changed."

Dyfrig's face crinkled here with serious consternation. "He professed words similar to what fall from the Merlin's lips, and men heard him and believed. A sect formed around Marcion, a sect based upon no sect. An organization based upon no organization. His cult came to detest all of the institutions and ordinances that have been the center, guidestone and devotion of our heavenly calling. These Marcionites threatened all established religion, rejected any priesthood or ecclesiastical authority, and radically encouraged individual study and an obsession that would have no man in Church on Sunday yet all paying lip service to loving the Lord. All centered on this notion, this *easy believism* they called *GRACE."*

The learned men were well-read and had studied Marcion and his heresies, but none had connected them to the Druid's disposition until Dyfrig illuminated the situation.

"Men will hear Merlin and should they swear by him or adopt his revelations, we will no longer have to worry about fighting Rome for paramount authority, nor for Land Grants or territories. Neither will Rome concern herself with making us drink of her cup." He looked sharply at the Catholic ruler, and his eyes met Cadfan's as well. "Why?" He asked the assembly and then answered his own question. "Because Merlin will have all men everywhere end all Religion. Theirs and Ours." He pointed at Meirchion and then to himself and Illtud.

"Surely you would not have us slay Merlin?" Saint Illtud the Wise at last spoke up.

Dyfrig clasped bony fingers together, rendering the tips red, and the knuckles white. "No, we shall not."

Meirchion rose in anger.

"Sit down." Dyfrig and Illtud were in unison, crisp and direct.

"As a Druid, Merlin never evangelized Arthur to be a Druid. As a… whatever he has become, he would not evangelize our king to be as he. Imposition is not part of his anti-establishment composition."

"However…" Dyfrig's hands motioned

Meirchion back down yet again. "The ancient ideas and customs of the Druids are part of our heritage and diminishing. The very mention of Merlin's new beliefs may sow seeds that we cannot accept."

"Wherefore," the bishop's words were careful, "I propose exile and strong encouragement for retirement. Let him share with Arthur over ciders and strong wine what he will, but let us greatly reduce audience time with the king. Let us forcefully encourage Arthur to name another Bard to balance representation at Court."

"Retirement, not tyrannical murder." Bedwini the Peaceful was happy. "This is a balanced and just move."

All of the other bishops agreed to this, unanimously overwhelming the hard position of Meirchion (and the soft acquiescence towards him of Cadfan). Merlin's mysterious new beliefs, shared so brazenly at Caerleon, warranted censor and control, but not death.

At last Meirchion's manners, subtle and serpentine, changed. "Very well. Control the rebel pagan and isolate him in his age." He finished with an empty sneering: "Please."

The assembly agreed to retire and discuss recommendations for the baptism of Saxon converts, along with attendance and worship requirements, in a fortnight (if victory was nigh) and to fast and pray until they heard of the final disposition of the Battle of Mynydd Baeden.

As they exited the house, Meirchion caught Cadfan clean at the elbow, jerking him close. Grave whispers ensued.

"Son of Brittany, Son of Llyn. You connect the

Blessed Isles to the Continent."

"I'm just a student of Scripture who finds merit in the Sacraments of Rome," Cadfan said, humbly.

"You have lands of immeasurable importance. Doubt it not." Meirchion was yet slithery. "Now listen. Retirement is fine for the Merlin."

"Oh?" said Cadfan.

"Men travel in retirement. They visit loved ones. They repose in the serenity of silent contemplation on any number of our daughter islands, mountaintops or caves. And *sometimes*," a near hiss could be heard now, "sometimes misfortune befalls someone not often expected or missed at Court."

A low growl answered him. "And if long time unnoticed, sometimes they are simply forgotten altogether."

Meirchion unclamped Cadfan, allowing him to leave.

Next the Old Crone-Stork validated that Vivien was lodging in Gwenhwyfar's white house, resting for the night after the meetings in Caerleon.

Boldly, and with poorly feigned manners, he encroached upon the door of her chamber.

"A few words, Lady?"

CHAPTER 13
Will I Now Lose My Final Son Too?

Returning straightway from the battle, Bedwyr was met with warm reception as he politely petitioned the butler upon arriving at the residence of Queen Gwenhwyfar ferch Cywyrd. Known as the white house of Gelliwig, it was immaculate from vault to floorboard. Of all the palatial abodes and small lodges where the queen now had 'homes', this great and safe place was in earnest her only 'home'. Securely nestled under the best vantage point from Lodge Hill, she truly loved the serenity, safety and familiarity of this place. It was, after all, her father's home and she desired never to live outside the cantref where she had been born, although she had used to enjoy travel.

At thirty and five, grievous sorrow had doubled her years. The queen was a woman with passion and expertise in the advanced arts and toil of the world's most difficult occupation: motherhood. It was what she had been born for, what she excelled at; she was mother first, queen second, and tertiary wife.

And this 'mother of mothers' had, in just the past three seasons, lost two young sons in the Saxon Wars. Presently she worried to distraction about the remaining two. As soldiers bask in the glory of battle campaigns, boasting boldly of scars, touting questing tales of damsels fair and dragons felled, there is but brokenness back at hearth and home. Brokenness of mothers and wives. Brokenness that exceeds the capacity of the spirit, leaving shards where verve once flourished.

Hour over hour, there is despair in the place of daily functioning.

To see one's babe grow to fourteen and then go off to war, and this without exception, without respect of station or privilege, engendered all the more hatred towards the Germanic horde – the invaders. The Cymry possessed respect for all children and mothers under heaven. For this cause, they never invaded anyone, save (with the hypocrisy not lost on the common person) their own rival clans.

The queen, like any other parent, was numbered amongst the broken.

Struggling to flicker somewhere well beneath the surface of her ghostly shell, Gwenhwyfar still possessed great beauty and authority. Her hair was long and red, full of curls that were corralled, braided and plaited. Her torques were petite, but ornate. Her long neck flattered and displayed her hair, ending in perfect soft 'L's, curving over soft, round feminine shoulders. Firm breasts supported her beloved green gowns and the freckles upon her chest and shoulders were an alluring, speckled and adorable garnish. Her cheeks were a bit larger than her chin, her nose was turned up just so; her face was symmetrical, proportioned, winsome and commanding, a striking Cymry woman.

The beauty was still there, except for the eyes. These were sunken into pits, always purple around the soft fleshy area as if she had been struck daily upon the nose.

Already fair-skinned, her depression took her pale but healthy complexion and made it look as spilled milk. Her face and neck were almost translucent. She ever chewed upon her fingernails and her promenade was not quite right.

And she loathed company.

The butler knocked softly at the door of her massive chamber, a 'house within a house', and then Bedwyr, her childhood friend, the one she had known seasons before she met Arthur and the man with whom the couple supped most often (especially before and between the Three War Campaigns), entered.

Bedwyr did not speak first.

"So." The dark-circled emerald eyes opened wide, causing the red lashes that were their canopy to almost disappear entirely within the folds of sad and swollen skin. "Merlin's magick could not save him. He told me as much."

Bedwyr opened his mouth. Some sound and throat-clearing ensued, some hand motion that should accompany speech, but words, the great Knight could form not.

Only just inside the bedchamber doorway, a calming hand appeared upon the knight's shoulder.

"It was wrong to ask you to deliver news to my wife, our queen."

"Arthur!" Tears sprinted down his cheeks. "But how?"

"I finished with Aelle with as much haste as I could and am here to be my own messenger to our Lady. I will apprise you on Aelle later. Please," Arthur hugged Bedwyr hard, "go now and rest."

Bedwyr looked briefly upon the Corpse Queen. He exited.

The simple blue tunic of the king then embraced the ornate green gown. Gwenhwyfar accepted the hug, as it kept her failing body together.

Arthur Pendragon, the great king of the Britons, began to explain the death of Gwenhwyfar's third son with brave and rehearsed words, making every effort to bring a peace that passes understanding. Knowing that rumor and whisper would deliver the dark tiding of the treachery of Llacheu to the queen's ears, Arthur could not but tell her the truth. From the gore and detail he spared her, even upon her wail and request.

They cried.

They reminisced.

Gwenhwyfar spoke loud words most foul.

They napped.

They kissed hard.

She screamed while he held her.

For two days they ate not and drank but a little water. Over and over again, questions were posed, the open wound, the needing to know.

The never seeing their boy again.

The toll of three distinct war campaigns.

Screaming at God.

Cursing the Devil.

Bargaining for a return that would not be. That could not be.

The weeping.

Throughout the wrathful grieving that immediately follows loss, the king did all he could for the Queen of the Britons, but felt as if he was failing to serve her.

King Arthur had learned love, and loved outwardly, as modeled by his father. Meurig exhibited a true and rare adoration towards his spouse and constant companion, which included: gentleness, compromise, leadership, sacrifice, humor, affection and recognition of a woman's soft wisdom. The more senior Pendragon's only error was in not emphasizing to Arthur that such a love occurs next to never in this fallen world. In the spiraling dance of romance entwining men and women throughout the dispensations of time, real love is rare. When it is present in the home, when you see it all the time growing up as a lad, the expectation may develop that *what mother and father have must needs be for everyone,* and *certainly for me.* But this is rarely so.

Arthur came to love *Love* itself and the art of it more than he did the actual women in his life. A connection to the person was lost, obfuscated or long ago given away to someone else somewhere in the king's distant past and, though never cold, he had not yet found the deeper links with his wife that he saw daily between Onbrawst and Meurig.

As a result, when Arthur opened a door, he did it for the Office of Love, not necessarily for his woman. When he rubbed her feet and served her mead or cider, 'twas for some unknown, immeasurable standard of Love, and not as the relaxed and natural extension of time spent with his mate. When he complimented her for her excellence in ever mastering the difficulties of governing the home, three plenary courts, and a myriad of administrative functions, the words of high praise were a performance to Love, and not a pouring out upon her. And when he ensured she was pleasured (even if he could barely walk from the fatigue or pains of war), it was 'for Love'.

Moreover, when Arthur spoke poetically and deeply of handholds hewn in heavenly molds wherein one would know their true love at finger's first clasp, it was for the Office of Love. It was, ultimately, not for the woman whose hand he held.

None of this did the young king do with intention to hurt Gwenhwyfar or any damsel, nor was he even aware of the fracture. Love itself had entered in and become a surreptitious idol to the king. His parents' unattainable, perfect relationship, along with an incident during the spring king making rites, created of Arthur a complex and, in many ways, abnormal man in matters of the heart.

Though given the choice and accepted without dissimulation, the marriage with Gwenhwyfar was political. By rote, Arthur was a wonderful husband, lover and partner. Tragedy unearths pre-existing cracks within, exposing them. And then it fissures the crust of the soul. Warm and friendly, Arthur, at the time when consolation and warmth was most needed, found himself just a little cold towards Gwenhwyfar, distant.

And there was more.

Arthur, when not on the field of battle or

dominated by moments of war and defense, was lately of a truth thinking about another.

A painted and dark someone else.

Even with his son dead and extant blood yet to let in order to root out the treachery from within. Even with mountains more of private anxieties and discreet pressures yet to shoulder. Even with major policies and so many sleepless (and perhaps sleepless and *alone*) nights ahead before his Summer Kingdom could in earnest dawn, his thoughts ran not to these things but instead to a delicious and shadowy distraction; to taboo acts, spiritual, fleshly and wrong.

A princess and daughter of a Giant, dark, painted, tiny. They had met while schooling at Llantwit Major. And she and the queen shared the same forename.

However, Arthur would not empower his lust to long burn, taking his thoughts captive no sooner than they formed; for no man that has ever lived, save Jesus of Nazareth, was honorable as Arthur the Silure.

He held his wife day after day during the tempest of dread.

On day three the queen began to consider matters outside the immediate sphere of her grief. She queried the king, "How did Merlin not see this? Was this part of his losing the Sight?"

Arthur knew not of what she meant.

"Can we please speak to him now?" she asked, with soft urgency.

"I don't know where he is," Arthur said.

"I see. Then let's decide what to do about our son." Gwenhwyfar made a sharp-turning subject change.

"Of our Llacheu? Gwen, as I've said, we–"

"Nay," Gwenhwyfar interrupted. Staring out of a window, she surveyed a blanket of January snow lightly layered with mist about the courtyard, covering it as a white cloth pressed hard against one's face after a warm bath. "Of Amr, our sole remaining son, heir to Glamorgan and Gwent, the Edling, and future of Britain." Her voice broke because it was filled heavily with obvious sarcasm. Obvious futility. She pivoted around slowly and said: "He is part of the plot too, is he not, husband?"

"The conspiracy to plunge our country deep into official Civil War goes above Caw and above religious disputes." Arthur joined her at the window. "Caw and the Saxons," and now he referred to what had been discovered when deposing Aelle, "are controlled by the same forces. By some Shadow Enemy I know not.

"Llacheu," Arthur continued, "Llacheu was meant to take my head or, alternatively, both he and I were to perish in the intrigue of contrived skirmish, and then…"

Queen Gwenhwyfar braced for the next sentence. There is no capacity for the tears of a grieving mother and now, after three days of weeping, more gestated, and streamed.

"Our inquiry confirmed that Amr was then to take the throne as a secondary plot, should Llacheu fall."

"You are sure of this?" screamed the queen. Stopping herself swiftly, she paused and answered her own question. "Yes, you are sure. Heirs to the Summer Kingdom when you and I go and sleep in the Lord, and for treachery they would have the crown now. Oh, the evil of power meets youth!"

"The sons of Maelgwn love me and the sons of Arthur hate me." The politics of north versus south were venomously worming into the sinews of the royal family.

Gwenhwyfar began to tremble, twitch and seize. "The Round Table Fellowship will not abide this treachery. They, or some of their own companies, will hunt down and kill our son as a Judas, a coward, a demoniac in league with the Long Knife." Taking both of Arthur's hands, she fell to the bed, screaming and screeching as a great owl. "Will I now lose my final son?"

The thunderous pain of the question rattled Arthur, yet he but looked at her, listening, temperate and warm, attempting not to break. Exerting force to peel back the vice that were her fingers in his, the Pendragon cupped his wife's cheeks. "We must save our people, though we lose ourselves."

"Let then it not be a Bard's song or the subject of boasting in some tavern, months or years hence. Do all to quietly remove him, that men may not curse him save by rumor in his passing."

"What do you ask of me?" said Arthur.

"Go swiftly, Lord Arthur." Ice replaced sorrow, but for a moment. "And quietly." Gwenhwyfar's upper lip bit down hard upon the right side of the lower. "Take Excalibur and kill our son. Yourself."

Arthur was agape.

"And then never speak of it before gods or men," she concluded.

A thousand thousand scenarios were weighed

and considered, filtered, mashed and reconfigured in Arthur's mind.

Merlin would know what to do. But Merlin was not there, causing the king to, in the corridors of his mind, launch a great counsel and debate with himself. In the end, he concluded that the queen's course was correct. Arthur shifted in countenance from grieving father and supportive husband to his office as king.

He rose.

"Amr was patrolling Ynys Mons with my nephew, Mordred, as of three days and more ago. I assume he remains in the North. I will go as a shadow and resolve this – in the shadows."

Arthur was a master of disguise. These arts he had learned from the Merlin. In an instant, he could transform from regal symbol of grace and splendor to black-cloaked night rider. He was adept at this and, under lighter or humorous circumstances, enjoyed putting a mask o'er the pressures of being history's most famous king. Indeed, he would often fool his mates and subtly attend a meal as a beggar or Bard, only to reveal that they had hosted an angel unawares the entire time.

This journey from Gelliwig up to Gwynedd would not be filled with physical danger. The Saxons had been vanquished. The challenge would be traveling near roads and villages where great celebrations of liberty and hope were breaking out, and ongoing. It was his adoring and happy citizens that presented danger of discovery for the king.

"Would you have me do anything else, my queen?" It struck Arthur as he posed the query that Gwenhwyfar now looked as if she were no longer there at all. Indeed, she was a shell and not there.

"Yes, please," she responded. "Immediately and with great haste, please have your sister sent to me."

"Anna?"

"Gwyar."

The request was greatly peculiar, for this sister and the king's wife were as oil and water.

However, he thought, *what has remained straight and logical during the crisis, here at the end of the Saxon Wars?* King Arthur opted not to ask why and gave his queen an affirming look.

"The Mistress of the Isle of Apples to your court I shall summon, with haste."

He then embraced the shell of the queen, feeling the madness absorbing its host. King Arthur knew this would be the last time he would interact with this honorable and good woman as husband and wife.

He would go do right but his wife could never look upon the executioner of her sons again. The marriage was surely now over; she already saw dead sons when she looked upon him.

Arthur fought back a rapid involuntary fantasy: *now I can be with the painted woman who tries to rule my heart when my head turns to lust.* Killing the thought, he sorrowed for the queen, for himself, and for his traitor sons.

The king, after three days of intense time with Gwenhwyfar, departed her side. Forever.

CHAPTER 14
The Loose Ends Ere the Dawn of Day

Before departing to execute his son, Arthur convened with Bedwyr as promised.

They would speak of many things. But the plan regarding Amr, he would conceal. This was his accord with Gwenhwyfar, and they would do all to make their son a missing person instead of a publicly slain traitor.

The two friends hiked up the trail, not far from Gwen's white house, to their favorite fort, Lodge Hill. From there, they could signal to any of the wheel of fortresses protecting the kingdoms. Within twenty minutes the citizens and livestock could flee danger through trails and well-designed pathways out of the valleys and up into Lodge Hill for safety.

Its military value notwithstanding, the hill fort also provided spectacular views. The River Usk could be seen in all her green pomp and glory, cutting through breathtaking Caerleon, pouring gracefully into the Severn Sea. Nearly the whole of the Vale of Glamorgan, with its hills and valleys, its sheep and song, its forests and ancient slopes, could be ingested and enjoyed.

There was a great sloping field just below the fortress where wild horses sprinted and toiled playfully for territory. Sheep grazed freely. The hill and fortress were all the diverse splendors of Cymru consolidated into one place.

Arthur truly loved Lodge Hill.

He inhaled, gulping thirstily a few draughts of the cool January air, and then began to recount for Bedwyr what had occurred shortly after the knight had left the battle camp.

King Arthur's personal physicians had attended to Aelle's minor wounds immediately after Arthur had removed himself from their initial brief exchange. The king deliberated most cautiously with his cousin, and in the stead of Merlin, primary counselor, Illtud. He had made haste to the battle site after the discourse with the other bishops and shared Arthur's worry and surprise that Merlin had been gone since the eve of Baeden.

Not willing to rule out foul and murderous deeds by Meirchion, Illtud broke the tradition of secrecy amongst clergy and shared some of the late-night discourse amongst the seven elders. They didn't dismiss the likelihood Meirchion had been personally involved, but he was accounted for before and after they had all seen the Wizard. However, he could have launched or coordinated a murderous plot with Caw. This all seemed most unlikely.

Or so Illtud hoped.

A cleric groomed for the Bishopric of Glamorgan and Gwent, Illtud was patient, humble, a devout student of Dyfrig, and no novice of matters political, philosophical and spiritual. Illtud and Merlin debated for hours, concluding always with a hearty hug and no mutual conciliation. Neither Merlin nor Illtud hated Rome or her Catholicism, as both saw great beauty amongst her traditions, and faithfulness and grace amongst her converts. However, they were in one accord regarding the Roman Church's ongoing tendencies towards statism. Both hoped to repel this peacefully.

Where Dyfrig had no stomach for pagans or Catholics and spent his time in ongoing communal contemplation with Meurig, Illtud was very active, ensuring that his cousin the king, now thirty and three, had what every king needs from his counselors – balance and perspective.

Now Merlin was missing.

Arthur had desired advice and to garner support for his desire to send a strong message back to all of Germania. But Aelle was a large bullish man, an old and very skilled fighter. Thus, there was direct and real risk in Arthur's proposition.

Urien, Gwalchmai, Cuneglasas, Cai and many others were against it. Illtud was in agreement so long as the crown would revert back to Meurig (for Llacheu currently lay upon sawdust and ice awaiting burial while Amr, although seventeen and older than his father had been when made ruler over his tribes, was no Arthur and would be considered too young by the Cymry). With significant reservation and much protest, the Round Table Companions yielded to the king's proposed course.

Arthur would engage Aelle in combat himself,

sovereign versus sovereign, thus officially ending the Battle of Mynydd Baeden and quelling the Saxon threat forever.

As Arthur was unscathed, Bedwyr knew the outcome was favorable and continued to listen, captivated. The king continued to describe what had unfolded next.

As noon had arrived that day the sun had dispensed its shards of glory upon Excalibur, unsheathed above the bent elbows of the stoic king of the Britons. Aelle was freed of his bonds and his battle gear fully restored. Armed with a number of diverse killing devices, he favored the short gladius: borrowed from Rome but modified, thinner, and curved. Aelle also used a great club, with hopes of countering the reach of Excalibur.

A hundred or more fighting men, not a few Bards and all the Round Table Companions, save Maelgwn, formed a great circle. In the circle, the two kings engaged.

King Arthur, as with all of his men, had adopted the fighting style of Maelgwn. With an angular discipline that would cause Pythagoras to marvel, the Arthurian warrior was never fully exposed; it was more a dance than a fighting style, a true martial art. The Lady of the Lake, who was Vivien the Breton, had learned and perfected this way from her ancestor Vercingetorix, the great Gallic opponent of Julius Caesar.

The Saxon, clumsy but swift, swung low. Arthur opted not to block the blow of Aelle's club. The Cymry Warrior's mind was trained to act contrarily to emotion or instinct; to move left when the mind begged to go right, to go towards a blow when the untrained emotion said to flee.

Sliding towards his opponent whilst the club was midflight with two aggressive inside shuffle-steps positioned Arthur to run Excalibur through the Boar's ribcage, below his left shoulder, and circle away, out of range.

The crowd gasped at the speed with which the Long Knife had been defeated. As soon as they gasped, however, there was collective repentance of the same. Arthur was the second greatest warrior in all the land (and maybe the known world), so now many men looked up at each other and laughed at the notion that they had gasped in surprise in the first place.

"It is mortal." Arthur looked round the camp, seeing again the remains of the greatest loss of life in a generation. "The money, the numbers, the magnitude! Tell me how you brought so many thousand thousands of men here and I give you my word that those of your kind settled on our coasts will be given mercy. Who funded you? *Who?*"

He moved close to the enemy, and by good fortune the words uttered were heard only by Arthur. "You will spare not your own sons. But you will spare mine?" Air pushed awkwardly out of the Saxon as he spoke. There was a fixed supply of it that would not be replenished.

Sons? Arthur noted that his adversary had used the clear plural. Even with poor Latin, the meaning was clear. The communication, both spoken and by gesture of face and tone, was clear. Arthur's sons were treacherous and the plot was not confined to an internal struggle of north versus south amongst the tribes. It extended to the commanders and elite within the invading horde as well. A conspiracy that transcended the war, and national borders.

(As Arthur shared these things with Bedwyr, he did not indicate that both sons were involved. Letting Bedwyr deduce this or not, Arthur was very selective with his words, providing the information whilst keeping the promise to his wife to kill Amr discreetly.)

Dark blood painted the Saxon's side black. And then he screamed, this utterance heard by all. "Heed me, Head of the Dragon. You and I are the same! Empty carcass used by greater powers! Empty carcass, empty carcass!"

Aelle made a desperate, manic lunge for Arthur. Excalibur halved the club, blocking the overhand strike. Moving to the left, the Iron Bear opened the Boar's throat. "Who?" he screamed one final time, grabbing the larger man by the nape of the neck, very close to the gash.

A shriek of proud agony ensued. Aelle let loose the words "Ask", then "Priest", and finally "Meirchion".

Arthur, circling once more to the right, flashed Excalibur, removing the head.

Reflexively, the Pendragon knelt to the ground quickly and grasped his opponent's sword to cast it away, as if his headless foe could still somehow do him harm with the blade. As he was about to fling it hard against the trees, King Arthur noticed a green plaid ribbon woven around the hilt, and from age, pressure and oil, now part of it. His thumb found an edge of thread and unwound the ribbon. A glare and grimace, paired with rage, rushed through his ferocious visage. *This is one of ours!*

And though the High King was emboldened in his righteous anger, the earth, filled with so much innocent blood, and especially of the children of simple coastal villages, roared in victorious thanksgiving, justice having at last been delivered by the Sword of Power and the Just King!

Recomposing himself, but still riled as a great bear, Arthur declared: "We will send it to his sons, with our ordinances, written in Latin, for West Saxons."

The princes and mighty men of the Britons, of Powys, of Dyfed, of Gwynedd, Cernwy, the Old North, Albion, Glamorgan and Gwent, the great men of the remnants of Lloegyr, the Irish and the Bretons all exhaled a unified and full exhalation of victory, knowing they were about to enjoy the first afternoon's rest in three generations.

Gwalchmai was first to respond. "We have no policy, lord."

"Not yet. And to that matter we must assemble soon, Hawk of May." King Arthur held his prize by the locks. "I must make haste to speak with my wife, then we will finalize those matters. We will decide on baptism and census and governance and all else quickly."

The eyes in the lifeless head blinked, now all nerves and no brain.

Arthur was eager for the children of the invaders to see the trophy, fresh and pitiful, and know that the Pendragon himself had finally removed the Boar's head from its thorny, black body.

"Too much deliberation and indecisiveness will render our message–" Arthur paused, as one does when attempting to avoid the impropriety of laughing at their own jest, "–unrecognizable, from decay, to its recipients."

The men laughed.

And so it was that King Arthur felled King Aelle with his own hand, thus formally concluding the Battle of Mynydd Baeden.

The Round Table Companions had broken camp to rest, and then soon to deliberate on the Matter of Britain: to find Merlin. To find Maelgwn.

After hearing all these things, Bedwyr asked, still considering Arthur's report, "What will you do with the day?"

"I need three days more to mourn the loss of my son." A vague yet not untrue statement by the king. "Please rest fully today, Bedwyr," Arthur continued. "Illtud and Bedwini would have us go the New Troy as soon as we are able."

"To Londinium? But why?"

Arthur actually blushed for the former part of the answer he made and then rallied with confidence for the latter: "There will be another crowning," he chuckled, "this time to include attendees from Loegria, some Pictish tribes and even men of other nations. Additionally, we will be strategically close to West Saxons to both communicate and implement our intentions with the remnants of the invaders."

"Makes sense, Emperor Arthur." Bedwyr placed a humorous jab into the rib of his friend.

Arthur laughed aloud.

"Please help with any preparations you see fit over the next few days, but insulate me from visitors. I require solitude."

"Even from Cai? He will not like not knowing exactly what you are about."

"Assure him I will be safe and, for once, desire and insist upon no company," replied Arthur, "even from my Steward."

The light mood was temporary as Arthur asked one more question of his most loyal knight.

"Merlin and Maelgwn?"

"Found them we have not, my lord."

Arthur had no choice save to compartmentalize his proliferating woe and worry for the two. Presently, his sole focus was serving his wife, now well sunken into madness and despair, and to rid the land of an eighteen-year-old assassin wrought from the king's very own loins.

At this, Bedwyr and Arthur hiked down from Lodge Hill.

The Pendragon then enjoyed an overly long soak in the natural spring bathhouses of Caerleon. While the sulfuric, healing waters soothed many hurts, creating deep temporal relaxation, his mind wandered to the dark female image and fascination of his youth.

Back to when he was fourteen…

Arthur killed the thoughts, arose and robed. Then he made ready his disguise.

He preferred to be cleanly shaven but did wear a short, stubbly beard during war campaigns. He kept the scruff. However, he darkened it and his wavy hair with a coal-based dye, some of which he added around his eyes.

Trading his beloved dark blues and reds for nightshade black, to include long leather gloves and a doubly hooded rider's robe layered over an also black tunic, the young king was seemingly transformed into night itself.

Like a raven flying at midnight, a black on

black shadow, knowing every hidden and short path, he rode until dawn. He passed through the forests of the Cornovii and then made hard north before sleeping, discreetly, in the woods, near the fortress of a chieftain called Ogyrfan Gawr.

That such a giant man had produced an equally petite girl-child was astonishing, yet on account of her power, she was no less giant than her father.

Ogyrfan Gawr was the father of Gwenhwyfar. The *other Gwenhwyfar.*

Arthur felt great guilt for sleeping under the shadow of the one who sometimes dominated his thoughts (and of late, increasingly so) while his Gwenhwyfar was surely playing out concurrent nightmarish thoughts, fighting impossible demons of dread. Yet, he wanted to be near the Gwen who was not his.

Was she making residence in her father's home this very night?

Against reason, was she thinking of the glorious king at that moment whilst he was but a stroll and staircase's climb away, sleeping sooty and destitute as a hermit in the wood?

A sleety, miserable winter rain had fallen and the night was frigid but Arthur managed to make a well-concealed fire and ate a few of the kind of mushroom that appears in an instant after the rain. He shut his eyes, thinking about her, enjoying the two to three hours of distraction that began as delightful visions and passed happily into sleep.

From Ogyrfan's fortress, the dark rider would continue north and then bank left, arriving unseen at last in Ynys Mon. At the northernmost tip lay Amlwch. Invasions were sometimes attempted through a port there that, if achieved, would grant wide open and easy admission to the Blessed Isles.

To protect this nook of vulnerability, by and through arts of engineering and architecture that could only have come from ancient, wiser times, or else by otherworldly helpers, the Cymry had been able to construct a port that could be reached with the greatest ease, but yet seen with the greatest difficulty. The location of the markers and use of angled embankments made navigation and landing at the place called Porth Amlwch easy if the routine of sea twists and turns was known, perilous if not.

Truly the harbor was at once inviting and lethally hidden.

Many souls littered the seas above Porth Amlwch, having known not how to make land. For this cause, young men could patrol the area with relative safety, as encroaches were rare. The northern patrol near the Caledonian Forrest was the most dangerous; the northern patrol near Porth Amlwch, the least.

The Prince Amr, under the guidance of Gwyar's oldest son, Mordred, could train and ride leisurely and lightly around the port area, enjoying strong drink, fair damsels and the infrequent and entertaining apprehension of thieves and rogues leaving the Isle.

Finding them was not difficult.

Arthur spotted the two, bundled in heavy, hooded cloaks but without armor, riding along a thin shoreline.

As was reported, the two were inseparable mates and Arthur, looking the part of a thief, of a dirty wretch or rogue, would need some fortune to separate Amr from Mordred. At a midrange distance, there was no chance the king would be identified, so, in the place of stealth, Arthur opted for an overtly obnoxious approach.

He dismounted and, with altered voice, began screaming profanities and goading words at the two boys.

"Drunkard." Amr tugged at the shoulder of Mordred.

The two made after the soot-smudged black-clad drunkard.

At that moment, Arthur heard, were it trick of wind or by some mysterious phantom emanation, Merlin's voice upon his ear. *"Patience, Bear."*

The teenage warriors were at full gallop now. *"Patience, Bear."*

Arthur heeded but dismissed the origin of the spectral voice. At just the right time he mounted up and ran hard upon Mordred's side, causing Amr to bank hard that way as well. Rapidly, the elite equestrian zagged back in the opposite direction, causing his pursuers to crash their steeds hard, shoulder to shoulder.

Mordred fell violently from his white horse, which stumbled heavily but stayed aright. Rolling twice he landed, flat-backed and staring at the heavens. Flipping his wolfskin garment out of his face and thumbing off the fresh, sticky blood on his upper and lower lip, he coughed twice and then released a bellowing jackal's laugh, screaming:

"Amr! Get him!"

The king galloped with urgent haste, as he had to create distance between himself and Mordred. But he also had to keep Amr close enough to make the pursuit worthwhile and not cause the boy to give up on the fleet-horsed fleeing vagrant. Arthur balanced the pace just so and Amr nearly met stride with him o'er a short ridge away from Mordred.

The king, in his guise still shadowy though it was day, did not unleash Excalibur as the two men rapidly dismounted. Amr, smaller than his father but sculpted, young and very strong, attempted to wrestle his foe to the ground.

Eyes met during the brief struggle.

"Father?"

Instead of an oratory of surprise, bewilderment or excitement following the identification, Amr, knowing the matter, unhanded the king and drew his sword.

There was no confession, no manipulation of words or effort of evasion. No adolescent lies. No plea. Rather, hubris filled the traitor boy's overly confident head, as Mordred was surely riding or running in lagging pursuit behind his friend.

Arthur drew his dagger, which was called Carnwennan. Its short hilt was white as the foam atop the Irish Sea, its blade dark, dark grey. As the wintry light of day touched upon the blade, somehow it cast a shadow upon Arthur larger than the breadth and width of what it ought to have done.

Nearly as sharp as Excalibur (which could cut steel), Carnwennan threaded Amr's winter layers as if a seamstress were carefully cutting and resizing the material. Cloak and coat were naught, and neither was flesh or sternum. Through the breast bone the heart was cleaved, and in one motion the dagger reappeared near the apple of the Son of Pendragon's throat.

Arthur was atop the horse and vanished so quickly that he was gone and out of sight before the body fell to the winter's ground, welcoming one more treacherous Briton into her callous and cold embrace.

As he rode, the scream of one word from Mordred was heard –

"Brother!"

CHAPTER 15
We Both Know He Loves You Most

Women know things.

Women have an intuition that men will never possess. In several stations of the human experience, they are simply wiser, smarter.

How they know what they know, in what corridors they glean and what circles they gather, and of their innate ability to read the motives, circumstances and the real story behind any matter (and especially where relationships are involved) is a mystery that engenders awe and can never be comprehended by men.

And, of the mysteries, motivations and true constitution of the Pendragon, as a man, as a friend, as lord and husband, Gwenhwyfar knew. For women know things.

A person being insane in general removes in no way their accuracy or credibility on a specific matter. Even one who is lunatic can sum one and one.

"Please, you are most welcome. Sit." The whole of the kingdom knew there was something different about Gwyar. Despite Gwenhwyfar possessing less fear than most for the king's sister and being brave (and mad), there was still a slight tremor in her salutation, though she was Queen and Sovereign and thus of the greater authority.

"How does your husband, Llew, sister-in-law?"

Princess Gwyar traced the rim of her teacup thrice clockwise, then paused.

Thrice clockwise once more. Gwenhwyfar wondered if this were some spell or enchantment being cast upon the room, but dismissed the thought as superstition.

Gwyar's hair, which was as black as a crow, was pulled back tightly, fastened flat to her head, and braided from forehead to end. She was wearing a knotted necklace made of black leather woven through three grey stones, two of which had a small engraving of the three rays, or Awen, and the third a beautiful etching of the four bear claws, the ensign of her Silure tribe. The necklace had no slack and Gwenhwyfar noted that it must ever choke its wearer.

In fact, all of Gwyar's attire was close-fitting. Her dark blue and grey dress, intricately laced along the ribs and at the bosom, seemed as if it were her skin and no garment. Although a mother many times over, she was youthful in form, a tiny hourglass like a faerie. Gwenhwyfar was bewildered at how beautiful she looked at certain angles and yet from other prisms, uncomely. She also seemed 'there and not there' when flashing a passing glance toward her, or away.

Lastly, to demonstrate respect and match the formality of the summons, the Princess had one gold torque orbiting her left arm and wore the simple silver circlet crown, humble yet powerful; a popular fashion piece amongst her tribe.

By contrast and irony, Queen Gwenhwyfar was in the same white gown in which she had slept and spent her days, certainly several times over. Her red hair was everywhere and nowhere close to regal in presentation. And she was pungent from a failure to bathe or pay regard to her hygiene.

In spite of this, Gwyar offered no return assessment and judged not the mad queen, but rather tried to respond with simplicity and grace. However, whenever Gwyar spoke it was with a quiet power, like a boiling kettle pot. Because of this she was often misunderstood.

"My husband, when not on the war campaign, is busy prattling about with the priests and bishops. Methinks he does flirt with becoming a Catholic. 'Tis rare we share a bed, my Lady."

"Oh, dear," Gwenhwyfar began. "If men on this Island weren't so addicted to the goings-on of the next world, perhaps they would focus more on making the present one less of a shit pile."

"Well. We are an island obsessed with the Spirit," Gwyar offered.

A curling smile formed about the queen's face. Her green eyes flickered and flashed as she relished the segue, allowing her to cut to the quick.

"So valid a point. So, so valid. To my own spirit I must attend, and the burden of Arthur's I now transfer. To you." Gwenhwyfar said these things matter-of-factly, a communication flowing in one direction like a decree, no longer a conversation. "Monasticism is no longer just for men. To a nearby cell I go to be with God and my own spirit, not to return."

Gwyar loathed everything about life at Court, about formalism, structure and authorities man-made. This was not an indictment of her brother, as Arthur himself was like-minded. She could avoid most of her duties; he could avoid next to none. He ever sought to keep government small, non-intrusive and mindful that its function, under God, was to protect rights, not usurp them. However, Arthur did enjoy romantic ceremony, parades and promenades combined with great music and Bardic tales, much more than did his sister.

Although, she admitted, she had her rituals as well. And she had other reasons for her monasticism and needful solitude with her goddess.

That Gwenhwyfar was on the verge of disappearing into the mist was clearly about to change two lives, and not hers alone.

"Before you protest and beg me to repent of this charge, I shall defend it preemptively," Gwenhwyfar began. "I love my husband. I made covenant between he and my God to be faithful, to honor him, to be his support and his friend."

The queen's face looked left of and over Gwyar, through a window that was in reality not there – a window to the past.

"He has vanquished the Saxon enemies but not those in his own house. He has proclaimed liberty throughout the land, but we all sense the grip of Rome is slowly closing. We stand at the door of an Age Golden but know such things are wrought through the personal destruction of those who wrought them."

Back to looking upon Gwyar, she went on: "He has your father, Meurig, still feisty, full of verve, limping about Caerleon bringing smiles and joy as he goes. But there are, sister-in-law, things a boy can't say to his father, a separation on private things that is natural, even for those as close as they.

"He has heroes, and mates and special men and true friends; knights for whom the Bards will sing for ages."

Gwyar carefully interrupted.

"And he has the Merlin."

"Merlin has been missing nigh unto a week and, if he returns, he is not the same." This the queen said on the basis of her interaction with the Druid at the conference preceding the great battle, and on her intuition. For women know these things. "He has changed."

"Missing?" Gwyar startled at this, for she had just seen Merlin on Ynys Enlli; he had come to visit her right before the great battle.

Did he not return? she thought. Making an attempt to go on further about this was pointless, as the queen was in full oratory stride, disregarding Gwyar's interruptions and listening to her not. Gwenhwyfar made a great orbiting motion with both hands. "He has all things. But what he lacks is the very fuel that could keep the dream of the Summer Kingdom aflame, the glue to bind the dream, a flickering of hope for Cymru."

Gwenhwyfar now drew close to Gwyar.

"For all the needs and wants of men, one is greatest. One paramount." And now Wisdom of the Ages came forth from the Mad Queen. "A man must have a woman that he loves beside and behind him. For the woman is the glory of the man."

Gwenhwyfar now grew bold, imposing years of observation, intuition, whispers, half-truths and blunt facts upon the Lady of the Isle of Apples. Without anger but with seething conviction she pronounced, "And we both know he loves YOU most!"

The enchantress's neck erected, as an adder's. She rose without speaking, intending to leave the queen and her outlandish statement without retort.

"You will not make your leave," ordered Gwenhwyfar. Her eyes now blazed, the green somehow brighter after releasing such a long-held suppression. "Sometimes, he describes you in his sleep and knows not that I know."

"It is not me." Gwyar, just above a whisper.

"You were both so young. Barely children."

"It is not me." A note louder.

"Merlin and the Lady of the Lake were managing King Meurig's abdication and attaining the glorious, gilded blade for Arthur. They made it back to the ritual late. They didn't know."

"It. Is. Not. Me." Teacups began to shake and two candlesticks buckled, and fell. The room grew callous; wind blew, of a source and force unnatural.

Gwenhwyfar marveled not at the otherworldly manifestation (but no longer had to wonder whether her speculation about the room being under the Sorceress's enchantment was unfounded), and proceeded. "The bishops couldn't care less about the spring rites, and demonstrations of virility or compatibility with the crops. They are clean of this as well."

CHAPTER 16
Not So There Is One He Loves Even More

"Clean of what? It is not me." Gwyar's disingenuous response fell to a whisper as Gwenhwyfar's missives drew her mind back to the incident that had shaped the future of all Britons, *nay, all men*, forever.

The Dynion Hysbys had made selection of a sixteen-year-old virgin for the rites.

There were local tribes that held to old ways, and even older gods. They would not accept a young king who did not pass the rites and demonstrate to them that the harvest would be ever reliable.

The king was one with the land, and the land one with the king.

Although elements of this worldview had been modified or rejected, trickles of it remained, adopted even amongst the bishops. Indeed, a king wounded in battle or unreliable in bedroom would die (often to mean retirement, abdication, selling or gifting of lands, or living in a cell or cave for a period of time) and a young heir would rise in his place.

The term 'death' meant many things to the Cymry.

As for the bishops, the right of kingship was based upon the royal bloodline, balanced with the consent of the people. A horrible, tyrannical or unjust man of high birth might be displaced by an honorable man of lower estate. On this topic, the bishops had a more reasonable approach than their pagan kinsmen.

Most of the ruling families or Royal Clans had adopted some form of Christianity, and even though Christ was proclaimed publicly and with liberty and comfort first in the Blessed Isles, the common man was slower to adopt the faith. Those who had not adopted the Christian faith (whether of the sect of Pelagius, or of the Primitive Church of the Britons, or of Romanism) still fought Cymru's battles, still mined her tin, still developed her coal, still tended and raised her sheep and cattle.

Their influence was yet a part of the fabric of the Isles. Rituals of season and harvest, of death and life and love, and of war and kingship were required to maintain their support, to mitigate skirmishes, raids, and rebellion and, moreover, to show respect for a policy of religious and spiritual liberty.

And, although the Bards held sway and authority in the plenary courts and palatial circuits, the cruel and nasty devising Dynion Hysbys lorded over the minds and souls of the middle and lower classes, often through dark arts and sinister black magick.

Raging with jealousy over the Merlin and

his softer and more enlightened approach to managing the transition from the old gods to the One True God and His Son, the Dynion Hysbys pumped chest where they could, asserted authority where they might.

Gwyar remembered well her brother had been in Brittany when she received the visit from the Dynion Hysbys. He had been pulled away, yet again, from school and was already earning a name on the battlefield, aiding King Budic II and his son Hoel Mawr in their fight against insurgents on the Continent.

The first sowing of Spring was nigh and it was made clear to the sect of Druid priestesses on Ynys Mon that they would need to be in Gwent for the arrival of the Prince.

Gwyar was away from her foster-mother, who was busy loaning Merlin the Sword of Power to give to the soon-to-be Boy King.

She was unusual amongst the young ladies and girls. Ever preoccupied by darker paths and arcane studies, she quickly mastered the spectrum of divergent Druidic theologies, and although she did not oppose them, she transcended them. Men feared Gwyar because she, like no other, seemed to be the same sort of creature as the Merlin. Outside of religion or sect, beyond classification, she was friendly to all gods but bowed to no God.

Command of herbs, poisons and the produce of nature she possessed. The mysteries seemed to flow through her and she was, by a very young age, viewed as one who hearkened back to those veiled times on either side of the Flood; those visitors to the Isles from the sides of the North, or else from the sky.

That her parentage was well-known didn't quell the speculation, though Onbrawst and Meurig were a picture of fidelity and loyalty.

When the Dynion Hysbys had visited the young priestesses, Gwyar recalled that she had been playing with other, younger girls, upon the pebbly Strait of Afon Menai. They were near the very spot where the Romans had come and butchered her spiritual and blood ancestors; their blood still cried for revenge from the soils of Ynys Mon.

Ironically, only certain sects of Christians and Druids had fallen to the sword of Roman persecution, which usually and almost unanimously left their conquered realms to their native gods.

There had been a time, five hundred years or more ago, when the connection between simple Christians and Druids was clear. This fact was, to most, now murky or lost, as if some dispute divided two old friends and now, many years hence, the cause of the dispute was forgotten but the chasm too deep to heal.

Conversely, the Dynion Hysbys hated anything that resembled the name of Christ. Nor did they venerate the elemental spirits of earth or water, of air or fire. Neither did they seek union with the divine inspiration, or Awen, that connected all Britons. Rather, they claimed to appease powerful fertility gods and a great cloven-hoofed, bovine deity whom they called Arddu. According to them, the horned (although he manifested oft as a winged serpent as well) Arddu was chief of the gods.

It was said that the whole of the pantheon of

deities such as Rhiannon, Arianrhod, Arawn and the Mighty Ones of the Cymry loathed Arddu and would neither acknowledge nor receive tribute or sacrifice from his Wise Men, though they hid amongst those who adored the gods and goddesses of Eire and Cymru.

Usually a Druid or small collective of Bards would accompany some of the Dynion Hysbys, but on the day they came to select a damsel for the rites, only they were present.

And they were accompanied by one man besides: a shadowy man who seemed to lead them. One whom Gwyar did not know.

He donned a many-layered black robe with underlying tunic of the same shade. Beads dangled and an inverted cruciform rattled, clacking against his sides as he walked, or rather glided.

Though his face was recessed too deeply into an overly large hood, and a black mask further made the actual features of his face unknowable, it was readily deduced that he was old, and not from the Isles.

Of Greece, or Italy, Gwyar assumed.

His fingers were plated with armor whose ends were metallic, pointy talons and his staff was not for walking, for it cast forth a vibratory hum that forced a bubble of separation between him and any who might approach him.

He and his dark companions made the pebbled strait a tessellated game board when standing amongst the Druid priestesses, all in dresses of pure white.

"A young prince will slay the White Stag and then become one with the land and you will be the vessel; the cup of that union." His voice was confident, but broke and scratched every few words. That Gwyar was the object of his pronouncement was clear as a single talon pointed directly upon her bosom, nearly meeting the skin.

"Do you fear me?" he asked.

"I do not," she responded.

"Of course not; you were before I am." The hooded shadow man was still addressing Gwyar, but was now speaking to someone or something standing behind her as well. "Some of you, at least, was." His look fell back upon her.

Gwyar did not see the red-eyed Lord of the Tylwyth Teg towering behind her.

"I am but sixteen and you are at least a hundred," came her youthfully rebellious bite-back.

"At least a hundred, little crow." Some teeth showed briefly as the hood shifted in the wind bellowing off the Strait. "See to it that she serves as actress in the rites."

He spoke but once more unto Princess Gwyar.

"In the rites, you are moon and the cup, the goddess. But this you already are, yes?"

She made no response as every tiny hair upon her arms, neck and shoulders stood and an icy wind moved about the whole of her body; at that instant she turned round rapidly.

Nothing.

The Man of the Fair Folk, the Fae King, was gone, or never there.

* * *

Gwenhwyfar reappeared in an instant. "Those nasty heathens and their godless ritual caused this; you are innocent."

The words refocused Gwyar's mind back to the present conversation (though Gwenhwyfar knew that further discourse may yet bring the entire palace crashing down).

Instead, and finally, a concession exhaled from the Princess's throat, for she knew more than most that *women just know things*. And Gwenhwyfar knew, or partially knew, something more than any other woman over the course of Gwyar's thirty and five years.

"Not even the Lady of the Lake knows that it was me at the Rites." Tears formed.

"Of course not. Merlin and Vivien would've never allowed such perversion." Gwenhwyfar was Christian; conservative and rigid. But she greatly regarded them as two honorable, special people, the last of a fading kind. Fading into the shadow of the Church.

"How did you know?" The confessing query finally came, and the shaking room settled.

Gwenhwyfar made a long, thoughtful response.

"It's remarkable how many years are uneventful or irrelevant, yet one year, or one moment, can change us forever. Though twenty years ago, that year of life, that one set of moons has impacted him, haunted him to this day.

"From the day he and I were wed, Arthur was very loyal, very faithful. Never did I worry about him wandering off to lay with damsels, dames or debased seductresses. His fidelity was a point of honor amongst gossiping women and pious bishops alike. But, from the beginning, even in our teens when you visited Court, I noticed looks, moods, temperature shifts, that flame of discomfort that must look and yet cannot look but will not look away.

"That a man would lust after his sister was unthinkable, unnatural.

"That the most honorable man that ever lived would, or could do so, demanded investigation.

"And investigate I did."

The queen rubbed her face hard with cupped hands, the crust of tears and sleeplessness crumbling and tumbling from her cheeks.

She continued.

"It was impossible to trace the exact identity of the priestess who had served as the Cup to Arthur's Sword in that ritual. Even upon aggressive, privy threats I could only gather that the participant portraying the goddess was young and dark."

Here Gwenhwyfar flirted with the Sorceress's hair, as a foolish drunkard makes for a wasp's nest with a stick or intentionally steps upon an asp, caring not for her own life.

"As the priestess is dark, and you are dark. And as he has but this heel of Achilles, this one weakness, that he calls out to one not there on some nights, that he looks upon some astral projection crawling along our ceiling of YOU and then ravages ME." Now anger and jealousy crept in again and the accusations resumed, more forceful than before. "It is you he was with, you he obsesses over and YOU who will serve him at this Court lest our Kingdom fall!"

The Mad Queen raged on, unable to cease

from visiting the matter, again and again assaulting Gwyar verbally, now accusing her of being Otherworldly to her face. "He thinks on a dark Fae that visits his sleep and seduces him. He plays again the ordeal and, at the moment of climax, confuses our names. He calls to–"

Suddenly, a raised hand stayed the queen's mouth effortlessly, Gwyar using her craft and power. "He calls to the Morgaine and he calls to Gwen," she said.

"Yes."

At this moment Gwyar could spare the queen, whose mind as well as heart (and soul besides) was as a broken looking glass, a clay pot dropped that could not be mended; or she could make an end of her with truth.

Knowing that Gwenhwyfar would have her will enforced by sword and permanent custodians if it came to it, and that her husband and Gwyar's brother would have no leverage to adjudicate an appeal, that Gwyar would now be away from her Isle of Apples and imprisoned to life at Court, resentment overruled grace as the Sorceress opted for cold truth in the stead of soft lies.

"You know much, yet not all, queen." Gwyar's eyes, massive and bronze-gold, opened extra wide to deliver this message. "At fourteen he did fall in love–" wailing now began, but Gwyar continued cold and unmoving, "–and he was poisoned by lust from what happened between us. However, Lady, you have conflated two events into one. At fourteen he fell BOTH in love and in lust and those two names he entwines, commingles, blends and emotes in the shadows, and at night."

"But he did not know me until *after* it

happened. I knew him not until he was fifteen, for we married the following Spring," Gwenhwyfar argued.

"He calls out to the Morgaine, and I am she." She pointed and rested her forefinger upon her chest, and at the saying of the name *Morgaine* a shadow of Gwyar, yet seven times her size, blossomed slowly and then overtook the greater part of the chamber. Real fear, and ancient power, blossomed along with the Shadow. "And he calls out to Gwen." The same finger started to point at the queen, then reversed its course, tauntingly. "But that Gwen is *not* you. In your queries and investigations and hunts, you should have started by seeking to find the object of his love, or lust, before the event, not *at* the event. You should have simply asked Illtud about Arthur's days in school."

Gwenhwyfar seemed lost and shocked at these words. So Morgaine made all as clear as the mirror of a still lake on a Summer day.

"I will stay at Court, as you will terrorize me to do otherwise, until he remarries. There is *another* Gwenhwyfar coming to Caermelyn, mark this. And it is *she* who he loves more! As I told you afore, it is not me! Or not me alone." A sinister stoicism now accompanied the verbal daggers.

The queen crumbled within herself, not having known that there was yet another rung left on her endless descent into living damnation. Had the king really been in love with another woman bearing her name? And before her? What of their two decades together?

Insult was her only recourse.

"You are a cruel witch, Gwyar. You would break

me with these words, knowing I have lost my sons." The queen stood and gathered herself again, and again was fearless. Her gestures indicated plainly that tiny Gwyar and the tall darkened spirit with her should leave. "May you never know the hurt of losing a child. For I have lost all, and one at the hand of Arthur himself. May you never know this. Take care of the king. Now leave this place."

CHAPTER 17
When It Comes Time to Do That

Merlin did not hire a ship, as it would have brought too much attention upon the covert travelers. Arthur's younger brother, Prince Madoc, was a master at sea and ever stationed at, or patrolling near, the ports. His skills with sword and fist were wanting, but his ability to scout, to chart, to organize and to know every detail associated with the vessels that both entered and left the Isles more than compensated for those deficiencies. Either by direct report, else by some seemingly organized orchestra of whispers, Madoc ever knew any matter of interest pertaining to the sea. And Britannia's most famous Druid and advisor to the king making off under cloak of night on hired boat would certainly meet the criteria for a 'matter of interest'.

And so, instead, Merlin and his travel companion paid, boarded, and blended in upon one of the supply ships, which sailed their routes late at night from Cymru to their cousins in Brittany.

Small iron cauldrons were aflame throughout

the concave hull of the vessel, allowing men to cluster round them on benches for warmth in the bitter cold. The seamen were ever scurrying to and fro, working. The passengers concentrated on not freezing to death; thus, the privacy was adequate.

As many of the battles of the Saxon War had been contested on wide rivers, great lakes and slivers of the sea, all Britons were well suited to harsh conditions on the water. Nevertheless, it was especially cold.

Maelgwn sat directly next to the Merlin, shoulder to shoulder, looking more a cuddling couple than two men of grit and war. A deliberate turn of the head was required in order to speak.

Ere Maelgwn initiated obviously forthcoming queries, Merlin took a moment to behold him.

Maelgwn.

The Lancelot.

The Bloodhound Prince.

The singular sentiment that coursed through Merlin every time he looked upon Maelgwn was *gratitude.*

Maelgwn, grandson of the mighty Cunedda. The strongest line of the remnant of northern kings that survived the treacherous Night of the Long Knives. Maelgwn and his Hosts, the most feared and elite cell amongst all the armies, could have overpowered and harassed Arthur to such an extent that they would have been a divided nation, an easy harvest for the Saxon sickle. Some reasonably speculated that he could have even defeated Arthur outright and installed himself as the Head of the Dragons (a position historically reserved for the Royal Clan of the Silures – never a Northman – but Maelgwn seemed to be the exception to all norms and customs). Instead, Maelgwn was introduced at age sixteen to Arthur, who was fourteen at the time, and in the twinkling of an eye, loved him deeply.

They were both pupils, schoolyard friends at Illtud's.

From the beginning, Maelgwn plainly declared that Cymru would be united: under Arthur as head. This news met with pricks and thorns from the other kings and lords in the Old North and such was the discord that Maelgwn left his lands, at first for fosterage, and then over the process of time permanently, to reside with King Budic II, who was sometimes called Ban, and his sister Vivien, over in Brittany.

His fame grew over on the Continent, where he became known as the Lancelot, which is by interpretation, *the greater who serves the lesser.*

But zealous devotion to his native lands in Gwynedd deeply tormented Maelgwn and the course he set for himself troubled him often, so much so that he would periodically break from the Round Table Fellowship (though he was their Champion) and go back home, intermittently reclaiming his lands.

He especially enjoyed a small farm set against the River Camlan near Dollglau. There was a great allure to the place that was at once sad and magnetic. In addition to the serenity of dark greens and blues that sat upon the river as a perfectly layered sweet cake, the surrounding slopes formed nearly a perfectly shaped 'V', creating Leonidas's Thermopylae effect; the Thermopylae of Britannia. Massive armies would be neutralized by the narrow valley, meaning those that had expertise of the terrain could defend against very many with very few. Maelgwn had rehearsed with his men how to take flight through rehearsed routes from a pursuing enemy and then slaughter them as they funneled into the field near the river, called Maes Camlan.

Serenity matched with remarkable natural defenses rendered this tiny spot in North Cymru precious to Maelgwn.

Soon after resettling and enjoying Camlan or any of the other countless majestic and romantic creeks, mountains, waterfalls, ancient lakes and beautiful estates and fortresses of Gwynedd, like some recurring cycle of cursed moons, inevitably the conduct and flirtations with treachery by other northern leaders, namely Caw and Meirchion, would wax great. Having no stomach to be around this, Maelgwn would go back to Arthur, or to Brittany, or to one of Vivien's Sacred Lakes in the south.

And then the sorrowful yearning for return to Gwynedd would return again.

Gratitude. Merlin had great empathy towards the displaced hero and marveled once more at the man comely as Adonis and skilled as Achilles, then readied himself to answer questions about the purpose of their secret engagement.

"Your strategy will live on through a thousand generations in epic poetry and Bardic ballads. My hosts salute you and I thank you. The Blessed Isles are free." Thus the conversation of two men, tall as trees but snuggled as children near the hearth, began with kind words from the Lancelot to the Merlin.

The congeniality was short-lived.

"Why am I here?" Maelgwn's directness returned.

Some frost and icicles formed and dangled from the old Wizard's beard, framing his mouth and making his speech look mechanical. It was very cold and the channel between Glamorgan and Brittany was troubling its seafaring passengers; at first gently, now with harassing force.

Considering his words carefully, Merlin opted for direct words that would both liberate the burden from their concealment in his bosom and impress the urgent necessity for his extreme mandate upon Maelgwn.

Though direct and calculated, Merlin ought to have begun with, "I genuinely feared that the Iron Bear's life was in danger." Instead he took the longer path, and tried to build the foundation first.

"I belong to a Secret Society." Merlin paused, continuing with simplicity rather than deep explanation. "Our Order is governed by another Secret Society, and that Order by yet another. At the very zenith of this… *pyramid*… is an assembly called the Counsel of Nine."

Maelgwn was always fascinated by religion and spirituality (as are all Britons), having the broadest possible exposure to variant Christian sects and of course having seen fascinating and arcane things with his foster mother, the Lady of the Lake, that would challenge any worldview. Therefore, Merlin's comments intrigued the impatient warrior.

"Are these men *like you,* Lord Merlin?" he asked.

Had he been with sharp-witted Bedwyr or

enjoying ale with sunshiny Gwalchmai, Merlin would have countered with levity, "There is NO ONE like Me," and enjoyed a hearty laugh. Instead he provided a mundane and standard description. "From the infancy of man there has always been a guild of the special, the learned, the good, and the wise devoted to liberty, fraternity and equality," Merlin answered. "And to unlocking the Sacred Sciences or secrets of the Cosmos."

Lancelot frowned, his lips pressed tight together ensued straightway by his perfect eyes and brow following suit; the protesting expression of disinterest.

"I know." Merlin gave an agreeing jest in response to the warrior's expression. "Sounds like the crafty, overweight and crooked sorts that sell old cows as studs to fools or the potion peddlers at the markets." Here the Druid humbled himself, his sigh of regret making a great cloud under the cold, evaporating and pushed up and outward into the sea by the fire cauldron. "And I bought the old cow. Drank the potion; a potion of lies."

Maelgwn at once re-engaged. "How do you know that what they teach is lies?"

"For many reasons now."

"Give me one."

"If the foundation be flawed then the building will fall. There are no *good men*," said Merlin with conviction. "Aside from any stated purpose, the Brotherhood convened magi and Wizards and diverse priests from religions the world over to learn the Higher Mysteries through a series of initiations, rites and courses that have spanned decades and decades.

"Some of these Mysteries we would take

home and blend into or use to enhance our native beliefs; others were considered secrets to fall under the moral and spiritual jurisdiction of the Society and our governing principalities alone."

Here Maelgwn interrupted. "Decades? Sounds worse than the memorization work demanded of our Bards. What mysteries could be beyond the grasp of men similar to you? What transition from milk to meat takes so long?"

"It's a ruse. The duration of learning the Higher Mysteries and the Seven Sacred Sciences makes the Teachers seem all the more impressive, and the students all the more filled with–"

"Pride." Maelgwn finished the Wizard's sentence.

"Aye." Another great sigh ascended through the flame and into the night. "We have been ever learning but never coming to the knowledge of the truth. Now, as my days are shorter and the setting sun of retirement draws near, it was communicated to me that it was my time to learn the final secrets and to graduate; to promote to the Counsel of Nine." Merlin was hoping to get quickly to the core of his purpose for bringing Maelgwn on this perilous and secret journey and at this critical moment he feared his audience was losing patience.

And that he was.

The towering warrior flung the coats and skins that had a moment ago been layered upon him, as effortlessly as a child flings sticks into a pond. As he rose, the flames illuminated his perfect form; harder than the statues of the Greeks and nearly as pale, this chiseled killing machine could pulsate his lean brawn in a way to intimidate men and wild beast alike. A living grey statue. An invincible man. One did not want to find himself on the wrong side of Maelgwn's disposition, lest he also find himself on the wrong side of his spear.

And yet it was rumored, and held true here, that Maelgwn never raised his voice. Some yelling is healthy: '*tis the quiet ones to mark and fear*. In a low, low voice just above a whisper, his frightful protest came down heavy on Merlin, who was still hunkered over the cauldron. "You left our most important battle, your country, my men and OUR Arthur for some pagan pride parade? For some ceremony to tickle your conceit!"

A form, rustle and disruption was seen and felt behind Maelgwn, then a shadow.

The two famous travelers were no longer alone. Merlin would give his answer to two inquisitors now, not just one.

Maelgwn's favorite weapon was instantly in hand and ready to dispatch any thief, pirate or unwelcomed guest. A unique killing instrument, the Lancelot's armament of choice was neither sword nor spear and yet both. Having no hilt or handle, it was a double-ended battle spike, the length of a sword, much shorter than a spear, and having one single crescent moon-shaped blade forming a hook to both guard one hand and serve as an extra killing option. Many Saxon and not a few Briton souls went on into hell on the other end of this famous killing instrument and the man who wielded it.

"Oh, put it away, Lord of Gwynedd." A familiar, pesky and irritating voice floated through the night, punching Maelgwn at once in both ears.

A figure stepped from behind several large

barrels housed on the hull and strolled right into the midst of Merlin and Lancelot as if he owned not just that spot on the vessel but perhaps the entire boat – or an entire fleet. A short, crook-backed man with knobbly walking stick, of small stature and great confidence. Precisely half the height of the other two, the hooded man, obviously a Druid, hugged Merlin hard, at his waist.

"Taliesin!" Merlin's great smile crackled, crushing and discarding the remaining ice chips around his moustache and corners of his mouth; and the joy of seeing his great friend and pupil (and teacher) caused Merlin to forget, but for a moment, the dire nature of his discovery by one who had obviously followed Maelgwn to the port. The bitter cold and sway of the boat impacted Merlin's brain, first with too many delays articulating the present distress to Lancelot, second in not immediately protesting Taliesin's presence.

"But wait. You cannot be here!" The Wizard recovered himself. "The entire nation save Maelgwn Gwynedd knows not my whereabouts, yet here stands the famous son of Ceridwen before me. I am breached!"

Unmoved by Merlin's concern, Taliesin responded: "King Arthur Pendragon has his Merlin; King Maelgwn has his."

"Whether I want one or not, so it seems," Maelgwn snarled.

Taliesin and Maelgwn shared a special history. Born in Glamorgan, Taliesin had been assigned to Maelgwn's courts in the North. Whilst all men greatly feared the tall King of the North, little Taliesin ever, instead, counseled, chastised, pestered and advised him. Merlin seemed to *see* that something tense, tempestuous and special would develop between the two and made use of Taliesin as an extension of his very own eyes upon the unpredictable warrior.

And Maelgwn secretly liked Taliesin *because* the little Druid feared him not.

He also, unknowingly, had the somber distinction of being the last person to ever see Merlin and Taliesin together, dialoguing, matching wit and enjoying each other's company, this side of the Afterlife.

"You followed Maelgwn here?"

"I did, and two of my men besides. We saw him break hard from the trails at Maesteg and, in light of *our* recent discourse, thought a connection plausible, if not probable. I thought you said you were done with the Nine, having no desire to have fellowship with the unfruitful works of darkness, knowing it is a shame to even speak of what they do in secret." A finger like a long knotted branch from a birch tree pointed up, up towards Maelgwn. "I agree with Goliath here; what matter have you with the naughty secrets of the religious elite? What have they to do with the Matter of Britain?"

"As I shared with you, I had no intention of completing the Sacred Rites, or learning the *Secret Teaching of the Ages,* as I too now find it to be folly. However…" Instantly, the conversation shifted from humorous barbs and sarcastic positioning to gravity unparalleled. Merlin, now fully warmed in brain and body, reassumed command of his surroundings and pronounced: "The messenger from the Nine indicated that King Arthur *was* the object of the final initiation and the *Secret Teaching of the Ages*. Not in allegory, not as a type, but that he personally was the subject and aim of prophecies and mysteries as old as the times of the gods."

Both listeners were silent.

Merlin continued. "As I continued to listen to the messenger, his aim was clear; the Nine's secret teachings had something to do with Arthur, and it was not safe, not positive and not good. There was malevolence in his voice that I have never associated with or heard from the supposed benevolent college of Seers."

Maelgwn's worldly wisdom about the nature of men and power resulted in thoughtful and true interjection. "They are about to initiate you into the highest levels of their Order, so their outward masks of White Magick and herbs and brotherly love is coming off. True power is what men of that ilk covet. They sound more like the dark Fae than men."

"Aye. Well said, Maelgwn. Discerning the change and potentially ill motive, combined with a recent conversion of–" Merlin looked at Taliesin, who smiled "–perspective in my own beliefs, I fear for our friend's life." The sadness of missing the great battle returned to Merlin at that moment. "And so, to reject the offer to join the Counsel of Nine, but to first learn, by guile, by magick or by sword, the meaning of the messenger's mystery, I hastened away from Caerleon, away from Baeden."

"And you summonsed the great Maelgwn as surety that your head would be attached to your neck long enough to do something with the information you will acquire." Taliesin confirmed the legitimacy of the Merlin's actions.

Maelgwn's angry disposition eased. "I now understand why we are here," he said, looking at Merlin.

Merlin then finished the warrior's sentence on his behalf: "But we don't understand why *you* are here." The focus shifted back to the one uninvited guest, warming hands and feet near the cauldron.

"As I said, I followed you here," he replied.

"Yes. And who in turn may have followed you?" Merlin continued to be haunted by an overwhelming feeling that, though Maelgwn was with him, he might not return from his dealings with the Counsel. "You are Taliesin and men will call you Merlin. This quest is not yours; my office you must soon take. You and your two men at the first port will disembark; Maelgwn Gwynedd and I to Broceliande will continue."

And then Merlin, feeling bereft of supernatural powers, still fully possessing the dominion of words and pitch, delivered a prophetic command upon Maelgwn, which at the time puzzled both hearers, being out of place.

"Lancelot. When it comes to the time to do that which you would do, for the sake of all free men, I beg you, do it not."

Merlin left no room for debate or further discussion regarding his utterance or the present quest, and limited the discourse to the pleasant conversation amongst warriors, men and friends. Taliesin and Maelgwn chose to accept and honor the old man's authority, although Maelgwn discerned that some great mystery was revealed from student to teacher and that Taliesin had said or done something to Merlin prior to the present distress. But sufficient unto the night was the peril of the dawn, and Maelgwn let the mystery remain such as they bade Taliesin farewell, making ground upon the Continent.

CHAPTER 18
The Present Sister

After delivering sorrowful justice to his son, King Arthur did not return to Caerleon. Instead, he and the twenty-six Round Table Companions, less Maelgwn, convened and lodged at Caermelyn, that famous yellow fortress woven forever into the Great Conversation through Bards' songs in epic poetry and prose and celebrated the world over, from queens in Africa to artists in Rome.

The shining city on a hill that could not, and cannot, be hidden.

Near the ancient city of Caerdydd and within the commote of Ceiwbr, within the cantref of Breinyawl, within the kingdom of Glamorgan, was the magnificent fortress found. The gilded warriors held court at a nearby small castle which was upon a meadowy flat land under the shadow of the fortress.

The castle's great hall housed the Round Table, with its set of circles within circles and pivots and rivets. A sacred dwelling set aside for the twenty-six to congress around legislative affairs, celebrate quests or debate matters of national interest.

In the Round Table hall in Ceibwr were great

scrolls affixed to ornate walls. They recorded the genealogies of the Cymry kings and chieftains from the present era back to Brutus, and upon some, back to Aedd Mawr who had lived thirteen hundred years before the advent of the Lord. The scrolls were scribed in three languages; Latin, Ogham, and lastly, the native alphabet of the Britons, which shared similarities with the scripts of the Near East. Additionally, elaborate stone cruciforms and memorials served the same purpose. The Bards would compete one with another; the selected player placed with back to the scrolls and reciting the lines by memory. The other Bards could randomly demand a 'switch' from paternal to maternal heredity and use other maneuvers of distraction and gamesmanship. Great laughter, greater concentration and, greatest above that, celebration of a special and unique people resulted from these and like games.

Harps and horns melodically filled the air, complemented by Illtud's perpetual choirs, constituted wholly of men rotating in shifts, ensuring songs and praises from eveningtide to first light.

Ever jubilant, the fortress Caermelyn, along with its satellite castles, chapels and estates, shone this day brighter than ten suns, a beacon of liberty to the whole of the world. For this was the first convening of the Round Table Fellowship since vanquishing the Saxons for good at the battle of Mynydd Baeden. The first convening of a liberated and free nation.

Old men were as young children, frolicking and hugging and wrestling about.

Young children were as old men, cheerfully

speculating about the future, talking for the first time of a bright tomorrow where the hope of *anything* was attainable.

Catholic priests embraced the Briton bishops, Druids hugged hard anyone who would receive their noble embraces and even the Dynion Hysbys were affable.

Men of the North supped with the Silures and the western tribes danced and jostled with the chieftains of Powys.

Arthur, flanked by Gwalchmai and Bedwyr (with Cai three paces behind, vigilant), entered the Hall.

Eighteen years and twelve major battles (when accounting for smaller skirmishes, successful defense of raids and minor battles the number was sixty and four) and so much burden, terror and sacrifice had forged this happy moment in shimmering Caermelyn. And not just in Glamorgan was this disposition present. Everywhere, the Blessed Isles were singing a collective song; one unified chorus at all hours and at all times for the past seven days: "Victory and Freedom, Victory and Freedom, Victory and Freedom!"

King Arthur was undefeated, save in his heart and in the corridors of his own house.

Queen Gwenhwyfar's seat was empty. All knew and none asked.

Amr was not amongst the young men who returned from the northern patrols. None knew and none asked.

So much external frenzied joy did not fool the wise king. He wondered how many of those singing and laughing and celebrating with such exuberance that their voices betrayed and abandoned them were like him… broken.

How many widows bottled, buried and died slowly from inside out from the pains of war? How many dashed souls locked away the caverns and cankers of loneliness? How many couples allowed distance to injure what Saxon blade could not? Eighteen years of parting kisses and too-short returns. How many writs of divorcement could have been prevented simply through that which was more valuable than lands or gold? Time. Family time. Couples' time. The Saxons had lost the war but drawn so many Britons into despair. How many were like Arthur and Gwenhwyfar in this very room, at this very moment? Real smiles and real joy lacquered o'er a cracked mirror.

Arthur was broken.

As the Sovereign's eyes were descending towards his feet, they fell upon a young child. The young girl was vigorously and victoriously waving a smaller version of a great war banner. A faithful and well-crafted replica of those used in battle. A child's plaything. Arthur saw her smile as she whirled the red dragon in circles dozens of times in but a few seconds. *And that smile!*

Arthur was unbreakable.

The child at once reminded him that the Isles had no more choice to sacrifice the current generation than a baker has choice to fling his eggs upon an invading thief. *The eggs are broken, but the kitchen lives on.*

Winning the Saxon Wars had been for this child. For all children. She would spend the next generation as a free woman, able to study and learn and pursue arts or commerce or become a great physician. Devoting her focus to herself, her

God, her family, her passions and occupations. And all without endless raids, invasions and repetitive, perpetual loss.

Art, science, spirituality, freedom of mobility. All the natural rights of man fastened strong by a grip called Hope to a torch called Liberty. Arthur and his knights, his Wizard, his bishops and famous women of renown had given the world a Kingdom of Summer birthed, like the king himself, in the coldest days of winter.

King Arthur professed and practiced transparency, often inviting and encouraging any citizen to listen to Round Table proceedings. However, he balanced this by making it clear that the Hall was not a public square for debate and continuously reinforced the law. Namely that chieftains, councils or kings ruled over cantrefs, not this centralized republican body.

On this day, with the buzz and frolic of celebration, Cai the Steward struggled to calm the crowds who were seated upon couches and rectangular tables positioned along beehive-styled stories running from floor to roof, allowing hundreds to see the noble assembly and hear firsthand of deeds fair, quests conquered and policies that might impact every hearth and home.

The assembly started with tidings that brought such a cheer and roar that Arthur forgot himself and joined the masses, fist pumping and feet jumping two and possibly three times, as a child leaps at the prospect of cake or confections.

"Maelgwn is found! The Lady of Llyn Fawr sends message that her foster-son has suffered a minor injury and convalesces under her care in Broceliande."

The herald, a Druid sent by Vivien, possessed no additional details and none pressed for them. How the Bloodhound Prince had been leading his hosts in delivering the final meticulous death strokes upon the enemy at Baeden and now, less than a fortnight later, was lain up wounded upon the Continent was, for now, irrelevant. He was alive and well.

Nor did any of the twenty-five use occasion of the good news as a platform to make inquiries about the bad. They would attend to the mystery of Merlin's disappearance at the right time and in the appropriate forum. Besides, the bishops and priests were already informed that Arthur would meet with them directly.

After several minutes of rapture, the Hall quieted and the Round Table fellowship entered into great discourse as continuation of making the final determination about governing the remnant of Saxons, Angles, Jutes and many other fatherless and brotherless disparate Germanic tribes, surely starving and frightened to fits along the Saxon shores of Lloegyr.

An enduring principle of the Round Table Fellowship was that 'all elbows are equal when resting on this table', and meant that much of the policy discussions and decisions were led by the great knights themselves, not Arthur, who respected and obeyed delegated powers. He participated as a peer (as did Maelgwn when present) and did not lord his office as Pendragon over any of his fellows.

Cador, Urien and other brilliant and heroic men, each deserving of tomes and poems for their mighty and good deeds, described how living Germanic males would be allowed to stay but would live under leasehold contracts, not being allowed ownership of Briton soil for nine generations.

Women, children and the elderly or infirm would be treated with mercy and kindness, and the local chieftains were charged with all the moral authority the Round Table could muster not to become the very monsters they had just vanquished. The Round Table could make no local laws forbidding the violation or abuse of women, especially for non-citizens. However, they did remind the chieftains and lords that they would periodically give ear to appeals where severe violations of the natural laws of man occurred and hoped greatly that they would never have to side with a Saxon bringing accusation of tyranny against a Briton; for they would side with right, regardless of race.

Moreover, the great sailor Prince Madoc would arrange a fleet of ships and repatriate survivors back to their native lands. This would be a perilous journey but, for the sake of right and good, one that the Cymry would sponsor.

As for those who remained, they could be freely pursued by any Christian sect but had to forsake their old gods and be baptized (in spite of what Merlin had pronounced upon the bishops, as he was not there to further formalize his protests), else be executed per the agreements of both the Romanist and Cymry elders. As these newly baptized Germans could not own land, the Religious Leaders shifted attention to placing lessors over them that could, seeking a double advantage of land grants and human capital.

Next, great announcements about the dissolution of the professional and full-time army and naval forces were delivered. Over four hundred thousand men had been succored by the people to fight the invaders for the past eighteen years. Four hundred thousand men would have to integrate back into the communities they had protected and bled for. Where lands had been lost during skirmishes, raids or fraud (for in the chaos of war, many professional criminals and baser sorts did harm to the soldiers, taking advantage of them), they would be restored and debts cancelled.

Men who had held sword longer than plow would now sow and reap, and the transition would not be easy.

Bishop Bedwini, whose speech never ceased to be soothing and seasoned with salt (a man who could deliver difficult truths with grace but conviction), made a formal oratory as to the *why* the military would be dissolved.

Using history to inform the present, professional soldiers were, as an organism, injurious to the liberty and often invented reasons to remain necessary, starting pretender wars. Or turning on the people. When being invaded, or for common defense, a terrifying military frightens the enemy. When at peace, it tends to terrify the people.

The Round Table Fellowship reduced the full-time army to one tenth of its size and dramatically reduced part-time or reserve forces as well. What remained of the armies under the direct control of the Pendragon would continue to secure borderlands and retain continuity of training, in the event that some unknown invader dared light upon Britannia's shores. In the Summer Kingdom, this was most unlikely.

Arthur personally asked for a full appraisal from his leaders and counselors relative to extant external threats within the borders of Cymru. The scope of his questions did not address internal conflicts, squabbles or rivalries with his countrymen such as Caw (who remained in the North, celebrating with King Llew) and Meirchion (who, along with his young child Mark, were present), but rather to pockets of Saxons, Picts or other threats that would require military action.

The Picts, an ancient people second only to the Cymry as settlers to the Isles amongst the Sons of Adam, continued to desire a marital alliance with the northern tribes and were a disruption, but no menace.

The puzzling West Saxons' king with a Briton's name, Cedric, had survived and escaped Mynydd Baeden. He led a peculiar band of Saxon, Briton and Irish rebels called the Gewisse. A persistent and valiant young king of similar age and disposition to Arthur, Cedric was formidable but had no strength of number or manpower (for most of his subjects lay in the field of slaughter or feeding carrion upon the slopes and crags of Baeden). He would need to be contained, monitored and ultimately killed or deported, but posed no real threat to the Summer Kingdom.

Prince Madoc's port guards indicated that Cedric had fled Cymru and was rumored as fugitive in the Emerald Isle. At the hearing of this, King Arthur turned towards the stories, seeking his Aunt Marchel. Married to King Anlach and critical participant in forging peace between the Silures and Irish, she could quickly wield her influence to flush out the fleeing invader.

Satisfied with Saxon policies of land ownership, deportation, massive reduction of the standing military forces and, hopefully, having struck a common-ground position to appease the grumbling factions within the church, the Round Table Fellowship shifted to discussions about what would become – *of themselves.*

The governance structure of local chieftains and their Druids or bishops ruling in diverse ways over local cantrefs (being approximately one hundred villages or large farms) worked as the best hope to check tyranny and preserve liberty and had long endured, through both the Roman and Saxon Wars. A Pendragon or High King protected the borders and solved major disputes and, if the Silure man was ineligible or infirm, he could appoint an Wledig or Battle Commander to serve along his side, or in his stead.

The notion of two sets of twelve knights and nobles in a type of 'government within the government' was a foreign concept but Merlin had forged it nevertheless, the extremity of the Saxon Wars demanding such a group be instituted.

With but a few detractors from the North, the consensus of the people was to retain the Round Table Fellowship. They would be greatly needed to stabilize and reconstruct a nation whose fathers and grandfathers and grandfather's fathers had only ever known perpetual raiding and then, all-out perpetual war.

Their ongoing existence delivered a message to future invaders and to the evils that still dwelled within the land (or any land): that Arthur and Lancelot and their mighty men could and would quickly activate when the cause was meet.

Questions of 'what will we do now?' frequented the gathering and King Arthur helped create a vision for them on how they would fill the void of war.

"Quest." Arthur let the powerful word rest upon its own pillars for a few minutes. "Without a quest, what purpose has a knight? And when all quests are fulfilled, what becomes of him?"

The twenty-four knights were enthralled at this saying. One of Maelgwn's sons, a young warrior not seated yet at the Table, was especially touched by Pendragon's words and committed, at that very moment, to one day being the greatest of the Questing Knights of the Round Table.

As for the types of quests relevant to a sitting body of heroes without a war to fight, Arthur gave examples.

"There are missing persons to find," (he spake of Merlin) "and there is much we don't know about the other creaturekind that shares habitation in this land. There are treasures, there are riddles, there are worthy commissions from bishops and Druids alike. We shall not serve vanity, but we shall find questing for good quests."

The king went on to say that the Round Table Fellowship would also be dismissed to spend more time with wives, children and friends, joining at Caermelyn only one time per new moon. And, as knights might be about a worthy quest, the number for a quorum was reduced from twenty and one to fifteen.

Having all these matters pronounced with

careful communication, edification and education, the audience in the small castle under the shadow of the great yellow fortress began to see Arthur's vision for the Summer Kingdom; *a unified Cymru with local leadership and small government. Of knights questing and seeking great and glorious things. An age of enterprise and freedom.*

As there was ongoing revelry and feasting to be had, the twenty-six save Maelgwn adjourned, but not before Arthur charged one of his own with his first quest.

"Hawk of May." Arthur warmly saluted Gwalchmai.

Gwyar, in accord with her dictate from the High Queen, was at court but in a high balcony, not yet reacquainted with her brother. Dressed in simple black garb, she was as a ghost during the revelries and proceedings. Although passionate about sovereignty, she was for the greater part ambivalent towards the banter about internal policies and certainly had no patience to suffer grown boys speaking of quests. But the mention of her son's name roused her from boredom. Alert, she listened hard.

"You will go to Broceliande and bring Maelgwn back to the Island." There was no option to decline, based upon the tone of the king. Joyful but direct, he continued. "Whatever evil befell him there, beware of and defeat. Go then unto the fortress of Ogyrfan. The two of you will personally escort his daughter, Gwenhwyfar."

Gwalchmai, not understanding the full wishes of the king, posed the question: "Escort her to where?"

"New Troy," the king responded.

Gwyar screamed "No!" as her own prophecies crashed upon her heart as great stones hurled by some giant down a slope. With the noise of the crowd she was heard not, but the Round Table vibrated and creaked. Few noticed and fewer cared, given the great happy frenzy of the day.

"If Maelgwn needs extra time to rest, give him some leave, but please ensure that you make as much haste as you are able. In a fortnight less a day you must have Gwenhwyfar ferch Ogyrfan to me. We meet at Ludgate." The king finished his charges.

* * *

Later that night the Pendragon struggled to find sleep. His heart seemed to desire to jump right out of his chest, pounding like a great battle drum. His shoulder muscles were stuck in a permanent 'shrugging' posture and he reassembled his pillows at least thirty-nine times.

Somewhere between wakefulness and slumber, with his senses compromised, she came.

Arthur's hands felt fastened, as it were by large iron nails, to the bed and he watched, or dreamt, as the shadow woman enveloped the vaulted ceiling of his bedroom and then slowly transformed, shrinking down to human size, hovering atop him. This he saw every detail of, yet he knew his eyes were closed.

The entity's eyes flashed gold mixed with bronze. King Arthur was aroused. Deep in the paralysis of the encumbered sleep, he relived the king making rites; the lust, the power, the communion with the heaven and earth through forces that paradoxically were in no way part of either heaven or earth. The aromas and lights in the cave. The masks. The location along a river and yet in a forest. The Stag. The memory of being presented proudly by Meurig like some newborn lion cub to the several tribes gathered in Gwent straightway after.

Now his mind's eye took him to Saint Illtud's, to school. "I saw her first," he declared, only half-musing, "I saw her first." Lancelot grimaced and his young sister Gwyar, in the anteroom and back of the chapel, cringed.

Reaching the pinnacle and release of his arousal, the Iron Bear's hands suddenly unhinged from their invisible nails and he reached for the feminine spectral haunting him. "Morgana! Morgana!" he screamed. A grave sense of danger prevented him from uttering the name thrice, just as always. His third and final nocturnal chant cried "Gwen!" at the precise second that the encounter *finished.*

Cai, stationed upon simple stool outside the room, heard some indiscernible disruption. A moment later he carefully and quietly entered the room and looked upon the king. All was in order, and the king soundly sleeping.

* * *

The following morning Arthur and Cai were enjoying a cold but sunny winter's morn, strolling through the market. It was busy with the enterprises of livestock, provisions and artisans. Hundreds bustled in the square. Peradventure chance brought them upon Princess Gwyar, doing the same.

"Sister!" Arthur, face to face with a sibling he had not seen in the flesh in a great while. "It has been so long!"

"Seems as if it has been but an evening ago, brother." Face to face with Morgaine of the Faeries.

CHAPTER 19
All Things Are Lawful Unto Me But Not All Things

"Nimue. Use the Sight. Find the Merlin," directed Vivien, who had had a large basin placed in an anteroom where she was lodging, four days removed from Merlin's tangle with the priests and bishops at the amphitheater, and the morning following her hosting the repulsive priest, Meirchion.

"I don't know if there is enough of him still upon me to accurately locate him, mistress." Merlin had given the young enchantress a soft, affectionate but appropriate kiss before he had stolen away in the night before the troops assembled at Ogmore.

Desperate to find him, for diverse reasons, Vivien had ordered her apprentice, the young priestess Nimue, to use the arcane art of scrying to locate the wandering Wizard.

Scrying is a form of divination whereby something attached to the subject is placed upon a clear pool of water filled *just so* in a special basin, pool or cauldron. By stirring the water thrice clockwise whilst saying the incantation, then placing the attachment (in this case the slightest remains of Merlin's kiss upon a handkerchief), then stirring the waters thrice clockwise again, the basin when at last still would form a window, or one-way mirror, between the diviner and the subject.

Per Nimue's worldview, that was supposedly how the process worked.

In reality, a familiar spirit must follow the attachment and, making sport of the enchantress, only respond if the words and rituals were followed. If the familiar spirit, a finite being with no powers of omnipresence, was not present then no reading would be had, forcing the diviner to suffer great embarrassment, speculate or guess. For this cause many enchanters and fortune tellers were reproved as pretenders and deceivers.

The waters stilled; the image of a man appeared! Nimue peered hard, hopeful. Looking and looking harder, she hoped to discover the subject, but – alas – raised her head from the Seeing Pool, dejected.

"He is…" Nimue did not quite know how to describe it.

"Describe," said Vivien.

"Shielded in white light. Yes, that is it. *Shielded.* I do not see Merlin; only the form of a man clothed in white light. I am sorry, mistress."

The Lady of Llyn Fawr forcefully, for haste and not anger, pushed young Nimue aside, wanting a closer look at the basin. As her head drew close, a necklace given her by her foster-son inadvertently breached the waters. Vivien saw even less than Nimue, finding only her goddess-like visage scowling back at her through the water. "My brother Budic is right. I am getting old." Laughter broke the intense and seemingly futile exercise.

Vivien paced away, mulling the words of Meirchion the priest-king, considering her course. A few paces more and she flopped down upon a slanted writing desk, made of oak and stained white; the kind used by monks and scribes. She mimicked them for a moment, drafting letters with her long fingers upon the desktop, distracted and thinking.

Then. Startled!

"My Lady. I find not the Lord Merlin but I see–" she triple-checked the looking pool for absolute verification. "Your foster-son, the great hero Lancelot. He just boarded a shipping vessel and sits next to the shielded figure."

"Nimue, you've done it!" Vivien stood, slow and authoritatively. "They are together. Has the Sight revealed unto you their destination?"

"The shipping vessel makes for..." Nimue became irony personified and her face a great beaming smile. "Broceliande. They are going to *your* forest, my Lady. Shipping vessels are slow and unwieldy, and make many stops. We can advance their arrival should we make our leave, right now."

"You must go alone, Nimue," and the Lady of the Lake delivered unto the girl her charges.

* * *

Broceliande was a magical forest, gargantuan in

size, which covered the whole of central Brittany. Entire villages and minor cities resided within its protective oaks, so tall that they blocked out direct sunlight, allowing only brilliant shards of light to enter in.

Its most efficacious point of entry for Merlin and Maelgwn was to trek through the ancient city of Rhoazon, and then bear southeast where old paths and star routes guided those who knew the coordinates to the Fount of the Lady. And near to that, the estate of Vivien, the Lady of Llyn Fawr. Legends and whispers held that she could pass effortlessly through underwater or otherworldly passages from her sacred lakes in Glamorgan to her estate in Little Britain. Water spirits were venerated above all other deities amongst the Bretons who, like their cousins in Cymru, were Christian amongst the royalty and heathen amongst the farmers and cattlemen.

Merlin knew the paths, as did Maelgwn, who loved Vivien as a mother.

Alternatively, a stranger to the forest would surely find himself prisoner to a labyrinth of trees and stone, an abyss of creeks and fissures, from which he would become disoriented and lost, and die. Or bewitched and misplaced by the Fair Folk without hope of retrieval.

Intending to lodge at the Lady's estate as two lonely questers, Merlin was astounded to see the small turret alight and a familiar shape waiting, leaning casually against the stone walls within the archway. Ivy had invaded and supplanted most of the stone and the scene of the exotic maiden against the beauty of the archway seemed as a painting to the Wizard.

He approached the painting, and the painting kissed him.

This time the kiss was beyond neighborly embrace, hard and wet upon the mouth. During the delivery she intentionally applied the lightest touch upon his fingertips and then clasped his free hand, the other dropping his walking staff at the gleeful shock of the exchange.

Knowing not how to evaluate the matter, all the wisest man in the world could do was toss forward a clumsy greeting.

"Oh, the folly of trying to sneak away, knowing you and the Lady can *see* me anywhere, anyhow!"

"But I did not see you, Lord," responded the innocent, mousey voice, its owner looking up at the tall Briton. "You cannot be *seen*, Lord Merlin." The smallest tone of accusation, and perhaps anger ever so slight, snuck into her tone. "But I did see *him*." A casual look at the other tall Briton.

"I thirst," was Maelgwn's only speech towards Nimue. By interpretation, it meant 'you two clearly need some time alone'. And into the home where he had spent so much of his youth training and playing and learning he entered.

Nimue reclaimed the hand she clasped and marched Merlin towards a secondary structure, a stunning little two-room cabin, used for highly regarded servants or guests requiring privacy.

Every man has a woman before whom he will crumble. Even unto every god or angel. Mighty Zeus had Danaë, David swooned at the bathing beauty Bathsheba and Merlin, an immovable man of principle and duty and unwavering focus on the mission at hand, melted o'er Nimue.

Reason knows not Love. You love who you love.

Nimue immediately disrobed with one hand, still holding Merlin's with the other.

Markings covered the young priestess. An owl interwoven in perpetual knots was centered on her back and Silure bear claws were spaced out all over her thighs and hinderside. Her arms were a sleeve of moons and black branches that brought out little alluring patches of her snowy skin. Like her mistress, golden hair, everywhere.

Nimue granted no mercy in mixing religious interrogation with lovemaking.

"Why could I see you not in my scrying basin, *cariad*?" Another hard kiss.

She allowed no space for response.

"Covered by your new God, Lord Merlin." A harder, nearly violent, kiss followed.

"Yes." Merlin drew upon a failing reserve of self-control, momentarily. "I am dead, and my life is hidden in Christ, in God. I am saved now," he testified.

Nimue: a creature seemingly created to seduce and manipulate men. A radical loyalist to the goddess Modron, channel of the familiar spirit of Queen Achtland (who could be pleasured by no man) and the water god Nodens, she typically felt numb when snaring men in their folly and cared not for their politics or religion. They were targets. Subjects. Victims. Yet at Merlin's words, Nimue was not numb. His words, his manner of speaking, were different. She was disgusted. Hate replaced apathy and vile enmity replaced the small measure of fondness she had always possessed for the Wizard, now turned Nazarene.

Though reviled, the seduction continued. Now as means of examination for purpose of gathering information. *Vivien and the Old Nasty Priest were right. He must not be allowed to live.* She convicted him in her mind.

She tempted and mocked Merlin's infant faith with questions of lust and sin, attempting to snare him in hypocrisy. And although Merlin did not ravage her and was fighting his flesh and seeking to suspend his burning towards her, he finally brought himself to simply state: "The flesh is dead anyhow. Don't you see, my love? All the land grants, the selling of this and the doing of that, the taste not, touch not rules of men cannot please a Holy God, else Christ suffered in vain."

"Then *do as thou wilt* is the whole of your law?" she asked.

"That is almost true, and yet a subtle perversion. I am not under law, but under grace," Merlin stated, as she now had him upon his back on the bed. Speaking through her skillful strokes and pets, he went on, "All things are lawful unto me, but not all things edify. All things are lawful unto me but not all things glorify God. All things are lawful unto me but I shall not be brought under the power of any. Do you understand?"

Nimue, a swarm of kissing bees hived around the Wizard's neck, popped up to reply. "Because you can do a thing does not mean that you ought to do a thing?"

"Exactly, *cariad*! What we do or do not do is a function of love, not debt, guilt and reward."

"I see why the Catholics want you dead, Lord Merlin. Will you teach these things to Arthur?" Nimue asked, then resumed her swarm of kisses and caresses.

"There is yet beauty in Rome. And not all

Catholic people are bad. We must always be careful to distinguish the people from their leaders. I long to see Rome. Paul was there."

"I hate Paul!" A visceral, loud objection. "He hates women and would subjugate us under the thumb of men as dogs or mules!"

"A common misconception by those who never read the man," answered Merlin, authoritatively. "Paul's letters must be read as such and he restricted the abuse of transitory signature gifts by women in a local assembly. Context drives meaning. After all, Paul had many women succor his ministry and it was he who pronounced words that would cost him his head, including the pronouncement that there is neither male nor female, as we are all one in Christ!" Merlin's words were masterful, given that he had not known a woman in years and that the very object of many nights of mortal self-indulgent thoughts was grinding upon his loins at the time.

But the words were lost on Nimue; she naturally could not receive them.

"Tell me that one part again, please," she requested, with an intentional erotic pant.

Merlin asked about which part, excited to share how Christ had died for her and reconciled with her personally two thousand years ago, and how the organized Church was the Devil's plaything. Playing a guessing game for a few more pets and grinds and jostles, she finally removed the last of the old man's clothing.

"Nay. The part about all things being powerful and such." She bungled his words with a purpose, begging his correction.

"No, lover." He tried to focus as she was on

the verge of forcing him inside of her. "All things are lawful unto me, but I shall not be brought under the power of any."

But you are under my power now. And Nimue seduced Merlin.

Many enchantments are made the moment a man's life-making essence is spilled, for several reasons. Principle among these is the fact that, more powerful than any intoxicant, a man goes into the nether world for a few short seconds; open, susceptible and vulnerable to other worlds, deception and manipulation.

As Merlin lay panting, happy, the portal for betrayal open but for a few seconds, Nimue rapidly handed him a chalice. A post-lovemaking beverage. Truly not able to think in his ecstasy, he received her cup, questioning not. In addition to unleashing malicious and murderous spells upon Merlin using ancient and dark carnal magick (she doubted in her mind that they would take effect, given Merlin's apparent special relationship with the Saviour Himself), Nimue served him a lethal dose of mandrake mixed with mercury and finished with purple monkshood. She masked the poison, rendering it as a gentle cup of tea tasting somehow precisely as the tea his mother used to serve.

Nimue had enchanted the famous and wondrous Merlin of Britain, and poisoned him that he might die.

CHAPTER 20
And What Did Paul Say to You?

Two sons feeding the worms. Newly single. Estranged queen in self-imposed exile. The Bloodhound found and soon to join the Bear at Ludgate in New Troy. Army practically dissolved. Knights excited to see their wives and move on from wars to noble quests. Saxon policies in order and insufferable denominations appeased. Country celebrating the birth of their Golden Age.

It was time to resume the matter of greatest severity.

It was time to find his Merlin.

Feigning a gentle knock upon Meirchion's door, coupled with a soft "Priest, a word with you?" No sooner did the door crack open than Arthur shouldered in with force and righteous anger and grace. Grasping the priest by the collar of his robe as one gathers and yanks the scruff of a cat, King Arthur suspended the scrawny, contemptible rogue three inches from the floorboard. "You urged for his death in your privy council."

"Apparently not so privy," Meirchion whined. "Illtud violated two hundred years of tradition gossiping with you as he did."

Arthur lowered his captive, glaring. "Tradition be damned when truth is at stake. Or my friend! Did you kill him? Kidnap him? Hear the severity and verity of my words and toy not. What hand had you in it?" The old Catholic was now witness to the ferocity of the king and the same look hundreds of Saxons had received, over the past two decades, immediately preceding imminent demise.

Meirchion calculated carefully his response. That he wanted the Druid dead could no longer be concealed. The precise nature, or the *why*, had to be distorted. Sharing that Merlin professed an end to water baptism, tithes and land grants, a reconciliation between Druid and the Briton's apostolic church and an unwavering conviction that Christ was all an individual needed and, topping all, that Merlin in his influence and brilliance as a speaker and leader would evangelize this 'good news' throughout the land, was unthinkable. For in sharing it, Arthur might find interest in the topic and his wanton neutrality over religion sway to this 'grace message' that would bankrupt Romanism's enterprise. Death threat from the High King or no, Meirchion offered half-truths to Arthur.

"In a moment of anger," he trembled, "I, amongst seven other aggravated saints, advocated for his death. It's true." At this saying, Meirchion thought he heard an actual lion's roar and hastened to continue his false account. "The Wizard had gone mad and, though confessing some heretical form of Christianity, sought to subvert all and slander the Church. We had been fighting long through the night about baptism and doctrinal authority over the Saxon remnants in the east and I forgot myself. I am old, young king." The tone shifted to contrived self-pity dashed with piety. "I know not where Merlin went; only that the heathen witch-queen had some notion of his goings." At this, Meirchion betrayed Vivien, with whom he had just freshly made an accord.

* * *

"I cannot stay, my lord, forgive me." Nimue greeted Merlin as he woke from his night in heaven; his one opportunity to have her. "My charges were to make sure you were well and report back to the Lady of the Lake."

Merlin stretched and yawned and laughed, and his joints and muscles reminded him that lovers were meant to be young. "But you didn't even ask me why am I here," he mused. Neither Nimue nor Vivien knew of Merlin's secret affiliations with the Brotherhood. Nimue had simply come to seduce and then kill Merlin and thus was caught in a brief tangle, failing to ask conjured questions about his mission.

Women know things.

A man freshly waking from passionate lovemaking is a fool, even one wise as Solomon, or the Merlin.

"I was so raptured in seeing you, having long suppressed these feelings, that I simply failed to ask. And now I am curious. Why are you and the tall killing device here in the land of the Bretons?" (She spake of Maelgwn, refusing subtly to even speak his name or acknowledge his personhood. Clearly, she was not fond of him for some unknown past wrong. Given his history and volume of women, surely there was a tale there Merlin had no desire to speak, nay even think, of.)

Her tactic assuaged any suspicion and now it was Merlin's turn to lie.

"The – uh – tall killing device over there and I had great cause to think that spies would grant the Long Knife access to our ports. From this very forest. The sensitive information warranted grave and urgent investigation. Better that the assembled armies fret about one old Wizard than a surprise threat to the entire campaign."

"Our victory suggests you quelled the threat, then?" she asked, half believing.

"The information provided was false." Merlin left it at that. "I am sorry my new faith troubles you, beautiful Nimue."

"It's as Arthur says, Merlin." Again, hatred had to be channeled into cunning words. "Let men worship what gods they will, *only that they don't kill their neighbors for it.*"

"I hope to see you again soon," said Merlin.

"I should like that, my lord." A parting kiss was exchanged.

Maelgwn presented himself, his mannerisms encouraging the two to leave. January rains are bitter cold, even in a magical forest. Validating that Merlin knew where the Council had stood up their portable tabernacle, they moved on from the Fount and the Castle of the Lady, deeper into the unforgiving, alluring heart of the Broceliande wood.

As the famous travelers progressed deeper and deeper into the wood, Maelgwn felt as if they were rather in a boat, floating towards the very heart of darkness. He also noticed that the old Druid's countenance had clearly changed. Merlin had hidden himself under the canopy of his grey hood for the sum of the day's ride, and a guttural cough had developed.

Maelgwn speculated that the wintry rain or nerves about confronting his former *Brothers and Elders* was causing Merlin to feel ill.

In reality, Nimue's poison was slowly taking effect.

* * *

At eventide, at the very moment they felt as if they could travel no more, they finally arrived at the temporary abode of the Council of Nine. As Maelgwn was the surety of Merlin's safety, he assessed the area and posed several questions before allowing Merlin to enter the edifice.

"If there is incident, how many men should I be prepared for?" he asked, rolling his shoulders and limbering for a fight after the stiffness of the cold ride. His unique battle spike made its first appearance.

Merlin turned to him, his wit, wisdom and humor overpowering the poison killing him from within. "Well, Lancelot, they are called the Council of NINE, so I suppose there are NINE of them."

They both laughed aloud. Merlin entered two folded curtains, each thirty and three feet in height. The entrance to the tabernacle of the Nine.

A stoic voice said: "Merlin. Enter. We are living in legendary and perilous times."

"Aye, of Biblical measure, yes?" contributed another. This one was less stoic and more mocking in tone and pitch.

Merlin made no response and continued to walk in, very slowly.

There he saw the civilized world's most powerful men sitting at a table within a trapezoidal hall fixed between two great obelisks. Dark without ceiling; ornate. Egyptian. The use of torches and great lanterns revealed the genius of the tabernacle's design, illuminating parts of the wooden, fabric and stone structure, veiling others.

The capstone was a glass pyramid, its masonry giving the illusion of suspension. Great lights descended on rods in six places, cascading independent streams of dusk's final light through the mist and clouds upon a great circular table, affixed in the easternmost chamber of the hall.

Many deities of Egypt presided over the hall in both paintings and stonework. *The Eye of Horu*s was, of all the relics and idols, most prominent. It sprawled across the span of the western wall in dazzling dyes contrasted against the sandy-colored interior. The place was as splendid as it was dark.

Two hundred girthy men could congress in comfort at the great table. It had a circular top fastened to a square foundation. Onyx busts served as lifeless but menacing watchmen at each of the four corners of the table. Their likeness was that of a man, an ox, an eagle, and a lion. Lastly, a winged serpent was suspended directly over the table. The design of the artwork made it look as if the winged serpent was chief over the other watchers.

Rattle and tap. Rattle and tap. Fingers plated with steel talons became a hand, became a wrist, became arms that disappeared up a black robe donned by he who wore a black mask and was clearly known to Merlin as the lead spokesman of the Nine (although on prior visits he had worn white or benevolent garbs and diverse face coverings). "I think you have something to say to us, maybe to show us?" the thick accent of Italy began. "Or shall we go first? You may choose, my student."

Though powerful men engender fear, often terror, Merlin too was a foe worthy of respect; one to be reckoned with cautiously. He was Fear and Awe in the form of a man. Advanced in years, mighty. Taller than the Britons but Briton through and through. His face was two ridges and an authoritative chin. His hooded garb revealed only the bottom crescents of his eyes. The oscillating flicker of light provided only a hint of the faded but proud serpent enjoining its own tail, tattooed on the Druid's long forearm. And he could answer menace with menace as needed. Instead, he chose respect. Respect and caution.

When given the option to speak or to listen, Merlin ever taught Arthur to start by listening, and to his own advice he here harkened. This would give him the advantage of considering, and then countering, their words.

Disquieted that the Merlin was outwitting

them from the start, and knowing that the Briton was the paramount debater and disputer in the world, the leader reversed courses, recanting his courtesy, replacing it with disingenuity. "Rather, you are the guest; pupil, we insist that you begin. I know there is something you want to show us. Show it."

Merlin measured every word and action. Although the sum of all the wisdom of men is counted dung compared to the excellence of God's good news through Christ, a lifetime of learning was about to be aborted. Should he offend them (and they kill him), he would never learn their secrets. And right or wrong, Merlin wanted their gnosis; not for ill, but rather to help reconcile his mind on the purpose of a life filled with lies. *And their initiations and secrets might reveal much about Merlin himself.*

But what choice remained? Somehow they already knew he had changed. And that the nature of the visit was not to become one of them. The tension and tones confirmed this. Respectful, firm truth seemed the Wizard's best, nay only, recourse.

From the folds of his grey robe Merlin produced a book; camel leather with metallic buckles. The cover was still decorated with a few specks of ink where once had been links in an ornate entrelacement of knot-work art that, in its original condition, had bedazzled any reader. Now only outlines of former art and thumb-worn smooth patches remained.

The words inside, however, were perfectly preserved. The vellum proudly declared its timelessness and resiliency to the reader. Such was the magnificence of the book that it seemed to be *alive.*

One of the Nine gently relieved it of Merlin's hands, covetously. He looked at it, agape, for what seemed forever, and then handed it to the Leader.

"Anything else in that robe?" Clearly the lump of a purse, holding cup or horn (or perhaps a weapon), lay across Merlin's chest, covered. After he declined to answer, the Leader of the Nine opened the book. The inscription on the sole blank sheet inside the cover he read aloud: "*In these letters are words that bring eternal life. Thirteen are to you and one is for you. Study. Pass forward. I love you, my son.*"

The design of the mask failed to cover the lower lip and most of his chin. A smile – a *concerned* smile – was evident. "It's part of a Bible," he said bluntly.

"To you versus for you; oh, the magnitude of distinction in those two words!" responded Merlin with passion. "Luke is written *for* us but these other thirteen are written *to* us." And now the unavoidable righteous indignation of any who is shown truth after being intentionally duped by systematized lies for years and years rose within the Druid, overcoming him. "We have studied all the great religions and given hundreds of hours to learning of the sects of Christendom. And in all those years, never once was there mention of *HOW* to study the Bible. How to note and apply its divisions. By what sorcery beyond mine was this simple truth hidden?!" Merlin found himself unintentionally yelling. He calmed himself. "Luke and his Acts of the Apostles are written for us but Paul, Paul is writing to us. The inscription to this blessed scroll contains more truth than the libraries of a thousand scholars."

"This book is over five hundred years old." The Leader of the Nine was gliding around Merlin now, analyzing and date-setting the small tome while the Wizard was preaching at them. "Where did you get it?"

The truth was that Taliesin, the Chief Bard, the future Merlin of Britain, had given it to the current office holder, and to Taliesin from his father and from his father his father, back to its original gifting. Without hesitation, to ensure Taliesin's head remained attached to his shoulders, and with unshrinking confidence and calm, Merlin lied.

"Mad Meirchion set ablaze a rival chapel in the South of Cymru. Most of the library was destroyed, yet I found this." A lie spoken. A seed planted.

The book was being passed around the Council of Nine. Many had never seen the letter to the Ephesians at all and fewer still a complete set of Paul.

After circling the room and coming back to the spokesman of the Nine, the book was shoved back into Merlin's hands, causing five hundred years of careful preservation to crumple and bend unwillingly. Merlin, a man of letters, cringed as if harming the book was as the injury or murder of a friend or parent.

"And what did Paul say TO YOU?"

Merlin gave a direct and thorough answer, telling the truth in love, flavored with salt.

CHAPTER 21
The Secret Teaching of the Ages Pertaining to the Souls of Men

"There is much to consider. The old Wizard… well," a shadowy figure released a bewildered laugh, "brought our wisdom to foolishness. And we are the illuminated ones!"

Another of the Brotherhood angrily turned his throne chair about, glaring at the three clergy sitting on a slab, palms in their hands. "Even our apostate theologians who have handled the Writ for a lifetime couldn't open up the Scriptures for us the way the Druid did!"

"Former Druid!" chided another. "What would he say to them?" Recalling the terminology the Wizard just used, "What did he say to us?"

"He said that the gospel is hid to those who are lost, that we are blinded by the god of this world," contributed another.

"Blind me with that *Light*." This speaker seemed to imbibe some invisible devilish milk, slurping it as he spoke, "but these clergy were supposed to have, well, aided us."

Though intelligent without equal amongst men (save, apparently, for Merlin), the Council of Nine placed in their employ fallen Christian scholars and scribes. Men of reprobate consciences who had forgotten their first love, they assisted the Council in understanding how Christians thought and the depths of Christian doctrine. Though the principalities that the Nine served guided them, there were things that they peered into and could not see. Through this combination of congress with Devils and false teachers, the Nine could quell and defeat any Christian teaching, save the one promoted by Merlin.

The leader notwithstanding, precisely four of the Nine knew some of what Merlin shared and four of the Nine knew none of it. The only man in the room not fully surprised nor confounded was the masked leader. The Adept of the adepts.

"Merlin's Mystery is not new to the enemies of the Cross of Christ. The Lord Arddu hates it above all doctrines and thus has worked hard to kill it in the womb, even from the Apostolic era. He conceals it from men and angels as he can. Our Lord is very devoted to keeping the Mystery of Merlin just that: a Mystery," said the leader. Four of the Brothers voiced agreement.

As the leader made manifest that he knew of the religion-destroying message, that God had already paid for the sins of all men living from Paul's day until the end of the age and that dead religion was of the Devil (immediately placing the Church in league with the aims of the Nine), some of his Brothers rose in anger. Clamor and yelling ensued.

Clearly compartmentalization existed, as it did

for all Mystery Religions and most sects, pagan or Christian, even at the very top.

Meanwhile, Merlin was standing there fighting the pangs of poison, having emptied himself emotionally, sharing his testimony and plans with dark, dark souls. *Men he had used to view as ministers of Light.* Nimue's tea was assaulting the base of his brain and pain, wrenching and writhing pain, was firing in each and every nerve in his head. Theology becomes irrelevant when a man is at death's door.

Hypocritically, Merlin had just professed Christ with his mouth (and with sincerity), but his flesh reverted to Merlin's otherworldly powers, trying to heal himself that he might live long enough to hear of their designs on Arthur. Additionally, Merlin hoped that the wisdom of the Ancients now verbally abusing each other in his midst could share some insight or information about what Merlin really was.

To Merlin's knowledge, the Nine were mighty *men* but, save perhaps the Leader, lacked the Sight, or shapeshifting, or elemental or any supernatural abilities. Over the decades, they had clearly been dependent upon Ascended Masters from some other world that provided them information. Their power was gnosis, not magick. That Merlin possessed both always made him their prized possession.

The Leader pounded fist against one of the obelisks, causing his beads and the inverted cross that dangled at their ends to rattle, clank and fall to the floor.

"Brothers!" He commanded silence. "I will tell you *why* some know of this and some know not in due time. But now…" He turned to the fading Merlin, whose magick was not working. "Let us give the Merlin what *he* wants."

Merlin continued to wonder how the Leader knew that he was there to disengage from the Nine but still coveted their knowledge. However discovered, the man was right, for these were Merlin's precise objectives.

The masked man changed countenance and asked Merlin to sit comfortably. This the masked man did as well.

Against reason, he gave the Merlin his wish.

"The Secret Teaching of the Ages has three spheres, student." The man motioned for water to be brought to the old Wizard, then listed the spheres:

"*The Secret Doctrine of the Ages pertaining to men's souls.*"

"*The Secret Doctrine of the Ages pertaining to the eschaton, or end of all things.*"

"*The Secret Doctrine of the Ages pertaining to the nature of Otherworldly beings, of Fae and Watcher, of Star and Dragon.*"

Additionally, he said, "And beside these are the *Seven Sacred Sciences,* many of which you have already mastered and know; but the Secret Doctrine of the Ages will clarify their import in the generations of man, or the *Great Conversation* as well."

"When you required I leave my king ere the battle for our liberation you said that the Secret Doctrine of the Ages involved him personally. Elsewise I would not have come. Was this a ruse?" The Merlin of Britain was bold.

"The Iron Bear born under the sign of the Red

Dragon." The masked man mocked Merlin for his boldness. "This is the problem with obsessively reading Paul; you need to keep reading through to the back of the Writ as well, yes?"

Some laughed.

"Your famous King Arthur is part of the doctrine." The man resumed a teacher's tone. "Patience. Listen."

At this point, although he did not unmask himself, the spokesman did remove his hooded robe along with his terrifying and foreign armor, which covered not just his hands but arms and chest as well, filled with serpentine fins and frightening spikes and hooks. Replacing these with simple tunic and trouser, he began to comfortably reveal the truth behind years of lies to Merlin. He began to teach the *real* Secret Doctrine of the Ages.

"I think I should introduce myself before I begin. Although we Brotherhood of Nine direct the Royal Bloodlines on behalf of our Ascended Masters and are pledged to a life of study and confinement to our mystical colleges, I will make an exception. After all, you've been with us for so long." A few protesting grumbles followed. Disregarding them, he said, "I am Simon Magus. Let us begin."

Without riddle or enigma, Simon Magus began to teach Merlin the Nine's doctrines pertaining to salvation. The lesson began with a declaration of a premise opposing the relativism taught at every other level of the secret societies, sects, neophytes and cults. An immediate validation that the top of the pyramid held far different doctrines than the 'regular folk' along the bottom and middle rungs.

"Every word of the Bible is true. Absolute truth."

Simon Magus paused. An impossibly long pause.

At last, he resumed. "Except for the ending of the tale. That God is assured victory is a lie. *We* will prevail. Elsewise it is all true."

Obviously Merlin could form no words in response to this. The same teachers who had taught that 'all the gods are one god', that 'man finds his own truth' and many other kindred worldviews was telling him that the group they mocked and derided the most in fact possessed the most truth! The Merlin vowed to just listen and not respond, doing nothing to endanger his quest to hear their aims on Arthur.

And continue Simon did, joyfully sharing the Brotherhood's fivefold plan to keep mankind lost and without God, without hope. He called it 'keeping the gate shut to the soul's salvation'. He went so far as to call most cults 'gatekeepers'. This involved, through false teaching, confusion and deception, finding just the right chapter of *The Great Conversation* in which to freeze a person, allowing them to proceed no further unto coming to the knowledge of the truth. Which gate kept a man locked unto damnation varied according to the individual.

The first gate of the lie program was polytheism, the belief in many gods. Many, many men would never see the real God whilst they worshipped the many gods of tribe, of stone, of stream, of season and circumstance. However, as men didn't see gods of rock and stone and merriment and season, they made idols. And idols didn't hug you, speak with you, or love you. You could neither be loved nor hated by a chunk of silver-decked wood. Moreover, the gods were cruel, contradictory, and often more of lower constitution of character than the men supposedly designed to worship them. Thus, men who seek truth sometimes conclude that polytheism is simply mythology; they open the first gate, searching for something more.

Convictions of silence gave way. Merlin had to interrupt. "That is not so! I personally HAVE seen gods and spirits aplenty, not just idols made by hands. What about the Fae?"

"The Isles, and this vast forest, are an exception," Simon Magus laughed heartily. "Ye know not what ye worship. Neither what you see. In any event, that will be covered in section three." Another chuckle, and emphatic request that Merlin hold questions until the teacher had concluded his presentation. He even said "Patience," speaking to Merlin as if he were a child.

Simon Magus explained that the second tier of deception was pantheism. The belief that God is *IN* everything. Those who rejected actual gods separate from the creation but who sought something spiritual gravitated towards pantheism. This form of worship resulted in either lasciviousness, where there is no accountability from man to something tangibly greater than he, or in fatalism, where man abdicates personal responsibility and effort, as the 'force' of which we are all part will be as it will be.

Those thinking and considering pantheism care-fully found that: "Man is God. Dirt is God. Man is–"

"Dirt." Merlin completed the line of thinking

at this point in the initiation. "Man is both nothing and everything under that system, and a meaninglessness ensues. The prison of reincarnation to return in a different form of the same 'force' is the only hope, but to what end? 'Tis a belief in absolute nothingness. It is not peace. It is prison."

"Yes!" Simon was as a proud father of a son who had just caught his first fish or hunted his first hare. Beaming, he said, "Yet we keep ten thousand times ten thousand and ten thousand times that under this system in the East." The lesson continued.

From this gate, Simon explained, some found the emptiness and went into dejection and rejection of the spiritual. To them, there was not a god behind every stone, neither was the tree itself God; having no introduction to Monotheism, they tripped into the pit of atheism.

As an aside, Simon Magus also explained that abuse by the Church under the name of God was organized and carried out to drive men to atheism, rebelling from God and anything remotely attached to religion. As this practice was only a few hundred years old, it had not formalized as part of the mysteries taught by the Nine, but was well on its way to becoming an additional gate.

"The fool hath said in his own heart, there is no God." Merlin again found himself speaking at the hearing of these intentional misdirections.

"Aye, in his heart, not in his head," Magus agreed. "Men in this gate look at the creation, the stars, the circuits of the sun. They behold the miracle of childbirth and they know in their heads that we are not here as a result of chance or random natural processes. They eschew accountability but they know that there is a God to whom they will answer."

"In this regard, there are no actual atheists," contributed Merlin.

"Again, you are correct, my student. Men toil behind this gate over anger, ill experiences and rejection of observable science, and replace it with a science of their own. A science falsely so called."

"What is the next gate?" Merlin was threading their strategy together and, although evil, it was fascinating and effective.

The initiator provided a brief summary, weaving it together again and again along the way. "There are many gods. No. God is in everything. This is not so. Fine. There is no God. That is not reasonable. From here…"

Magus paused again and Merlin could hardly contain himself. Again, he seduced his hearer with summary. "Many gods, God in all, no God, transitions to *I am God*."

The structure and sensibility of this continuum of deception made absolute strategic sense to Merlin, the great strategist. When man knows that there is a spiritual reality but rejects or graduates from systems that do not hold under the light of scrutiny, what is left but to venerate himself? Especially for the atheist. If man graduated from primordial simple components to his present condition, why would he not then progress unto deity?

One of the Nine actually mocked this concept (perhaps he was the very one in charge of seeing its growth and popularity) and chimed, "From goo to you, through the zoo! From slime to divine!" The entire council laughed and even Merlin found himself amused at the ridiculous emptiness of atheistic naturalism.

The leader, Simon, brought the Brotherhood and their 'once gilded pledge and most promising student, turned grace believer' Merlin back to order. He reminded the assembly that, although naturalism and atheism would be mocked on the Blessed Isles where obsession with the spirit and the afterlife was paramount, it was vastly popular amongst the Greeks and other cultures and had kept many souls gated from pursuing a relationship with the One True God.

Merlin again, feeling somewhat more comfortable during the discourse, inquired. "So, the Secret Doctrine of the Ages for men is that you know the truth, but lie anyhow?"

Simon Magus confirmed, even his laughter thick with the accent of magnificent Italy. "Yes." Asking all to resume sitting, he concluded the first of the three great spheres of the Nine's quest. Again, he opted for summary as a powerful preaching conduit of his false gospel:

Many gods.
All is God.
No gods.
I am God.

A person of intellectual honesty, he postulated, could no more think himself a god than a cat could think itself a hummingbird. Each star had its own glory, each element differed from another. Those who thought themselves a god did oppose themselves. A man was a man and a god was a god. And thus, after a season toiling under the weight of self-deception that they, a finite being full of flaws and scars and sickness and infirmity, were likened unto Zeus or Poseidon, they faced the fact. There was a God. And they were not Him.

"And what becomes of these?" asked the Merlin.

"They make it to the final gate. That Satan is God."

This booming statement shocked and confirmed what Merlin already knew. The Council of Nine formally and officially were in league with the Prince of Darkness.

Simon smiled. "When you reject Christ and determine that all the false doors are that, what door remains? These set aside the followings of polytheism, pantheism, atheism, self-deification and any other 'ism' I have forgotten besides and choose rather to follow the one god that makes sense; the god of this world."

"How much do you really control this journey into finding your Lord?" asked Merlin. "And why do you care if men choose Christ or Rhiannon or Bel or your god Arddu? What matters it to you?"

"Excellent questions! The right questions!" Simon Magus always and ever marveled at the genius of Cymru's greatest mind. "Men are blinded by unbelief by nature, but by nature seek the true God. Because of this paradox, all we do is give them a nudge in the wrong direction. We plant certain thoughts in leaders in cults and churches and sects. We publish certain writings and we watch and influence 'big issues', but the greater sum is just enjoying man doing what he does best; rebel."

"And the why?" the Druid pressed.

"As to 'THE WHY' we seek to keep men lost, it has everything to do with the *End of Days*. And much to do with your King Arthur. Are you ready for the second sphere of the Secret Doctrine?"

CHAPTER 22
Tⱨe Otⱨer Antichrist

In the days when Saul of Tarsus (who would later convert to the Faith and become the Apostle Paul) persecuted the Messianic assemblies, causing them to scatter abroad, Mary the Mother of the Lord and Mary of Magdala came, along with other noteworthy followers of the Lord, into Gaul.

Magdalene took a husband, one of Jesus's brothers, and bore him a child. A contention over certain sacred relics arose between the two Marys. So severe was the dispute that they parted, unreconciled: Magdalene unto the caves of what later became southern Little Britain, and Mary the Mother of the Lord unto the Isles, where she tangled with Anna, also over the matter of certain relics. By the time, three decades and more later, Paul finally visited the Isles, Mary was long since retired to the Isle of Apples, under the care of her guardians, the Druids.

After learning the Brotherhood's first great secret, how they intentionally developed false doctrines to doom and blind men when they in fact knew the truth but hated God too much to accept it, the Merlin girded himself to hear about the second sphere of the Secret Doctrine of the Ages. Based upon the allusions provided and from what Merlin had begun to comprehend from rightly dividing the Scriptures, he was fairly certain that the subject would shift towards politics.

Night had fallen and, outside the massive curtain doors, the blackness of night was thick. 'Twas the type of night where one couldn't see their fingers, though they wiggled them two inches in front of their face. Yet, within the great temporary structure, strange and awesome blue and green lights filled the chamber. The illumination of the all-seeing eye was beautiful art made ugly to Merlin for what it stood for.

Although he was certain there were servants or soldiers (or both), Merlin had only seen the Nine, robed and hooded, save Magus, who was still in his leisurely attire and serving his brethren tea.

Merlin felt better when standing as the poison navigated his veins, destroying them as it traversed. He was content that his curiosity and academic need for their final set of secrets was more than satisfied and, were it not for the bait they had dangled before him regarding Arthur, he would have fled the place at once, having no need of further lessons. Instead, exercising the haste of a dying man, Merlin vowed to himself that he would just stand there and listen, saying nothing, arguing about nothing.

Simon Magus rose, speaking dramatically with his hands and head, deeply enjoying his own lecture. Although Merlin had been lured away from the most important military conflict of the age by a grave beseechment about the end of the world, his *teacher* rather started, to the dying man's chagrin, at its beginning. Before its beginning.

Magus spoke of God's eternal purpose for the Ages. Again, he bluntly proclaimed his unwavering loyalty to his god, the angel Arddu, and his plan and program for thwarting the Creator. However, he had so mastered the truth, and was so articulate in explaining it, that any hearer would become captivated and bewitched, slipping into moments of confusion, thinking the man was Moses or the Apostle Paul, and not the Devil's most important human agent.

In the most unadorned declaration, he stated that God's eternal purpose was to glorify His son Jesus Christ, the possessor of heaven and earth. It was noteworthy that there were no hisses or protests at the mention of Christ, or of God's eternal purpose concerning Him. Nor were there jeers or curses when Magus confirmed plainly that Jesus was Himself God; distinct in personhood, but equal to and one with God the father (Merlin had no need for explanation of this, for the Druids had well understood the triune name of the Hebrew God for generations).

The protest, the vitriolic fang-baring, claw-scraping hatred came when the Leader began to teach on how man, originally created in the triune image of the Creator, had been chosen to be God's agency to rule and reign over these spheres. Yes, Satan had wanted to be like the Most High, but that was in his connection to be promoted over man, not serving him. Yes, he had coveted a throne above the Lord's, but this only at hearing that he would bow down to Adam. Satan was man's adversary, not God's. As if God could have a rival. That man was the heir of salvation, that man would inherit everything good and wonderful in creation, that man was in a special relationship with the Sovereign ignited Arddu's rage, causing iniquity to form within him.

When Adam was about one hundred and thirty years, the great cherub could no longer contain and rebelled. Since that very day Arddu had ever sought to dispossess man from his place as agency for Christ, from his dominion. If man was disqualified, ineffective and lost then God's purpose would be thwarted and God, a relational being by nature, would have no choice but to turn to the angelic hosts to replace those roles.

God had greatly duped Arddu by concealing a great secret for four thousand years. It was ever known that Christ would rule earth through men. God would outmaneuver His enemy's aims on Adam, and then (after Arddu did his greatest work on the other side of the Flood), Noah, the Patriarchs and ultimately Israel, with whom He made His covenants concerning the Land. That Israel would inherit the kingdom was no secret (though Satan believed thoroughly he would still win in the end), but no mention was made of the other half of the Cosmos – heaven.

Though expelled from the upper heavens and though engaged in perpetual war with God's faithful angels, heaven belonged to the hosts. The luminaries declared God's message night over night, the Moon gave her glory over the night as the Sun his during the day. Heavenly thrones, powers and principalities held control over the governance of heaven. Satan had access to the Heavenly Father, even after the Fall. Satan was the prince of the power of the air, even after the Fall. Satan's legions controlled the nations through influencing corrupt men from their territorial domains which remained unchanged, even after the Fall.

In the heavenlies, the war was as it had been from the foundation of the world. Angel versus angel. Man, that worm and ape, toiled on the earth and Satan had many, many strategies for foiling man down there.

Again, as Simon Magus told the story of the generations of men (and angels) he would oscillate in tone and pitch and emotion and at times it seemed that he sincerely championed God's cause. At other times there seemed to be pity for the Devil. *Because truth engenders passion, those who have rejected it can still be convicted and tormented by its fire*; this was Merlin's only conclusion as he listed to the Sermon unfold. Simon had sold himself to the Devil but could preach and teach the truth.

And because of the little book and *how* the simplicity of Christ and what He was doing in the dispensation of grace was shared with Merlin, he knew the next part of the glorious story and eagerly wanted to join in telling it.

Simon continued. When studying the Scriptures, he shared, the theme was the same from beginning to end:

From Adam to Noah is about dominion over the earth.

From Noah to Abraham is about dominion over the earth.

From Abraham to Moses is about dominion over the earth.

From Moses to David is about dominion over the earth.

All the Prophets are about dominion over the earth.

All of these, he explained, spoke of a coming King, a Wonderful Counselor, a Mighty God. And surely this King was from heaven but the theme of the Scriptures was the earth.

Merlin fully agreed. Merlin could have given this presentation and, thus far, beyond the pure demonic hubris of intentional aims against truth, was learning nothing new. The old Wizard now wondered if Simon Magus may have been educating his brothers, countering the Merlin's testimony, which already had covered these grounds. *No, he is leading me somewhere with this; keep listening*, Merlin concluded.

Then Simon Magus transitioned to the four gospels. For in these four books and their correlative Hebrew Epistles do both Rome and the Britons draw their doctrine and enslave men. The great themes of the gospels are the deity, humanity, kingship and servant aspects of offices of the Lord Jesus Christ. However, the theme never changes where God's purposes are concerned. They still deal exclusively with Israel, from whom the kingdom is taken and given to Peter and the Eleven, who then take the name of the Little Flock or the Israel of God. To them is given a special inheritance, a great city that comes down from heaven. From this city, the twelve will reign over the twelve tribes of Israel, who will in turn reign over the Gentile kings and by extension *the earth. Still the focus on earthly.*

"All the teachings about cutting out one's eye, or selling all possessions, or being water-baptized as ceremonial washing for priesthood functions. All the rules and regulations were given to the Jew. Yet your priest and bishops appropriate them and Jesus wouldn't have even spoken to a Gentile in His earthly ministry!" Simon was disgusted at the ignorance of the professing Church.

And on this point, Merlin agreed with the Devil worshipper.

The Brotherhood's masked master concluded the summary with doctrinal precision and accuracy.

"The earth. The earth. All the way through the 'Book' 'tis about the earth." He then looked up through the pyramidal glass ceiling. The wintry night in Brittany was still of the darkest pitch. And then, the thick overcast parted and a few stars emerged, then a few more, then the clouds at once dissolved and hosts and hosts of luminaries could be seen, orbiting around the still earth. "What about them?" he asked, still stargazing. "What about heaven?" And now his look fell back upon the dying Wizard. "The Creator reveals His twofold purpose, of possessing earth and *HEAVEN*, right from the first Book of Moses, but then fades to overwhelming silence on the one half of the cosmos. Why?"

Merlin, newly immersed in rightly dividing the word and understanding God's diverse programs and strategies, was full of the hunger and zeal of a newborn and could not contain himself. He had the answer, and *made* the answer.

"God did not want the Devil to know that it was always His intent to fill the heavens, demoting the angels and having Men be his agency there as well. Thus, he kept the battle focused on earth until the fullness of time, when the Lord Jesus did something unique on that Cross, allowing for the making of a New Creature; men who would fill up a Body in heaven and displace Satan there too, making his demise and defeat complete."

Here at death's door, Merlin, the most legendary of all save King Arthur Pendragon himself, the legend amongst legends, he who had fulfilled quests, conquered foes, explained dragons to architects, mapped the heavens, performed signs and wonders, seen things with Vivien that were unlawful to utter and, above all, raised, mentored and advised the Once and Future King of the Britons, had saved his best words for his final breaths.

His conclusion was equally astute. "Because God's heavenly program was a secret, there is very little information, as the Devil knows the Scripture better than slovenly and lazy man, who does not study. For this cause, we only know that entrance into the heavenly body is wholly based upon grace and that heaven will be filled with low-down Gentile dogs like us, with no preference for Israel, or rich, or poor, or man or woman. God picked the murderer Saul, the chief of the rebellion against God, and saved him for this heavenly calling. No religion, no works, all focused on the Cross!"

"Yes, we have heard this before ten times

tonight!" one of the Nine rebuked Merlin. At the hearing of the name 'Paul', the disposition of the room became an anger, thick and foul.

"So, you know God's Mystery. Are you ready for ours?" Simon was smiling, little drops of perspiration forming where mask met skin.

"Yes." The dying man's insistence and confidence was waxing whilst his life essence waned. "What does all of this theological diatribe have to do with *my* king?"

"There are nine of us on this council." Simon's hand made a sweeping, circular motion, passing by each Brother seated. "Why nine?"

Merlin, an adept at the meaning of sacred geometry and the mystical association of numbers, answered immediately. "'Tis the number of wisdom and initiation."

"Very good!" The Italian accent was thick when Simon was excited or happy with Merlin's answer. "However, there is more. We are, in reality, two groups of four, with me as a sort of mediator or facilitator." An arrogant smile pushed the mask up nearly to his nose. He enjoyed being the leader of the world's most dangerous cult. "And the number four, Merlin?"

"It speaks to completing a path or to being comprehensive," he responded.

"So wise, Druid!"

"*Former* Druid." The agitation towards Merlin had not abated since the mention of Paul and the Cross and grace.

Simon resumed teaching.

Merlin's numerological deduction was precise. Simon began to explain that the Council was divided into two factions with paradoxically contradictory objectives. He called them *Immanentizers and Delayers.*

Finally, he began to speak of the end of all things, and how the Nine might fulfill their purpose: how they might immanentize it.

First he provided instruction about how Christian leaders must never read Paul and be thoroughly confused about the End of Days. Using as a pattern that contemporary eschatological doctrine espoused by Augustine of Hippo and earlier *Church Fathers*, they used their influence to ensure that the influential believed that the Resurrection would be preceded by a Golden Age lasting, figuratively, a thousand years – really, an unknown amount of time. Some Christian sects would be instructed to teach that only in this reign of the saints Christ would return; still others held that Christ would return in the heart of the believer and no more. The orthodoxy of the day rendered prophecy fulfilled in AD 70 and the Church as the New Israel.

On the basis on these teachings, the Council of Nine labored to build an anti-Golden Age. Looking like the real millennial reign, and duping souls until the prophesied One would yield up to Lucifer and his consort all things that he might be all in all at the end of the aeon. Where this translated into politics, the Immanentizers ever sought to build a world government by goading nation states into conflict. Through loans and debt-slavery they would create a drunken and power mad leadership with one hand and deceive the world into thinking they were living in the Millennium with the other.

After a world leader would rise, convinced that

he was the long-promised Messiah, the Church would be discarded as a harlot is beaten and thrown to the streets when her use is completed. The holy land and Israel would be restored and the world leader would run the world from that coveted city on seven hills.

The Immanentizers, every day and night, labored only to bring about world government, to foment war and peace, and to create every criterium requisite for the Apocalypse.

"And yet…" Simon noted Merlin was in shock at what he had once been a part of, once very nearly joined. "Why would we want the End of Days?"

"You already told me; because you believe Satan will win. That the whole of the Book is true save the end," Merlin answered.

"The Book says that when such things come to pass our Master will be filled with great wrath," and now in a whisper, "knowing that his time is short."

"You know he will lose, hence the whisper!"

Simon Magus struck the tall Briton square upon the nose, splattering famous blood everywhere.

In an instant, the greatest Wizard and advisor to ever live was joined by the greatest warrior. Lancelot appeared, watching all somehow (but hearing none due to his vantage outside the great folds of the tabernacle). Of equal surprise, thirty heavily armored guardians appeared in an instant.

Sopping blood with the sleeve of his grey cloak, the Merlin followed a frequent custom: using jest instead of panic. "Sorry, Lancelot. I undercounted."

"Yes, you said nine!"

Merlin believed the Round Table Companion's return volley also full of humor. The guards chased Lancelot out of the Tabernacle into Broceliande's haunted and enchanted night.

Physically, Merlin could slay the Italian with no effort. Merlin was not some passive advisor; he was a Cymry warrior in his own right and many had fallen to his blade and staff. However, if Merlin was to die of poison, he would know of the plans for Arthur first. And, through whatever means necessary, keep his heart beating long enough to warn his beloved friend. And so he stopped the blood, pressing thumbs hard into nostrils, and sat down, calmly.

"Because the Lord Arddu is not here I will tell you that, though you blaspheme, you may be right. We believe he will win but our preference is not to immanentize." Simon now looked upon the four who served the obverse purpose. "Our preference is to delay."

The lesson continued.

As both Merlin and Magus had shared in their exchange, God was filling up a heavenly body with (primarily) Gentile believers to reign in the heavenly places. This meant that the Powers, Principalities, Thrones and Dominions currently running heaven (the Fallen Ones) would be expelled, dispossessed, and replaced with New Creatures from amongst the saved of the sons of Adam. This reconciliation of heaven could not be achieved until the Body of Christ was full. Thus, the plan was to keep men lost and blind. At first it had been thought that this would only last a few years, but the Church had fallen asleep after

Paul. "Let them sleep while we feast on their immaturity!" Simon cried.

Working in concert with the Immanentizers, Magus explained: "Our Dark Lord wants man dedicated to kingdom building. A kingdom without a king. He has already defeated Christendom in the same way he has since the Mystery was gradually revealed – with works-based institutionalism."

Although always having to deal with a small group of the faithful, an endless kingdom where the Adversary was god of this world and prince of the power of the air would suit both he and the Nine well. Driven by a never-ending lust and covetousness for more, Satan would one day be compelled to battle for complete control; but he relished the great measure of control he already possessed.

Compelled by the dual command to convince man to 'put off' salvation whilst always having an Antichrist candidate ready was life's mandate for the Secret Societies.

"The second Secret Doctrine of the Ages is that you are both working to bring about the end of the world *AND* prevent it?"

"Aye," laughed Magus.

And then the part that was not humorous ensued.

"We have two candidates for the Antichrist, should your Lord tarry. Childibert, son of Clovis, who ever fights with your friends Howel and Budic, is one candidate. He is of the Merovingian line and his lineage runs all the way back to the brother of the Lord. The one who looked just like Jesus. The one who had lain with Mary the

Magdalene. He will be passed off as a child of the Christ; the people will devour the lie! And," Simon again performed his unnaturally long pause, inhaling through his nose and exhaling dramatically, "your King Arthur Pendragon is our other candidate for Antichrist."

Simon let the plan settle. "Born on the Mass of the Christ, under the Sign of the Dragon, named after the Bear. Don't just read Paul, dear Merlin, read John the Revelator. Arthur *is* Antichrist! The world already loves him."

"The Merovingian or the Pendragon. Why else would we visit this damnable freezing forest in January?" one of the Nine grumbled.

"Arthur will never follow you. Never. Never!" The Merlin seethed with energy meet for defending his king, his friend.

"He doesn't have to," said Simon, sighing at the Merlin's ignorance of the matter. "If he has some secret sins, we will extort them. If he has loved ones, we will threaten him."

"He had sons, and we turned them against the famous king without complication," contributed another.

"Moreover." And now Simon revealed highly guarded secrets, "all he must do is suffer a grievous head wound, then will we be able to insert the spirit of Judas Iscariot, who is in his place in the Underworld awaiting that day, into him. You know we are in league with entities that can do this."

"The Dynion Hysbys." Merlin's face was as a ghost.

"Aye." Simon was gleeful at this point. "When your king was a boy I personally selected his first mate. Let us describe it thusly: we found one who opened a channel in Arthur for us to work with."

Neither Merlin nor Simon Magus, there representing God and the Devil, knew that it was Arthur's very own sister selected for him at the rites. Merlin, however, again felt the unknown pains of deep regret about those events, nearly two decades ago. That the Dynion Hysbys had aided this collected assembly of the world's most influential villains whilst Vivien and Merlin were busy preparing Excalibur to gift to the young prince vexed him thrice over the poison in his veins.

"And if he will not be your King of Kings, what then?" asked Merlin.

"As we said, we have the son of Merovech. But we prefer Arthur. He will join us, or we will wipe his lineage from every history book and every poem. He will be a myth. A children's nighttime story until, at some later time, should we delay and not immanentize, we will resurrect him for some future generation."

Merlin found himself looking at the author of the Saxon Wars, the puppet-masters of generations of distress, destruction and devastation upon enchanted Cymru. These men had worked out not only a well-constructed plan but a secondary plan, a tertiary plan and a fourth and fifth plan besides. Despair was swallowing Merlin; he was drowning, and his hope in peril.

However, he still managed a "You will fail–"

Before the sentence finished, Simon interrupted. "There is still the third sphere to cover, Merlin. You came here for the Secret Teaching of the Ages. Your despair for your friend is boiling on the kettle of the despair for your own soul; we've not even poured into the pot. It is time for you to know *what* you are, Merlin."

CHAPTER 23
The Lady of the Lake's Fateful Alliance

The Lady of Llyn Fawr galloped through the mists, weeping.

Dignity. Majesty. Self-control. These were the attributes to which she anchored a life of service to her deities, to her people. Spanning from Albion in the North, Lloegyr in the East, her cousins from the great kingdoms in the West Country to those who lived in the horn of Britain in the South and, of course, her own kinsmen in Less Britain, Vivien loved her people.

For them, the preservation of their customs and ways, for their heritage and the very survival of her great goddess, she had authorized a diabolical plot. Her anchors now jerked violently from the seabed of conscience.

Dignity in murder?

Majesty in seduction?

Self-control in enraged political posturing?

That which serves the people is moral. Murdering served the people; therefore, murder is moral.

The dangerous and faulty sophistry of her thoughts was swept quickly away along with the tears, streaming along the windblown slopes of her perfect face. Returning her hand to the harness she galloped, harder now.

The shoreline wound round a beach from which Britain could be seen. She turned south and rode hard into Broceliande, stopping at a great freshwater pool, seemingly placed by the gods themselves for private reflection, intimacy or mourning.

Would she make it in time to stop Nimue?

Fae of an outwardly benevolent but somber disposition scurried throughout the trees, gazing upon the solitary Lady. Tiny beings whose stars covered their little bodies, they were as fireflies gazed upon round a fire. They loved the Lady for her kindness and they swarmed near, concerned greatly for her overwhelming distress.

She was Lancelot's mother in every way save blood. A pillar of invincibility. Powerful beyond measure, yet feminine and soft. Vivien, the Lady of Lake, the most beautiful of all the Britons. It was a comeliness from within and external. Clad in her elegant garb, the flowing white dress, pillowed sleeves and hooded cloak, she was invisible against the snow save the golden glisten of her legendary hair. But the Fae were able to see her. Eyes elliptical and emerald, skin transparent, Vivien was the vicar of the goddess on Earth.

"To defeat the enemy from without." Soggy twigs and snowy brush shifted audibly beneath as she approached the Lady of the Lake, still atop her mount, "we must first defeat the enemy from within."

Vivien gathered herself in an instant. "And who is the enemy from within?"

"My Lady. We heard what was said at Caerleon ere the battle of Mount Baeden." There was no mercy in the words from Nimue, who had clearly completed her mission. The little faeries recoiled, scattering at her appearance. "The Druid turned Christian who would betray our sacred knowledge, even the Mystery!" Escalating, her voice was venomous, metallic. "Because of your bravery and decisive action, we will never bow down to the Bishop of Rome and our mysteries will never be shared or defiled. Never!

"And what's more," she continued, "his recent conversation constitutes a dereliction of office. Not only was he distracted so close to receiving his final initiation, he had become – dangerous. I, like you, loved Merlin, but he has," she searched for the word, "changed."

Vivien considered her response. For the first time since living the legend, a legend that for her had begun with giving Merlin the Sword, she saw something hitherto undetected in the young enchantress. Hate. Nimue now, perhaps had always, shared the same flaw as her enemy. Similarity breeds contempt.

Vivien could not punish or rebuke Nimue for carrying out the very direction given to her by the Lady herself. But the joy with which she had performed the dark task gave Vivien great pause.

After Merlin had brought to ruin the hierarchical Sects of Christ with his words at Caerleon, Vivien had felt betrayed. Merlin had spoken of a Mystery and of an end of all the devices of man-made religion. In her hurt she had become selfish. With Merlin's fame and popularity, his turning to the Christ would result in the same for what remained of the small numbers of Druids left on the Isles. The common man would trust Merlin where they distrusted and despised the priests and bishops, and the whole of the Island, save the nasty Dynion Hysbys, would turn to Christ. Merlin, when passionate about any matter, was the Great Strategist, the Great Orator, the Great Evangelist.

The night he had said these things, in her hurt she had mourned and pondered in her chambers… and then the knock on the door.

An unwelcome guest.

On her worst day Vivien had tenfold the wit and one hundredfold the wisdom of Mad Meirchion. But that night had not been her worst day. It had been worse than her worst day. Merlin's salvation was Vivien's death. Death of relevance, death of influence, and perhaps death of liberty. On this day and this day alone, the Majestic Lady had allowed herself to be duped.

Meirchion had pointed out that the Church of Rome was much kinder towards the indigenous faiths of her vassal kingdoms. The shrines of Ephesus, the pagan faiths of North Africa and even the tolerance of Mithraism near to the Holy See in Rome were used as examples.

By contrast, the Cymry bishops were antagonist towards other paths, often deliberating on diverse ways to separate the Lady's head from her shoulders. They planned a kingdom of priests and kings where the entire nobility would rule using Christian precepts with an iron fist. Catholicism, by contrast, was open to plurality and freedom under the wing and protection of Mother Rome.

Moreover, there was a great gulf of animosity between the Druids and the Church of the Britons. It did not manifest often and many Bards were Christian. Surface level handshakes and embraces abounded at festivals and meals but, amongst the higher ranks and at sundry times, a great anger existed over some wrong perceived to have been done unto the Christian sect. Knowing this secret was part of Vivien's rearing in her own mysteries. Yet, in the process of time, of fighting the Saxon Wars, of exhausting endeavors to temper northern versus southern conflicts, she had forgotten all about the origin of their old hurts. *Had she remembered, Merlin might not be lying dead or dying presently.*

Merlin was becoming one of them, though different, and they hated her. Moreover, when Merlin shared that he would openly tell Arthur of the 'mystery', Vivien the Wise became a Fool: committing the sin of assumption.

However, even in her compromised condition that fateful night, she still clung to what all Britons cleaved unto; the threat of Rome upon Cymru's national sovereignty. Historically, the Romans and Silures fought to a draw many times and Cymru was ever a rival and equal of Rome, never bowing a knee; even whilst they paraded the great Caradoc captive around her capital, the Sword of Caesar plucked right from his very hands was on display in Lloegyr.

Meirchion, freshly come from a privy council with the bishops, had openly called for Merlin's head and was desperate for an ally in hopes of retaining his own. Thus, to quell the concerns of the Lady, he used the very name of the king he loathed to comfort her. Indicating that neither King Arthur nor the Round Table Companions would ever yield the sovereignty of a nation to a foreign king or potentate after fighting for so many years to win and protect it, he offered Vivien the illusion of a perfect picture of her future. The future of her kind. Her help in assassinating the Merlin in exchange for an alliance against the bishops, and a vow that her goddess and the old gods would be protected as the country continued its transition to the Christian Religion.

And so. Here she was. The plot activated.

Nimue had a few days' lead time on Vivien. Her repentance had been too slow. Her arrival to arrest the scheme too late. Her coming to her senses delinquent.

Meirchion officially had the Lady in a vice. If she honored the deal, what surety was there of Rome's help for her people, and at what cost? If she confessed to the Round Table that she was in league with him, even if pleading that she had taken leave of her senses due to grief, she would die the *Triple Death* reserved for traitors (a complete or threefold death required for complete justice of the condemned). Her only escape, her only recourse, was to ensure that Merlin *did not die*.

If he yet lived then there was no murder to confess, no collusion with the Swine Priest. Merlin *must live*.

"Nimue, we have violated the very thing that our High King champions. That men serve what gods they will, only that they don't kill their neighbors for it."

"He was a traitor. He was to reveal our mysteries."

"A mystery," Vivien interrupted. "There are many mysteries. I agree that Merlin has turned from our goddess, but we are wrong here."

"You have become weak and sentimental, Lady." Hate had fully consumed the young priestess.

Vivien looked to the snowy forest and a swarm of the celestial little beings at once enveloped Nimue, poking, pinching and stabbing her, causing her to flail arms in the air and run blindly. There were so many of them that she was as a torch, an aimless whirling torch.

The Lady of the Lake uttered ancient words to a nearby stream. The waters immediately organized themselves into a well. The faeries manipulated the panicking Nimue's course, causing her to stumble and fall, head first, down into the infant well, born for her death.

"The goddess will not receive one so full of hate and murder as you. She demands works. May Merlin's new God accept you by the grace Merlin is now so fond of." Vivien spoke again her ancient incantations; the well at once become a fount, and Nimue's tomb.

Vivien hastened into vast Broceliande, hoping to find and save the friend whom she had betrayed.

CHAPTER 24
A Good Secret to Replace a Bad Secret

While the merriment of free Cymru continued, the Pendragon labored to find his old mentor and friend. He honored the bishops and priest Meirchion by allowing them to convene amongst the wild horses and majesty of Lodge Hill.

Cai joined them.

"We are now ten days since seeing Merlin. Ten days! Maelgwn and Gwalchmai will return soon from Brittany and then we are all traveling to New Troy. When standing upon the platform under banners and trumpets, MY Wizard had better be standing next to me." The Bear of Glamorgan's patience over the matter was officially spent.

The clergy, all grown soft and given to pampering, stamped their feet under massive coats, attempting to stay warm; the Usk river's frigid waters, paired with gusting winds, created a freeze that climbed all the way up the hill.

"Oh, Cai, please help me build these delicate souls a fire." Arthur was never too proud to aid in that which he requested of others, always showing hospitality (even when full of anger and dismay). As the king knelt to gather sticks, he noticed that one was missing amongst the shivering bishops.

"Where is Cadfan?" he asked, disappointed at their failure to meet his expectation that *all* present at the privy council meet him.

Arthur stood ere they answered, dropping the sticks.

"One who should be here is not and one not expected here is," he said.

Gwyar presented herself, emerging from one of the mid-level ridge trails in the fort; clearly on a morning walk. Mutually startled, they both laughed.

"The children of Meurig love this hill!" they cried in unison.

She was clearly upset over being displaced from Ynys Enlli and he was on the brink of unraveling at not knowing what had become of his friend. When not at war, Arthur loved the solace of the fort. When visiting family, or trading in Caerleon, Gwyar would leave the markets and come to this very spot. No matter what perils, quests, marriages or adventures separated them by distance or years, *Caerleon was still their home and this was their hill.*

"Are we so predictable, sister?" Arthur and she laughed again. They shared a light moment.

Illtud was intrigued by Gwyar, the rest feared her and Aiden, whose intolerance was burgeoning, loathed her.

"One witch is absent from Court," (he spoke of Vivien, reportedly caring for Maelgwn and yet in Brittany) "and another appears. You know what the Writ says about their kind, my Lord?"

"*Suffer not a witch to live*," Gwyar responded for her brother. She twisted hard upon her forearm and spoke an imprecation. Where she twisted and torqued corresponded to the spiraling crackle of bones seen and heard at the very same location upon Aiden's forearm. The pious preacher crumped in agony, crying curses at the king's sister, before shock caused him to pale and swoon. "Should any of you desire to enforce that part of your Book, here I am."

Frightened and powerless, they all spoke of Jesus's love under the new covenant; tolerance was restored.

Arthur clasped his face with both hands and exhaled, frustrated. "Cai, take the bishop down the hill. Sister, control your gifts. And *someone* tell me where Cadfan is immediately!"

Gwyar, moderately embarrassed, lowered her eyes, but her smile she retained. A smile soon to vanish, visage to become cold as the Usk's winds.

Meirchion stated, "Cadfan is in the North. He is blessing the foundation and flooring for a new chapel there."

"We were aware of no such chapel scheduled for erection," Dyfrig said, puzzled, Illtud's comments matching those of the more senior bishop.

"It's a little endeavor; 'tis nothing." The scheming Meirchion was enjoying the enigmatic discord. "It was fully authorized by Einion, the chieftain of Llyn, the son of Owain Ddantgwyn, an upright man who reveres the Bishop of Rome."

The Llyn Peninsula formed the northwest 'arm' of Cymru. And beyond the fingertip of the peninsula lay the Isle of Apples, the abode of treasures and secrets and Gwyar's orchards contained in the castle made of glass.

"Where in the cantref is the church to be built?" A pit of betrayal was sinking within Arthur's sister.

"The Bishop of Rome says Enlli is a Holy Place, visited by many renowned Saints and champions of the faith. Cadfan will be inserted Bishop of Ynys Enlli."

If words could be sharper than Excalibur, these were. Inside of a fortnight drawn away from her Isle, shackled at Court per the dictate of a mad and broken queen, the Church had pierced its talons into the heart of Gwyar's world, changing it forever.

The princess could not act upon her desires to kill Meirchion. In so doing, her husband Llew and Einion ap Owain would surely put her to death and the Silure bishops would be gleeful to see them do it. Traversing from powerful sorceress to begging relative, her voice became as a whimpering puppy as she appealed to Arthur.

"I cannot interfere with this, sister. I'm sorry. Llyn is in Gwynedd and the local chieftain makes such designations for places of worship. It is not my place and would be an abuse of my power. The Summer Kingdom must not suffer corruption so soon after it has been born. Yes?"

Gwyar felt helpless and drew Arthur away from the gathered bishops, yet complaining and railing about the cold. Walking a short distance into the wood, with the fortress just overhead, the two spoke. For the first time in many years, really spoke.

"Bear." An affectionate opening. "You remember what is on the Isle of Apples, the secret I told you. The good secret we shared to replace the bad secret we conceal?"

"Of course." Arthur embraced Gwyar as if he were his namesake, a great bear. "I have been fond of Mary since I was fifteen because you shared this secret with me. Look," Arthur reached into his satchel, producing one of his favorite shoulder fitted sigils, "she was with us at Baeden."

Gwyar smiled.

The Druids and primitive Christians had once been great friends. From the very beginning, however, the Jewish Little Flock of Peter gave themselves over to idolatry. They boasted of their position and inheritance and, when the world did not end, began to assert their claims by venerating relics associated with their firsthand time spent with the Lord. And they began to worship and elevate people too.

After the Apostle Paul's visit, the Druids came to the aid of the mother of Jesus (who had seen the corruption) and hid her, and the ark, and the cup. As the Jewish assembly died off, their doctrines and ways survived in the form of the Apostolic Church of the Britons. Try as they might, they could not discover the relics or the tomb of Mary, and they hated the Druids for it. This conflict became a whisper with a fissure, a rarely discussed point of contention that floated like lake moss, ever just beneath the surface.

"They must never find Mary, Arthur. They will desecrate the grave, raise a shrine and make her a goddess, thus blaspheming everything the Blessed Lady stood for. She only ever wanted to live out her life with her foster-son, John."

There upon Lodge Hill, two famed heroes shared why the pagans and Druids and heathen sects hated the Church. It was because that institution, in all its forms, was an insult to Jesus and those who really loved him. Gwyar did not hate the Christ; one of her many sacred and secret obligations was to forever hide the tomb of his mother. She hated the men who were *fake* Christians.

"Even if they put a chapel on the Island, I trust that your magick will conceal the Lady and keep our good secret intact. Leave Gwent and return to the place you love." Arthur was an exceptional brother.

"I cannot," Gwyar wept. "I am bound here to support you behind the throne."

"Bound by?"

"Your queen."

"But why?"

"She thinks she knows that you love me."

"Well, I am glad you are here. Just no more arm breaking whilst you stay." Arthur tried to solicit a smile from his distraught sister. Then he offered some help whilst adhering to his own laws. "I cannot stop a local chieftain from building a church. But I can intervene if any of our national treasures are in peril. I will need cause. Then the Round Table Fellowship will respond."

"That form of justice is reactive, and will be too late. They must not intrude upon the Isle of Apples!" Gwyar was not angered with Arthur. She gave him another tight, tight embrace and ran from the scene. She paused and turned back to the King.

"Do not marry the other Gwenhwyfar! And please stop ever putting Gwalchmai in danger!"

These were the types of requests said with a smile that overlay a warning, even a threat.

Gwyar vanished.

Arthur resumed his interrogation of the remaining bishops. They were most offended that Merlin had declared that one did not have to give land to the church; neither was baptism required, for the soul's salvation. His words were dangerous in their ability to control the nobility through land grants and the purchasing of heaven. The Pendragon cared not to delve into the merits of the theology from either faction, or from the secondhand account of Merlin's words. Rather, he wanted facts.

Shattering the tradition of the secret conferences amongst bishops and elders, the truth surfaced that the Britons favored asking Merlin to retire and that Meirchion had threatened his life.

Meirchion immediately provided an alibi for his comings and goings, before and after the great conference before Baeden, and made it clear that he had been arguing religion with Vivien late into the night and had no window of opportunity for a plot.

That Vivien knew he had spoken only in the anger of the moment and could testify of this satisfied Arthur to an extent. "I will have to validate this with the Lady of Llyn Fawr," he proclaimed.

"Upon her return, of course," responded Meirchion with feigned respect.

"Still, you threatened the life of one of three Chief Counselors to the Pendragon. There will be consequences for this." Arthur chose irony. Fed up with talks of gifts of land and tithes and gold for clergy, he decreed the following. "You are expelled from Glamorgan, forever. Your lands will be gifted in penance to your rival Illtud and, as he sees fit to appropriate, to the See of Llandaff." Arthur loved Illtud and Dyfrig but was fatigued over their constant wrangling for possession and material comforts, or gold. Here he chastised them as well. "That should be enough spoil and expansion to satisfy your greedy guts for a while, yes?"

Meirchion left Lodge Hill without lands or a home. Arthur left Lodge Hill still without his Merlin.

Gwyar purchased the fastest steed in Caerleon, plus the employ of a servant. She clung on to the servant and slept as he rode without resting, making their way to the highest point in Glamorgan: Craig Y Llyn. When exhaustion took him she flung him from the mount and took the reigns, then climbed on foot to the zenith. Peaking higher than even Caer Caradoc (where the nobles had been slain at the hand of the Long Knives so many years ago), she felt as if she looked down upon all the kingdoms of the world.

Below Craig Y Llyn was Llyn Y Fawr, where Vivien resided when not in Brittany.

Gwyar had not come for the scenic appeal. She had come for the power of the high mount and the lake. The moon cast her light upon Gwyar, whose arms were extended slowly and then clasped above her head. Calling upon elemental spirits from an older Age she commanded them, along with the spirits of the waters of the lake. At the same time, she called unto the dragon who ruled the high Mount.

The holy mountain and the lake. The mountain was heaven and the lake the primal earth covered in water. The mountain was Ynys Enlli and the lake was the ocean surrounding its shores. Gwyar was transformed into the great goddess of destruction, ready to deliver death from above.

"Morgana!" Once, at a whisper.

"Morgana!" Once more, louder.

When she finished the summonsing, the thing that the King of the Fae had put in her, nay, made part of her, took form in the sister of Arthur as never before, causing thunderbolts and visible glowing red illumination to outline her tiny form.

The next morning two supply ships and her passengers made a watery grave of the short channel between the tip of Llyn and Ynys Enlli. The dolphins swam against the current, seals protested loudly and birds were everywhere out of season. The whole of the Island was covered in mist and an unnatural force surrounded the place.

Intruding upon the place that the Bards called Avalon would not come without much peril to Cadfan and his Catholic pilgrims.

CHAPTER 25
I Will Go All the Way to The Bishop of Rome With My Mystery

Although the thirty guards were chasing Maelgwn, he was, in reality, in total control and may as well have been chasing them. When finding the clearing he desired, the Bloodhound Prince engaged.

The battle spike quickly felled two who rushed foolishly head-on at the knees, and a third who attempted a cowardly rear attack position. Maelgwn was said to be able to see in all directions at once. He was a poetic killing instrument, moving with great haste for concern over the old Wizard whom the masked man had smitten upon the face.

As he would run one guard through the chest, two or three would attempt to tackle the Cymry warrior. Thus, he had to remove the battle spike quickly, avoiding any scenario where two men could bring him to the ground and, because of numbers, smother and slay him. Rather, he would kill and then run a short space, kill and run some more.

By twos and threes, and no more, he created killing spaces in which to engage them. Soon fear found fertile ground and the remaining guards fled. Maelgwn had ended above twenty men in half an hour. But, he felt, one moment was too long.

He raced back for the tabernacle.

"I know you are going to try and make a monster of my beloved king; what needs have I to hear more of your lies?" Merlin surveyed for more guards, looking for a window of escape. Of hope.

"Most appropriate that you choose the word monster." The Italian accent relished the unwanted invitation to share more. "And you know the information I have given you is truth. We use it for deception, for the Lord Arddu, but no lies have been told this night, Merlin, save for the one you have shared about your salvation."

Seeing no escape and knowing his travel companion would soon return, soaked in victorious blood and ready for more, Merlin had little choice but to indulge him. "The third sphere of the Secret Teaching of the Ages it is then." A dramatic exhale pushed out as the Wizard sat.

Simon Magus went to it directly, giving his third sermon. This time the subject was an exposé on the reality of otherworldly beings. Merlin had admitted that he did not know where the gods came from save from 'the true North' or from the sky and Simon confirmed this, stating that it was presumptuous to think that many of the gods even knew of their own origins.

As with his instruction regarding the salvation of men's souls and the end of all things, he asserted the truth of God's word. Then he told the tale of Azazel and two hundred angels that had been charged with teaching, enlightening and watching over men.

This they did, but soon became corrupt and entered into a pact to go down amongst the daughters of men and take them for wives. The incursion began in the generation of Jared about four generations before the days of Noah. The first prophecy in Scripture, he explained, said that the seed of the woman would bruise the head of the Serpent. For this cause, the Jews reckoned their genealogies through maternal lines, but the blood came from the Father. Thus, the Devil launched a plot to fully pollute the seed of the woman, defiling all flesh, leaving nothing but corruption and abomination upon the face of earth.

With all of mankind corrupted, there would be no possibility of a Savior to come through the seed of the woman, and nothing left to save.

"Beyond this, the Watchers simply lusted after the daughters of Adam. They looked upon them, filled with lust and envy, and had to have them." Magus here emphasized that often the Dark Lord used everyday motives like lust to slowly guide his larger agenda, often keeping it from his very inner circle.

Magus taught Merlin how the sons of God had entered into the daughters of Men, resulting in demigods, Giants and other monstrosities. The act of procreation furthered the Watchers' desires to be like the Creator, so they brought forth all manner of abominable hybrids. Where the Lord

God made a horse, they added wings to the horse. Where the Lord God made a leopard, they added bear claws to the leopard.

What Merlin was hearing was the explanation for every ancient religion from Babylon to Egypt and from Germania to Africa. The ancients were worshipping these angels, or gods, and their progeny.

But there was more. Many of these angels had repented, but God had spared them not. The first few generations of these fallen ones were good, save their desire for worship. As their blood mixed with sinful man, the creatures became monstrously corrupt. Often demigods would kill the more foul or bloodthirsty beasts, becoming the heroes of legends of old.

When the corruption reached its climax, God's long suffering had come to an end; He flooded the whole world. In creative cruelty, He made the Watchers observe their offspring's destruction first hand. Azazel was made the Scapegoat and fastened to the luminary hunter, Orion. The others were bound in the Underworld until the end of days.

As these Giants and monsters perished, their animating principles became known as *evil spirits*. Most were tossed into the Deep that surrounds the world (which was why all demons hated water, save the elemental water spirits who were commissioned to help manage the currents and sciences of water), but the Creator left one tenth of these to roam the earth.

"Why?" Merlin inquired.

"The Seed of the Woman had to come, or God's plans for restoring heaven and earth through the worm that is man could never be. So much did He love His son, and so much glory did He desire for Him, that He left these unclean spirits and let them manifest powerfully when He was come into the world: as a sign of His coming so that He could defeat and make a showing of them.

"They," Simon continued, "of course gathered round Israel, concentrating their power on foiling and disrupting the Covenant People and the Promised Land." Now Magus returned to an earlier discussion about polytheism. "So, yes, Merlin. Zeus, Poseidon, all your pantheon of gods and Fae have their origin on the other side of the Flood."

"If God destroyed them all, then besides these ghosts that He left to be made an example of, how do all these beings exist now *after* the Flood?"

"Merlin, ye know not the Scriptures; for does it not say that in the first Book of Moses there were Giants in those days, *and also after that,* and does not your Paul tell the women of Corinth to cover themselves *because of the angels*?"

"So the Watchers came back?"

"Nay," Simon patiently answered. "Those original two hundred are still bound. Other fallen ones made a similar attempt in Sodom and the displaced spirits found a way, through divine fornication, to bring their essence through the seed of men. Occasionally you will see a star fall from heaven, and isolated cases of rape occur where a fatherless child is born. Thus, it still happens, rarely, in diverse ways."

Simon directed one of the scribes to hand him a large Bible written in Latin. His mood shifted from educational to sinister again. He explained that life was in the blood and that the blood was passed from the father, not the mother. This was how Jesus had been able to come into the world, fully God, yet take on Mary's humanity. He had the mother's traits and the father's blood. It was the same for these gods and their offspring. As they continued to procreate and cross-pollinate, only those whose total paternal lineage was of the Fallen Ones were beyond redemption. If mother was the child of a Fallen One and father was mortal, the child would have supernatural powers but be yet human. If father was the child of a fallen one and mother was mortal, then the child was *a child of the damned.*

"The great tragedy is that, with whole races of Giants and faeries and elves created and crossbred along with other angelic activity, it is often nearly impossible to know if one, even one ten generations removed and with very diluted devil traits, is damned or not.

"Many races of otherworldly beings do not know this history but some do. And imagine their toil, their dread! They love Jesus more than you do. Devout, tirelessly charitable, not knowing, not knowing."

Merlin could not believe this. "More lies, Illuminated One."

"Let me read it to you." Magus went to the place in Isaiah and read the words that damned these woeful creatures regardless of their deeds, or their faith.

"O Lord our God, other lords beside thee have had dominion over us: but by thee only will we make mention of thy name.

"They are dead, they shall not live; they are deceased,

they shall not rise: therefore hast thou visited and destroyed them, and made all their memory to perish."

The 'they' in the Latin text was clearly the Raphaim, a race of Nephilim or Fallen Ones. Giants who ruled as gods.

"They are not men," said Magus, "and they are not angels. Where have they to go? They will live an unnatural long life and good or bad, ill or grand, go into an abyss of nothingness. Outside the saving blood of your Lord Jesus Christ. The woeful and sorry damned. No more redeemable than the waste of a dung heap... no matter how beautiful your Lady of the Lake is."

"No! The Lady's father lay with a Fae, so her blood is mortal; you do lie again, deceiver."

"Very well," dismissively. "Perhaps you are right about her, Merlin. But I ask you..." Simon now stood (causing Merlin to do the same) and encroached upon Merlin, drawing nigh. "Who is your father?"

Merlin's long years flashed before him in an instant. *Is it true?* The priests called him 'Child of the Devil'. *Were they right for once?* His mother had overcompensated with a guilty love over Merlin his entire childhood and adult life. She had lain with a Devil, had been seduced mayhaps. Merlin didn't know and yet knew it to be true.

"Your grand journey to understanding God's plan for the Ages and the simplicity of salvation, and it's not for you. You are just another god, who will die like a man! A man with a soul beyond redemption."

Another of the Nine stood and reminded the Merlin that he had betrayed the Brotherhood, and all secret societies, by profaning their Secret

Doctrines with his promotion of the false god Jesus Christ. At this moment a group of monks entered the Tabernacle. And Maelgwn had not yet returned.

Clearly Roman Catholics who had been turned and corrupted by the Brotherhood, Merlin ignored the hideous truths hurled at him by Simon Magus and the Nine.

"Brethren, forget not the beauty of Rome. The greatest and most lovely of all Christians come from there and the inspired letters that save men today were written from her palace and prisons." It then dawned upon the Merlin that, if he were a child of the woeful damned, his mind was simply under the power of suggestion and that his magick was fully intact, just under self-imposed dormancy.

He was compelled to try.

Soon a vapor filled the large Tabernacle hall, making possible an escape in the misty confusion. Through the haze, determined to live, determined to defend the gospel of grace, he cried out: "I am the Merlin of Britain. I will take my truth, my mystery, to the Bishop of Rome; a great and honorable man by reputation. He will hear me, and the world will change."

The metallic glove with talons startled Merlin, clutching the tall Briton's throat. The masked face appeared, and the grip was sure.

"You will go to the Bishop of Rome?" He turned his masked face sideways, like a stalking predator playing with its prey.

With his empty hand, Simon Magus removed his mask.

"I AM the Bishop of Rome."

Maelgwn finally rushed in, screaming for the Merlin to identify himself. Magus's final words to the Merlin (accompanied by a chorus of accusations of being a traitor to everyone on all sides) were, "You are John the Baptist. You pointed the way to the Messiah, who is Arthur. You must decrease and the Pendragon must increase. I feel the poison in you. One third of the traitor's death is already upon you. In you. Today. You die."

Maelgwn's battle spike came down hard, cracking through the armored glove, spraying the Pope's blood onto Merlin's beard and face. Magus recoiled in pain, relinquishing his grip.

Maelgwn grasped the poisoned old man by his robe and ran the two out of the Tabernacle, into the forest.

The monks and guardians gave chase and Maelgwn fled, at times nearly carrying Merlin, an awkwardly tall load.

*　*　*

Dawn approached. The snow was lightly kissing the treetops and the heads of weary fugitives. At last they came to Vivien's estate. The small guest house was nearest and easiest to defend, so Maelgwn carried the Merlin inside, laying him upon the bed. They could *feel* their pursuers close by.

As they neared the guest house, Maelgwn could identify some of the monks as his own kinsmen, Ravens from the North. And many of them were soldiers. The Roman faith was encroaching steadily there and clearly they had been involved in the plot to lure Merlin to this fateful initiation. Maelgwn knew not the greater portions of what had been shared, but he knew it to be pure evil. Broceliande itself was rejecting them and moaning that such vile men trod on its paths and drank from its streams.

Maelgwn confirmed the count of the swiftest of the manhunters: three. "Easy enough; they should've brought more."

"Lancelot. Please come close." Nimue's concoction was about to render Merlin unconscious. "Thank you so much for being here."

"I have my Merlin, Taliesin, and Arthur needs his; happy to do it. I will defeat them and then we will find help for you. This forest has healers in many forms, Lord Merlin."

Merlin was not consoled by the glad tidings, but he appreciated the softness of the oft cold and unpredictable warrior. The old Druid politely disregarded him and continued with a final admonition. "Lancelot, your son is what is best in all men. Protect him at all costs."

"Yes, Lord Merlin."

"Lancelot, when it comes time to do that which you would do, for Arthur's sake, do it not."

"Yes, Lord Merlin." Lancelot now had to hold the head of the Wizard, who was quickly fading.

"Lancelot. The Wars are not over. Tell Arthur–" Merlin coughed violently. "Lancelot, tell Arthur to kill the Giants! Every Giant. Kill them!"

Merlin passed into unconsciousness.

Maelgwn turned quickly to the door as the enemy fast approached.

Then it happened.

The undefeated warrior, who was unscarred (save a scar he had earned fighting Arthur himself) and had suffered barely a scratch over twenty years of war. A man who was invincible, who danced and flew when he fought and who escaped any predicament with calm followed by athletic ferocity. The best of all fighters by chance stumbled upon a shoe left behind by Nimue. The fall was hard as he was caught unawares, failing to brace for the impact with his hands. The knight's beautiful face struck violently against the baseboard of the door frame, rendering him, like the Wizard he had joined a few nights earlier on that cold boat, unconscious.

"Wake him up for this." Magus, now fully armored, masked and full of self-righteous victory, commanded.

They shook Merlin awake. As soon as half an eyelid was opened the noose was around the neck, placed by one of the monks. A sloppy noose, one designed to strangle, not break bones for a mercifully swift death. Dangling from a tree, he was stripped naked to shame. The guards carelessly cast his garments and satchel into the wood, not seeing the cup he bore. They mocked him. "Poisoned to death. Strangled to death. That's two, and one remains."

They beat his lifeless body, and his form was more red than flesh-colored, stained with blood.

They spat upon him and plucked at his beard.

"To this Fount bring *The Wizard Turned Grace Believer*," Magus ordered, hissing, laughing and cajoling.

"Hear me, Merlin; for I know you live."

Merlin was unresponsive.

Simon Magus plunged Merlin's head into the Fount. He felt several nervous jerks, complaints and twitches, and then nothing. Magus continued his overkill, shoving a short blade into Merlin's kidneys, continuing to drown him.

The Fount became all blood.

"Merlin the Magician. Poisoned, I assume by one of your Druids; Hung by priests; Drowned by the Rulers of the World. O, how you would have been the greatest amongst us... but you would not."

During the head Devil worshipper's oratory, the Fae concealed Lancelot, wanting no more legends and heroes to fall this day.

Simon at last pulled the Merlin's head up out of the water.

The Merlin was as dead...

EPILOGUE I
The Golden Age Begins Evil
Present from the Beginning

Vivien arrived at her Castle several hours later.

Her foster-son's head wound was already bandaged and hot tea simmering at a low boil, filling the room with aromas of healing and love. He slept, breathing patterns normal. She thanked the Fair Folk, but saw them not.

Soon thereafter she found the Merlin. Weeping, she held him for but a few moments. Then as women, who are stronger than men, do when mourning or crisis is upon them, she took care of the necessities. She cleaned and dressed his wounds and found his clothing with the contents of his satchel, covering his nakedness, providing her friend with dignity. Much of his blood was on her hands. *Figuratively and literally.*

His life essence touching her enlightened a partial vision, for she loved him so and possessed the Sight. "You are still covered in light; I can barely see you, love." To herself she said, *I am a sorrowful child of the damned.*

Vivien took Merlin's body to an oak tree older

than the Flood and used a wand to burn a door into the tree, and to hollow its center. She placed the Merlin in the Oak and then shut the door. And sealed it.

* * *

Retired King Meurig, the Pendragon before Arthur, was the type of father who ever had his arm around his son's far shoulder when talking to him. A perpetual hug, and perpetual lecture.

"I'm not like you," Arthur protested, unable to escape the paternal grasp. "You found your one true love as a young man and are blessed. Things have been…" the younger Pendragon, ever seeking to be respectful of women, was no less so regarding his estranged former wife "… less successful for me in this category."

"But we are but a month from Baeden. You just put your wife away and now are to court with the intentions of marrying a new wife. A new Gwenhwyfar, no less!"

"I am about to be handed the second of the Three Swords of Britain. There are tributaries and clerics and tribal leaders from the whole of the Island, other nations, and even Cedric has agreed to terms. Having a betrothed by my side will show strength." Arthur now didn't mind the hug and nudged into it, hoping his father would accept the rationale of his response.

Meurig was not to be fooled by the lad. He could outwit the Boar and command the tribes, but he could not dupe his da. "So, it's a political arrangement then? You know what they say about her?"

"Father, I don't care. No, it is not political. I love her."

"You've not known her since you were both fourteen! How say you that you love her?"

"How old were you when you loved mam?"

Meurig put both hands hard upon his son's shoulders. "Fourteen." The Uther Pendragon was a wonderful father. He had made his protest known, had heard his son's heart and now it was time for him to support the one who had brought peace to the Isles and joy unto his people. The War King was about to be made Emperor. An Emperor with a policy of no Empire. *Merlin would love that!* Meurig thought.

* * *

The Sword of Caesar, called Angau Coch, or *Red Death,* impaled an archaic anvil used by blacksmiths. *Excalibur could cut right through this,* Arthur mused. This special blade had been stuck in the shield of a prince called Nennius when he engaged Julius Caesar in combat. The Briton had never relinquished the sword and it had become a symbol of the Briton's resilience against all invaders.

Old Dyfrig was there in the courtyard of Saint Paul's church at Ludgate, in New Troy, which is Londinium. The aged bishop had crowned Arthur in the forests of Gwent at fourteen and was pink for laughing and smiling at the honor of crowning him at thirty and three; this time not as King of Glamorgan and Gwent, but as Emperor.

Arthur clasped Angau Coch's hilt with both hands and freed her from the stone, waving the sword high. Rays of sun fractured and showered the myriad of guests with light.

Gwalchmai held Excalibur as unspoken signal that he was to be Arthur's heir, and Bedwyr held Arthur's spear.

The sea of people parted, making a pathway. Marching regally through an archway of countless swords, then torches, and then birch branches came Maelgwn, tall as a mountain, shimmering armor glossed and clean as it had been in the days ere the Saxon Wars. At his elbow was a woman of identical height to Gwyar and of similar form and presentation. She differed in overt seductive appeal and she was painted, bearing tribal marks upon her neck that disappeared into her dress, causing all men to chase the designs' origins and twists and turns about her body. *She liked to be looked at in this way.*

Maelgwn presented Gwenhwyfar to Arthur, and the crowds exploded in cheer and jubilation.

The Lancelot's eyes never met Arthur's. As he placed her little hand upon the palm of the Iron Bear his low, mannish voice spake but four words: "You saw her first."

Gwenhwyfar's father, Ogyrfan the Giant, looked on, enjoying the ceremony.

Author Profile

Author Zane Newitt is an American-born Cymrophile and Theologian who feels 'more at home than home' enjoying a tea or cider in Caerleon. An ancient and medieval history expert with an emphasis on the British Isles, the father of three enjoys traveling, speaking and teaching engagements on an array of subjects, coaching, running a number of businesses and challenging friends and strangers with wit, love and unashamed irreverence tackling taboo, politically incorrect and sensitive topics – just as Merlin would do were he here today.

Publisher Information

Rowanvale Books provides publishing services to independent authors, writers and poets all over the globe. We deliver a personal, honest and efficient service that allows authors to see their work published, while remaining in control of the process and retaining their creativity. By making publishing services available to authors in a cost-effective and ethical way, we at Rowanvale Books hope to ensure that the local, national and international community benefits from a steady stream of good quality literature.

For more information about us, our authors or our publications, please get in touch.

www.rowanvalebooks.com
info@rowanvalebooks.com

Lightning Source UK Ltd.
Milton Keynes UK
UKHW04f0958310718
326554UK00001B/128/P